Ticket
to
Minto

The

Iowa

Short

Fiction

Award

University of

Iowa Press

Iowa City

Sohrab Homi Fracis

Ticket to Minto

Stories of

India and America

University of Iowa Press, Iowa City 52242

Printed in the United States of America

http://www.uiowa.edu/~uipress

Printed on acid-free paper.

The publication of this book is supported by a grant from
the National Endowment for the Arts in Washington, D.C.,
a federal agency.

Library of Congress Cataloging-in-Publication Data

Fracis, Sohrab Homi, 1958–

   Ticket to Minto: stories of India and America /
   by Sohrab Homi Fracis.

         p.   cm.—(The Iowa short fiction award)

      ISBN 0-87745-779-4 (pbk.)

      1. United States—Social life and customs—
   20th century—Fiction.   2. India—Social life and
   customs—Fiction.   I. Title.   II. Series.

   PS3606.R33 T53   2001

   813'.6—dc21   2001033590

01   02   03   04   05   P   5   4   3   2   1

. . . the other *story—the woman's story,
the black story, the immigrant story, the
homeless story, our own story reimagined, the
daunting freedom and responsibility that a
reimagined self would demand.*
—JOHN EDGAR WIDEMAN,
The Best American Short Stories, 1996

*. . . our innate curiosity to know what blood,
clan, country, street, mental, emotional,
or psychological predilection claims the
Unknown One in our midst.*
—E. ANNIE PROULX,
The Best American Short Stories, 1997

Contents

ACKNOWLEDGMENTS

I once thought writing was a solitary activity
and a book an individual's achievement. Well,
to an extent they are, but this book at any
rate is a product that owes its final shape to
many more minds than mine. First, I must
thank Frank Green and his weekly creative
writing workshops around Jacksonville,
particularly the morning church group,
for hearing first drafts of my stories and
providing instant feedback, a hard thing to
do. Kathy Hassall provided guidance, at the
University of North Florida, for the creation
of a core group of stories in this collection,
when she graciously chaired my 1993 M.A.
thesis committee. William Slaughter and
Allen Tilley were encouraging members of
that committee. Prasenjit Gupta, Howard
Denson, Sunil Misra, John Hunt, Judas Riley-
Martinez, Marty and Becky Khan, Khurshid
Mehta, Jim Wilson, and Charles East each
provided valuable insights on a number of
stories and on how *Ticket to Minto* worked as
a collection. I'm further grateful to so many
family members and friends and colleagues
for their feedback or help on individual stories
and to so many more who were wonderfully
forthcoming with encouragement. It kept me
going.
Research information from Cyrus Wadia of the
Forty-third East Bombay Troop, from the
Muscatine Center for Tourism, from Suresh
at the Hare Krishna Center, from the public
relations division of Air India, and from
student residents at Minto Hostel was greatly
appreciated. The Florida First Coast Writers
Festival awards and the publication of early
fiction by *Other Voices*, *India Currents*, and

the *State Street Review* gave me none-too-soon and much needed affirmation. Encouraging and constructive feedback from other magazine editors also contributed to many a story's development. Welcome validation then arrived in the form of awards and acceptance for publication at *India Currents*, the *Antigonish Review*, *Weber Studies*, and the *Toronto Review*, as well as the collection's selection as finalist at the University of Georgia Press's Flannery O'Connor Award for Short Fiction, 1999. The 1999–2000 Florida Individual Artist Fellowship in Literature/Fiction was a great honor. And, of course, nothing that came before compared with the Iowa Short Fiction Award, 2001, from the University of Iowa Press.

My deepest regret is that my dear father, mother, and grandparents will never see this page. I trust they sensed that I would some day realize just how much I love and owe them. This book is dedicated to them.

Ancient Fire

A fire burns on the hillsides of Khandala every December. The hill station's farmers survive the way mankind has done since prehistory: by the earth's provisions. They cultivate millet and root crops on the hillsides near Rajmichi Point in no fear of drought—between June and September the monsoons bring torrents of rain to Khandala, steaming the summer heat out of its air and soil, turning it a glistening jade. Months later in December, before next year's planting, the farmers set fire at night to the underbrush choking the slopes, burning it off and leaving fertile ash in its place. Somehow, trees in the fire's path never catch; they just remain to grow taller, their foliage more unreachable. Townspeople stepping out of their bungalows to take the cool night air get a whiff of the brush burning and look up. In silhouette against the indigo sky, a long, low blaze creeps across the top of the hills, hugging the dips and crests like a luminous serpent.

The fire can be seen from the broad, rear-facing dormitory windows of St. Mary's Villa, a century-old, barrackslike structure that serves the lower end of the tourist trade, either families unwilling to pay hotel rates or groups of schoolchildren from Bombay and Poona accompanied by their teachers. For years, the scout troop at Campion, an upper-class boys' school in Bombay run by Jesuits, has held its annual camp in Khandala. Normally the camp is timed for the monsoon holidays, so rather than pitch tents for three slush-ridden nights, the scoutmasters book the villa, knowing the rambling old place is large enough to stable forty to fifty colts. Over the years, the troop's activities in and around the villa have evolved from experimental to repeated to established to traditional, barely short of ritual, until somewhere along the line it became unthinkable that the camp should be held anywhere other than St. Mary's. So when one of the scout-masters came down with malaria during monsoons, the year after the Indo-Pak war of 1971, and the camp had to be shifted to December holidays (when Khandala is cool but dry and quite suitable for tenting), the villa was booked anyway.

On camp day the Screwvalas of Bombay drove to Campion after a lunch of Parsi sali-boti and coconut prawn curry with rice, prepared Goanese style by Lucy, the cook. Pesi Screwvala, like his father at the wheel of the Herald and his sister on the backseat with him, was silent. His mother was speaking quietly but insistently, her intestines well up to the task of digesting the meal without an after-lunch nap, something he knew his father often craved but rarely had time away from Ahura Chemists for.

"Pesi, the last thing we want is you falling sick again. There'll be a nip in the air at nights, so make sure you wear your sweater to sleep and cover yourself. Sit close to the campfires when you're outside. If any of the scout activities makes you too tired, remind Mr. Garewal that you had typhoid just a year ago and excuse yourself—after his malaria, he'll be the first person to realize how much it takes out of you. The sweater is right at the top of your haversack. And I've put six pairs of underwear inside, just in case you need more than one every day."

Two undies per day. Stifled giggles came out of his elder sister, Soona, like bits of steam bursting musically from the bathroom geyser.

"I want you to promise me that you'll say your kusti every morning after your bath—your prayer topee is inside, folded up in the corner. I've put in a sadra for each day, so your khaki shirt will stay fresh over it even if you're running around. Yezdi, will you please speed up? At this rate, the bus will be at Khandala before we get to Campion."

His father's face registered some subtlety of expression, but the Herald seemed to actually slow through the tricky Eros junction before picking up its pace. The wispy-mustached mongoose face was as composed and mild as ever, and Pesi felt a swelling of annoyance with it in anticipation of the annoyance he knew his mother would feel at the lack of a response. He remembered the time she had told him privately that sometimes Daddy acted like such a martyr she felt like slapping him.

"I don't know if I was supposed to put on my uniform for the bus ride, Mummy," Pesi said, leaning up against their backrest. If Carl Fontaine or Manohar Bhandari saw him dressed in daily clothes when everyone was in uniform, he was destined for sneers and some merciless arm twisting. The tiny interior of the car seemed armored and cozy at the thought of three unbroken days around those good scouts.

"Did you ask Mr. Baptista?"

"No, but I think last time we went in uniform." The previous summer the family had journeyed to Aspi Uncle's house in Bharuch, so it was now two-and-a-half years since Pesi's last Khandala camp. He was only a cub scout then, and it was a haze of rainy treasure hunts and coastguards-and-smugglers games outside the chapel, in his mind.

"It doesn't matter. We'll see now." Nadia Screwvala turned her dark-haired but light-skinned Mediterranean features smartly to the front as they passed the bandstand and paralleled the riding path around the park.

They rounded the bend toward the Cooperage stadium and approached a red-and-white school bus parked below the similarly painted school building. Around the bus spun dozens of students and parents, and he saw that all the boys were in brown, wearing their khaki scout uniforms.

"I told you," he cried. "I knew we had to wear the uniform."

"You didn't know, and you never told us," said his mother, as the Herald lined up at the curb. "Put on your haversack and come with me now; you can change in two seconds."

She took his hand and strode along toward the entrance steps, smiling and waving at parents she knew from PTA meetings, an attractive woman, assured and strong, in Western dress among mostly sari-clad mothers, her calf-length skirt flaring a little. Her heels clacked up to the foyer, paused a second at the base of the central, impressively broad stairway, then moved past it, and he went despondently with her, knowing it was too late—he must have been seen by half the troop already.

"Where is the bathroom, Pesi?" she asked.

"In this building? I don't know," he said. "Our class is in the next building."

"Even then, isn't your lunchroom here?" she said, as they came to the side staircase and the lift. "Come on now, get your uniform out; this is good enough."

And she moved underneath the first flight of steps and began to unbuckle his belt. He cringed as it became clear she meant to help him change right there in the open, covered by only a stair-way, just yards from the side entrance. It was an accepted practice up to the third or fourth standard for mothers to change the clothes of little children whenever and wherever necessary, but he was in the sixth standard now, eleven years old. Off came the terylene anyhow, and on the khaki. She was buttoning his shirt while he stepped into the shorts when another mother came through the sun-laden side door and stared briefly at the tableau, her face a shadowed mask. He stared back open-mouthed at her, the shorts still well below his underpants. Then she turned around the way she had come. As the stockings and broad leather belt came on he could only thank God in a daze that her son had not been with her. Even worse, what if Carl or Manohar came to know? There was a thick layer of dust on the underside of the steps, and he felt a tickling in his nose. His mother twirled the scarf into a long cylinder of red and white peppermint, arranged it around his neck, and slid the leather toggle up around the ends. She folded his discards into the haversack in a minute, and they walked out into the sun, back to the bus. It was almost ready to leave.

"You look smart now," his father said, clearly not noticing he was in shock, and his sister looked coyly up at the senior scout on the rear ladder who slung Pesi's haversack up to the carrier. His mother bent over for him to kiss her. He pecked at her powdered cheek, then climbed up the bus steps. The rows of dark blue-bereted heads inside seemed to be looking at him and talking about him at first, but after a second he could tell it was a more general buzz. In one of the front seats Mr. Garewal, still a bit thin and shaky from the malaria, motioned him toward the rear, and as he pulled himself along the aisle by the backrests, a space opened up between Carl Fontaine and Manohar Bhandari.

Years later, when he understood himself better, Pesi would come to believe that each person's universe contains its share of demons, real and imagined, each child's more than its fair share. His incorporeal demons in childhood did not erupt out of flames. Rather, the Screwvalas' ancestral community, the Zoroastrians of India, held fire sacred, had done so for thousands of years starting in ancient Persia. So, conventionally demonic settings did not inspire fear in Pesi's imagination. If he dreamed of monsters, they were more likely to inhabit bleak, odorless landscapes of perpetual rain, lurking behind the gray sheets of monsoon downpour that enveloped his world for months each year. Strangely, the beasts in his mind were indeterminate not only in appearance, shapeless forces, but also in intention. At times he felt that, more than harm him, they wanted to make him one of them.

As to corporeal threats, for almost two years Carl Fontaine had traversed Pesi's universe as chief demonic body. He was big and ruddy and foreign, old enough to be in the eighth standard, boyishly handsome and freckled enough to be a Vienna choirboy. His actual nationality Pesi did not know, just that his parents had transferred in to work at one of the Commonwealth consulates. Clearly accustomed to making a place for himself in new schools, he had quickly allied himself with the bigger boys in class and brought a dormant taste for domination to life within the group. Pesi, who used to stand either first or second in class at the time, was a natural target, but something beyond that about him, something to do with his fair skin—only a shade or two darker than Carl's, without the ruddiness—and sharp Persian features, the tinge of foreignness of his own, seemed to make it imperative for Carl to draw a line between them, a line that, as it cast Pesi out, kept Carl on the same side as the darker-skinned majority.

During recess, if they found Pesi playing table tennis in the basement with someone, Carl and Manohar would lean over the dark green table and flick the ball out of the air, crunch it beneath their Bata leather soles, pick it up and send it cracked and skittering across the table at him. If he was out in the back gardens, crouched over a marble pressed against the tip of his left middle finger, aiming it, Carl would come up from behind and push his face into the dust, then catch hold of him if he sprang up and twist his arm up behind his back till he was arched backward and on his toes to minimize the pressure. He held off from pleading as long as he could each time, but the feeling of impending fracture would finally crash through his armor, an armor Carl was aware of and eager to pierce.

Once in class, not long after Carl joined Campion, he had pressed the point of a compass into the back of Pesi's hand, pinning it to the desk. As Mr. Baptista spoke of fractions and Pesi stayed motionless, silent, the point pushed deeper and a bright bead of crimson welled up by its side. But Pesi hadn't moved or given sign of pain, and a minute later the compass was withdrawn and a whisper said, "You're a freak; you don't feel the pain?" He had smiled in a small triumph, yet to understand his adversary's nature (later, he'd look on sickly as the same compass point dismembered wriggling, wingless flies), revealing a shield in boasting of it: "I do, but I'm able to stand it somehow." So when subsequently he held on to his silence, he found his arm jerked ever higher with each refusal to voice submission, feelings of impotence, pain, and alarm mounting until they broke through in garbled, shrill utterances. Carl would smile then, a confusingly seductive smile, and Pesi was left to nurse the fire in his head and arm.

Before the typhoid, he had tried to match up to his enemies by increasing his size. He envied them theirs. Pull-ups, he'd heard, could make you taller by stretching your spine; push-ups made you stronger. From only half a struggling pull-up, hanging off the doorjamb, and five push-ups at a time, he'd got to fifteen and seventy, when the illness hit. Two-and-a-half months later, when he flattened to the tiling and tried to lift, he barely made it once before he dropped, his head spinning, and next morning the beginner's ache was in his shoulders all over again.

Now, as the bus moved out for Khandala, Carl smiled at him, all poisonous charm, and said, "Did you kiss Mummy bye-bye like a good boy?"

Pesi edged away distractedly, but Carl pulled him down. The two bigger boys' uniforms were crisp and smelled of starch.

"So sweet, Baby Screwvala kissing Mummy Screwvala."

And Manohar, his voice almost adult-deep, said, "The whole screwy family was there."

Pesi hated his surname.

"I saw them." Carl's blue eyes searched Pesi's armor for new chinks. "Mummy Screwvala's all milky white and bigger than Daddy Screwvala. Isn't that nice? Mummy Screwvala screwed Daddy Screwvala and Baby Screwvala came out of Mummy Screwvala's cunt and kissed her. What did you see while coming out, Pesi-Waysi?"

Pesi was fuzzy on the scenario Carl had painted, but, like his mother, he wished his father's family had never made screws and never acquired the appellation. Yezdi Screwvala's changing tack, so to speak, from the family business to running Ahura Chemists had unfortunately had no impact on the family name, unless, as Nadia pointed out was a possibility, a few generations down the road they came to be known as the Pillvalas. She made no secret of her disaffection for her married name; her maiden name, Deboo, had lacked the sophisticated and powerful ring of a Commissariat or the rich sound of Readymoney, but anything was better than Screwvala.

"Forgot how to talk, Screwvala, just like you forgot how to read?" Manohar Bhandari leered at him. "What happened to all your marks in class? My rank's better than yours now. Some of your screws came loose?"

Pesi stared sullenly back, refusing to comment on the precipitous slide in his class performance after his battle with typhoid.

"Why don't you open your mouth?" Carl switched off his smile.

"You think we're talking to the air? Think you can insult us like that?"

"What am I supposed to say?" Pesi muttered, barely audible above the bus. "*You* insult me all the time for nothing."

"Oh, acting tough now," said his freckled tormentor, who clearly had no intention of either being appeased or conceding logic. "I'll teach you to act tough with us."

And in a jiffy he had Pesi's arm jacked up between his back and the thinly cushioned backrest. Not enough to arc Pesi out of his seat, but the leverage was sufficient to keep him captive.

"I don't insult you for *nothing*, Screwvala." Carl yanked up on *nothing* for emphasis. "I don't *have* to have a reason, and I don't *have* to tell you, but bloody simple—I feel *better* when you feel *worse!* Like my reason?"

For the two seconds before he sensed the next yank coming, Pesi considered asking *why* it made Carl feel better, then bobbed his head quickly. He suffered a final yank anyway, but was released to ponder the simplicity of it all in Carl's mind even as the bus rounded the Dadar Train Terminus circle and rumbled out on the highway. Mr. Baptista started up "She'll Be Coming 'round the Mountain When She Comes" in a robust baritone, and soon the whole troop was chanting "Ai-yai-yippee, I come from Mississippi." After Panvel, they wound slowly up the Western Ghats to the tunes of "My Bonnie Lies over the Ocean" and "When I Get to Heaven." The bus, its engine straining to do number two, dropped all the way into first gear to crawl up the steep bends.

"Coming to the mandir," Mr. Garewal shouted from the front seat. "Get your coins ready." The bus grunted past a miniature Hindu temple set into the hillside, pitted stone showing through thin coats of blue and yellow paint, and everyone crowded over to the inner windows to toss five- and ten-paisa coins into the arched opening for luck. Pesi moved quickly up to one of the seats vacated in front and slouched in it so his head was invisible from the rear once everyone settled back. Bhushan Sanghvi started up "Rolling Home" and was shouted down—the song was reserved for the return trip—so they sang "Oh! Susanna" instead, and Pesi joined in for the first time with a lighter heart. Once or twice, he was surprised by his voice dropping in pitch, and shouted all the louder to see if he could crack it for good.

The oldest boys in his class had voices that had either broken already or cracked frequently, and he felt there was a connection between that and the strange things they spoke of at times. In moral science class they had often argued with balding, honey-haired Father McLeary before he returned to Ireland.

"Noo, noo," he would insist, soft voiced. "Masturbation is a sin before God."

"But why, Father?" Manohar Bhandari would say, winking at the others, a broad mixture of Hindus, Christians, Muslims, Parsis, and Sikhs. Pesi envied his sangfroid and his popularity. "What's wrong with it?"

Father McLeary would not elaborate, however; he only turned the discussion gently to less mysterious sins: lying, stealing, disobeying your elders. . . . When Pesi asked Robin D'Sousa what masturbation was, he laughed and shook his head. But Sharukh Billimoria, the other Parsi in class, spoke confidently of what to Pesi seemed the rather bizarre and unlikely practice of men peeing into women, even sometimes—and this had Pesi's mind in a spiral for weeks—into women's mouths.

The bus had been stiflingly warm when they began, but gradually, as they climbed the Ghats, the air whisking in through the windows acquired a brisker edge, and the skies turned a watercolor blue. Almost four hours after it had started from Campion, the bus entered Khandala to maneuver the narrow, autoriksha-cluttered streets of the old British hill station. Then it turned past a painted plaster statue of virgin and child into the grounds of St. Mary's Villa.

Bunks were quickly assigned within the huge dormitory wing. Through the vertical bars of the broad rear window behind Pesi's cot, as he pulled a T-shirt and pair of shorts from his haversack, he could see a range of hills miles away. They looked rounded and soft. Once everyone had washed up and changed, the scoutmasters divided the troop into several duty patrols, and Pesi found himself on the campfire preparation patrol, searching the grounds for deadwood.

Lines of trees fronted the three long wings squaring off the courtyard; red-flowered creepers twined up the tree trunks. He slipped beneath the volleyball net strung from one of the trees to a wooden post and moved along the dining wing, picking up fallen branches, feeling their roughness against his arms as the pile took on volume and weight. Rounding the far corner he saw, set against the short wall, a statue of Jesus Christ in plaster and paint. Jesus stood, child-sized, in full robes on a cross-embossed pedestal, pointing to his heart with one hand. Pesi put his wood down to step up and investigate: with the other hand, Jesus had uncovered his bare red beating heart, and out of it burst petals of flame and a cross.

The image captivated Pesi; he stood staring at it. Christ had mostly been an abstract figure, a prophet of the priests and some of the teachers and boys at Campion, except when moral science classes—taught now by Father Coslo, the principal, an indigenous product with a full head of very black hair and a cold, thin smile—developed somewhat on the lines of sermons. But here was something that reminded Pesi of his own Parsi fire temples. In the fire that sprang from Jesus' heart, he could see the crackling blaze in the great silver chalice at the Wadiaji Atash Bahram. His parents had taken him there early in the year to give thanks to Ahura Mazda for lifting the typhoid that had kept him on his bed for two months all told and almost taken his life. His mother had on a lacy white sari instead of her usual dresses and pulled its top fold up to cover her neatly permed hair as they climbed the steps into the front hall. On the opposite wall was a gigantic, almost floor-to-ceiling, framed painting of the white-robed, full-bearded Zarathustra, his index finger and eyes raised to a sky done in muted, dark tones. Pesi's father helped him adjust his prayer cap, and they followed Nadia into the inner sanctum after removing their shoes.

"Thank you, Zarthust saheb," she'd said in an uncharacteristically lowered voice, "for sparing our dear son so he can grow up and have Parsi children himself, in your honor. As you know, Yezdi and I are too old now to risk having more, even though we are worried about the way the community is dying out after all these thousands of years. But now Pesi can carry on the family name"—he noted that she did not actually say Screwvala—"and both he and Soona can have many good Parsi children who will carry on your teachings."

She had then recited Ashem Vohu and Yatha Ahu Vairyo in the original Avestan, nudging them to join in. They fed sweet-smelling sandalwood sticks to the sacred fire and threw ash into it that sent it sparking all over the somber inner room. Legend said the fire had first been kindled more than three thousand years ago in ancient Iran, when the Persian Empire was at its mightiest and Ahura Mazda the most venerated God on the face of the earth. Today the Parsis were only a tiny, dwindling community in India, self-exiled from Islamic Iran since before the second millennium began, but they had escaped conversion, kept the sacred fires burning. The deep hush and dusky corners around the central orange glow had sent a dreamy peace into Pesi, and as he offered the ash in approved fashion, between two fingers and thumb of his right hand, elbow supported by his left hand, he'd felt a warmth course through his arm and engulf him in its strength. . . .

Across from the little statue of Christ was the chapel wing. Stepping down finally, Pesi picked up his growing pile of firewood and moved along the wing, looking for more. At the far corner of the villa, resisting the attraction of a small cannon on wheels set halfway to the entrance—probably a relic from British days or even Maratha wars when, he'd learned in history class, Shivaji's forces had fought a pesky guerrilla action in the hilly, wooded terrain, against the powerful Moghul emperor Aurangzeb—he turned back toward the center of the courtyard where the older boys were using hand axes to split large limbs into small logs and kindling. They sent him off again to collect bark and husk for tinder, and that night after dinner served up by the kitchen duty patrol, the troop sat cross-legged around the tepee-shaped pile of wood lit and nursed into red, flickering life by Pesi's patrol.

The chill night air made all the cozier the warmth radiating from the campfire, and he planted his palms in the dirt behind him and leaned back as Ismail Khan, the school captain, struck up a breezy song on the mouth organ, lank black hair flip-flopping over brown forehead, and people clapped in time and sang along. The raspy strains seemed to reach Pesi from a distance, as if filtered through the fire, and when the entertainment patrol announced they would next perform a short play, he didn't catch the name.

Through the haze around the fire he could see three actors mouthing lines, but it took a familiar voice pitched higher than usual before he leaned forward in confusion and disbelief for a closer look. It could never be, and yet . . . it was! The slender figure, smallest of the three, clearly a junior among senior scouts, dressed in a belted, flower-patterned sheet for a gown and a scout scarf drawn over curly brown hair like a bonnet, was none other than Carl Fontaine! The face beneath the bonnet—how had this escaped him before?—was exceptionally *pretty*, a natural choice for the female role in an all-boys' cast.

"I'm sure you can convince him, dear," said the figure, simpering through cherry red lips at a taller personage bulked out by Mr. Baptista's coat, and Pesi began to laugh hysterically. The coated one hesitated and smiled uncertainly out over the fire, while the bonneted face turned blazing cheeks toward Pesi. But he could not stop, though he knew he was a marked man—some other boys had started tittering at the mistimed outburst, but he was the only one having a fit.

"I see you have great confidence in me, good woman," said coat, carrying gamely on.

"Only speak to him, my love," said bonnet, stammering painfully over the endearment, perspiring rouge to reveal freckles, and Pesi fell over sideways, shrieking uncontrollably.

Something poked him through his shorts pocket, and he straightened up, gasping and snorting, to fish it out, even as Mr. Garewal got to his feet with a finger across his lips. It was the box of Wimco matchsticks Pesi had used to help light the fire. Coat launched into his mission to convince, but Pesi, recovering his composure finally, would never learn what the purpose was. As bonnet retired hurriedly from view, the bit part done, and the senior actors' voices receded again, Pesi stared absently into the increasingly vigorous blaze and found something companionable in the warm arms it reached out to him. It danced and crackled with brisk cheeriness, strong and strengthening, battling the night for yards around with its luminous color.

Later that night, Pesi the smuggler crouched shivering behind the small cannon on wheels, waiting his chance. His assignment: smuggle a paper-wrapped Cadbury's chocolate éclair, caramel toffee shell around a soft chocolate center, past the coastguards spread out around the courtyard and into the dormitory wing. The campfire was out. It had bothered him to help splash water on the smoldering embers as they struggled to breathe, glowing brighter and larger with each puff of air, then dying inward again. When they were all out, he had run his fingers through the wet ashes. Still warm, they were flaky and blackish, not finely powdered and gray like the loban in the fire temple. But he liked them better: his own hands had worked the transformation.

A cold moon was full in the air, and the chilled, smooth iron of the cannon, moist against his cheek, brought back the ackack guns firing up into the night sky at a squadron of Pakistani bombers that had somehow penetrated all the way through to Bombay in the third week of his typhoid, sending his parents into a wild, stumbling run switching off lights as the air-raid warning wailed over the city. Darkened beyond normal already because of the blackout requirements, Bombay descended into utter darkness. A week before, he'd watched from his sickbed as his father nailed black cardboard over the windowpanes, each hammer blow clanging like a gong on the inside of his head. Now, all the excitement and the pitch black had him sitting up for the first time in weeks, and when the artillery began to hammer away at the unknown he begged to be allowed to open his window and look out. So they all sat on his bed and watched the stutter streaks of hot yellow light lance repeatedly up into the sky, though of the planes they saw nothing.

When the firing ceased and only stars were visible, cold and permanent night-lights, he'd broken the silence to ask, "What if the Pakistanis win? Will we have to run away to another country?" He imagined millions of Indians fleeing in wooden ships the way the first Parsis had fled Iran a thousand years ago to escape conversion, carrying the sacred fire with them, shielding it from wind and sea.

But his mother said, "No, of course not. Nothing will happen. Everything will just go on like before. You lie down again now and rest and get better. Enough excitement for one day."

And in a sense, nothing had happened. That was the first and last raid to reach Bombay. The Indian army had swamped the Pakistani forces in a matter of weeks, and the river of East Pakistani refugees flowing into India could return to a newborn country of its own, Bangladesh. When Pesi's typhoid abated as well, his temperature normal for days in a row, his parents took the illness to be over and sent him in to school. He sat through classes and breaks in something of a daze, heard classmates boast of having run to the Colaba harbor the day after the raid, finding enormous shell casings and bits and pieces of wreckage. But by the time his father came to get him after school, he'd practically collapsed. The typhoid had returned, a relapse said the family doctor, and he was confined to his bed once more. This time his temperature raged past 104 to hover around a blistering 105.5, reducing his speech to feverish babble, ice packs to water, drugs to placebos.

Dr. Bharucha, stooped and graying, was openly worried. If the boy's temperature reached 106 he would not recover, he warned; as it was, his brain cells were burning up at the rate of thousands each second. Pesi had a vision of his individual brain cells catching fire, sprouting tiny flames, and spiraling down in smoke one by one. His mother filled a fresh hand towel with ice cubes and laid it across his forehead, then went out for an hour and returned with a china bowl containing something that looked like a gray-brown jellyfish floating in brown water.

"What is it?" he had asked, and was told it was a special food that would take away his fever. Pirojabai from Ratan Tata Industrial had told Nadia some days ago of the woman who prepared it and prayed over it, then gave it away free to those who were sick. Pirojabai knew of many, many cases where the patient had been cured after eating it. So Nadia had taken a taxi to the woman's house, where she was assured that the food worked very well in cases of typhoid, and no, there was no payment to be made; God in his mercy had spared the woman's husband from bone cancer, and she had vowed to help other sick people without taking a single paisa for it.

"It looks very bad tasting." Pesi screwed up his face.

"You eat it now, like a good boy," his mother said in a no-nonsense voice.

She spooned it into his mouth, and it went slithering down his gullet and lay coolly inside him. Every morning after that, while his father was at Ahura Chemists and Soona at school, Nadia made the trip and brought back more of the substance. One day, however, after about a week of the new diet, she left later than usual for the woman's place and did not give the jellyfish to him when she got back around lunchtime. His father came in for half an hour as always, had a rushed meal, then sat on Pesi's bed with a bowl of hot chicken broth. He helped Pesi up against his pillows, put a hand to his forehead, and asked how his boy was.

"Drowsy." Pesi leaned forward to sip at the spoonful of soup held out for him. "How come no jellyfish first?"

"Jellyfish?" his father said, tipping the spoon into his mouth. "What has he been eating, Nadia?"

"Nothing." His mother set the clean lines of her jaw—his first indication that he'd made a mistake in mentioning the daily meal. "He's just rambling again. Eat your soup, Pesi."

His father took one look at Pesi's suddenly wary face and, still as mild as ever, put the bowl down and walked past his wife toward the kitchen. Throwing a grim look at Pesi, Nadia Screwvala stalked out after her husband. From the kitchen Pesi heard first the sound of the refrigerator door popping open, then his parents' voices, his father's muted but unusually firm, his mother's insistent.

"What is this dirty thing, Nadia? Don't tell me you have fed the boy something like this."

"It is not dirty, Yezdi; don't talk nonsense. Many people have been cured from absolutely their deathbed by eating this; ask Pirojabai at RTI. The woman who prepares it is a very saintly person and spends hours and hours praying over it."

"It looks like it is some sort of mold, some fungal growth. God only knows what it will do to him in his condition."

"It is doing him good already, I can tell, and I am going to give it to him until he gets better."

"No, Nadia, don't insist on this." Even in his dopey condition, Pesi was upset at his father's stubbornness; it was only going to put his mother in a bad mood. He knew she must be already irritated that he'd gone and had a relapse after they'd spent over a month getting him well in the first place. "Our son will get better without any of these dangerous superstitions."

"All right; I'll ask Dr. Bharucha tomorrow if it is safe to give him. Satisfied?"

"No, don't do that. I don't want it going around the doctors that the owner of Ahura Chemists gave his son some ignorant sort of miracle food."

There was a short pause; for once, his mother was without words. Then she found some. "If he dies, Yezdi Screwvala, you can tell all your customers how much good your tablets did for your own son. Then tell them that you stopped me from giving him something that *everybody* said would make him well."

And she marched off, flushed with anger and frustration, through the children's bedroom and into hers. Pesi heard something being washed down the sink, knew it was the jellyfish. Then his father came back in, gave him his soup and sweet lime juice and pills, put a fresh ice pack on his forehead, and went off to work, leaving Pesi to toss and fret and ponder the implications if all his brain cells burned up and he died. He wondered why his life should of all things be ended by fire. Eventually he decided he didn't really care. Even if he survived, he would only end up on the pavement once his parents got a divorce.

That night he slept as if dead, but in the morning when his mother took his temperature it was 102. She cried out something garbled and gathered him up, hugging him hard and long, her face moist against his. When at last she straightened up, her eyes were streaming. It was the first and only time he'd seen her cry. Then she went off in a great rush, calling to his father and sister in the dining room, to show them the thermometer. Dr. Bharucha, clearly pleased when he came in for his morning visit, declared that the fever had turned and Pesi would definitely recover from there on, though they must take care this time not to tax him and risk another relapse. His mother wore a knowing look through the instructions and, relating the news to his father at lunchtime, hinted broadly at the role the special diet must have played in the sudden recovery. Yezdi Screwvala responded only with silence.

Stillness had spread over the villa grounds. Pesi's thigh was cramping under him, and he pushed against the cannon to stretch the leg. Golden specks pulsed at staggered depths in the dark air about him, mirroring the stars. Now might be a good time to make his run, and he decided to avoid the coastguards waiting to intercept smugglers in the square by going around it through the chapel and dining wings.

The corridor was much darker than it had been outside. As he felt his way nervously, shivering again, past the chapel door, his hand encountered something projecting from the wall, a thin encircling edge. His fingers slipped over a smooth but rippling concavity into the sudden chill of water. He snatched his hand out as if from an electric shock, and suddenly the darkness around was full of shadowy demons waiting to engulf him. Heart thumping, he forced his hand back, adjusting to go beneath the projecting object. Its underside was rough with ridges and small, hard pimples, and he recognized finally a large seashell of some sort set into the wall, functioning as a holy-water container. He slipped ahead, wiping his hand on his shorts. Everything, now, was dark and cold and scary. The statue of Christ was a shifting, nightmarish outline, its heart extinguished by the night, poised to pounce as he brushed quickly past it.

He crouched and stole along the dining-wing corridor, pulling the éclair from his pocket, then sprinted through to the dormitory wing unchallenged—to find the game was over, the front corridor crowded, and everyone lined up for a bedtime mug of hot cocoa! Pesi leaned unnoticed against the wall until his heart had stopped pumping double-time, then joined the line. When he got to the front, Mr. Baptista poured cocoa for him. He clutched the steel mug with both hands above the cocoa line and sipped. The sweetness trickled soothingly down his gullet and a warm flush spread from his stomach to his brain, leaving him drowsy and limp, ready for his cot.

Changing into pajamas, he looked out of the brown-grilled rear window immediately behind the head rail of the cot and saw a misted line of hills rolling slowly across it. There seemed something motherly and protective about them. He wondered if the troop was to climb that very line on the next day's trek. Then he got under the cover, pulled the pillow in place beneath his head. Within the musty pillowcase, it separated almost evenly into two large lumps of hard cotton; he settled into the softer space between them and dozed off before lights-out.

He woke gasping, something vile and pasty in his mouth, a burning up his nose and then in his eyes. Sputtering into the dark, he felt hands shoving more slippery stuff on his face, heard a familiar voice—on key again—say with muted savagery, "Laugh *now*, you gaping hyena! Laugh again, let's see. Thought I wouldn't know who it was, wouldn't get you for it? Don't think you can get away with laughing at me *any*time. Never, never, never! Next time you act tough I'll make you eat more than boot polish, I'll make you eat cow dung. I'll put chilies up your nose, not just toothpaste. Laugh. Laugh. See what happens—just laugh again and see. . . ."

The outpouring was punctuated by rhythmic smearing passes and stabs as Pesi flailed ineffectually about, and then he was left to sit up and rub at the muck clogging his facial openings. It came slickly onto his hands and pajama sleeves, and he stumbled off in the dimness to the shadows of the bathroom wing, to wash it off as well as he could.

———

In the morning when he got his turn at the basins, there were still traces of shoe polish to be soaped at. The lavatories stank from overload and the water sitting in steel buckets in the bath stalls was too cold to bathe with, though he could hear other scouts sloshing away. It was not just the temperature: his mother had often accused him of hydrophobia, rightly suspecting deception once the bathroom doors shut between them, depriving her of direct knowledge of his doings. Only partly undressed, he'd dip into the bucket and splash mugfuls against the coral pink tiling, carefully interspacing lulls to represent soaping activities. A face wash, some wetting of hair and towel, and he was out, nodding earnestly to her "Did you wash . . . everything? Properly?" At camp there was no need to even fake it, no need for the slyness. And since his kusti had not been undone in the first place, in order for him to bathe, he didn't have to say his prayers and tie the creamy goat's-wool band around his waist again— thrice girdled to represent good thoughts, good words, and good deeds.

After flag break and breakfast they changed out of uniform into T-shirts and shorts for the hike up Sausage Hills. It was a dry, cloudless morning, the sun uncovered and unseasonably hot.

They filed across the market road in twos and threes, Pesi strag-gling, having noted Carl and Manohar at the front. To the left of the stores, with their steel shutters rolled up and storekeepers idling half in, half on the steps, a high running wall hid most of a stone and brick bungalow. But a little girl in a lavender frock peeped over the wall at the procession, and Pesi wondered what held her up. They came to a small lake by the side of thatched shanties, and alongside half-submerged black buffaloes he saw brown-bodied children swimming, jumping off an isolated section of iron pipe as wide around as they were tall, walking naked among the green rushes of a central islet. And he wondered what *that* was like, to go unashamedly naked in the world, no underwear even. The file of scouts turned, chattering, over a bridge above railway lines to the side of a hill, climbed up past an old railroad siding, and Pesi, laboring a little now, wondered why the steep stretch of track curved up the hill like a giant children's slide in reverse, then broke off abruptly, arriving at nothing. At a catch-ment full of green water, Mr. Baptista let them bunch up and de-livered a dry lecture on hydroelectric power. When he was done, they shed their listening expressions and continued up a steep, winding dirt path flanked by dense shrubbery. Forest odors flowed thickly about them; their feet rasped over pebbles and earth.

Again Pesi watched for Carl and Manohar to go ahead, then trailed the pack. It was hard going; his breath quickened as they climbed past enormous bamboo clumps with stalks crisscrossing densely, dried to yellow, and he began to hear his heart over the trilling of birds. Even the slight breeze twirled warmly about him, and a fine film of sweat sprang out all over his legs and arms. In a while he could no longer hear the others climbing ahead and started to feel the onset of nausea that, ever since his illness, exertion brought. Now, too late, he wished he'd done what his mother had told him—asked to be excused from the hike. His head had begun to go around. He was ready to drop where he was, when within the tall shrubbery and dense foliage to his right, several paces off the trail, a hole opened up just above ground like a whirlpool in a swirl of green, light filtering through from the other side.

He veered off without a thought and crawled through the short tunnel, his T-shirt catching on twigs. Branches caught at him, scratching his face and hands, but he came out into a flat area flanked by clusters of brown, twiggy plants holding shriveled bellflowers. The ground was strewn with thick droppings of long yellowed leaves like dried corn husk, as brittle under him as straw as he labored toward a gnarled fig tree to collapse at its base, breathing raggedly. There was a sort of inaudible drone in the air that he could only sense, not hear. Now the sweat began to flow, and between its streams and puddles a large red ant scurried up his arm. When it stopped to sip at the perspiration, he wondered what might happen if it kept coming and crept in through his ear to the inside of his head. Then he flicked at it and watched it tumble lightly to the bark, whose cracks and ridges were alive with other ants. If it had reached into his brain, what further damage might it have caused, how many more ranks would he have slid?

In the weeks following his typhoid he'd come to realize that something had changed within his head. When he sat with new textbooks to catch up with the rest of class, he found that after just one or two lines his attention drifted off into long reveries, out of which he woke with a start to read over, before moving on, only to drift off again. Each page took an hour or more. In class too he drifted in and out of daydreams, remembering little he had read, following little that was taught. During library class, Miss Fernandes set up a reading experiment in which she had them read a long passage to themselves, going as far as they could in five minutes but making sure they followed everything they read. Pesi read carefully along, but, six or seven lines down the first page, broke into a sweat because he couldn't remember what had gone before or how it connected up with the sentence he was reading. So he went back over the introduction slowly, mouthing the words, engraving them on his mind. In this painful manner he moved along, back and forth, feeling surer of having an answer to questions. But when Miss Fernandes called time, she explained to the class that the experiment was meant to gauge, not their comprehension as he'd thought, but their reading speed.

"Let's see," she said, sending a bright, tastefully lipsticked smile around the classroom. Miss Fernandes was a Goanese Christian, sweet-accented and given to wearing short skirts. When she walked out to the back gardens, older boys dropped casually to reclining positions on the ground in hope of catching a glimpse of her underwear above smooth, lissome brown legs. Pesi, his eyes often magnetized to her gentle features and liquid black eyes, wondered at the difference in looks and station between her and the Screwvalas' Goanese cook, Lucy, bent and pudgy, humble preparer of prawn curries. "How many of you read all four pages? Wait; let's start the other way. All of you, I suppose, got through the first page?"

And she waggled her head confidently at them.

But his hand had gone slowly up, and he managed a hesitant "No, Miss."

"Oh, Pesi," she'd said, looking sadly at her once-upon-a-time star pupil. "How far did you get?"

"Half the page," he admitted, glancing furtively down at the passage, hoping she'd ask him some questions next.

But all she could manage was another sorrowful "*Oh, Pesi,*" and there were snickers around the classroom and raucous bursts of laughter from Carl and Manohar.

When report cards came in, he had plummeted twenty-odd ranks, a fall that entertained his tormentors considerably.

"Screwvala is not so smart after all." Carl had sneered, popping the back of Pesi's knee in assembly line. "We all knew he's mentally retarded."

But little by little, Pesi's mental strength returned, as if his brain were gradually building alternative pathways to those that had gone up in smoke. Though the dreaminess remained— his intelligence a slower one, his concentration fragmented—his ranking had climbed almost halfway back. It was as if his mind had been forged again, in some natural furnace. And now, miraculously, his corporeal monster, his tormentor of over two years, had turned kittenish by firelight, his callow prettiness no longer camouflageable by aggression. In fact, Pesi realized, Carl would not have reacted half as violently to Pesi's laughter had he not felt its power to melt the compass point that had pinned Pesi like a fly to his desk for so long.

A stinging sensation was spreading on Pesi's inner thigh. An ant had crawled up his leg into his short pants and bitten him. He squirmed to his feet, brushing grit and ants off the shorts, encountering protrusions in his pockets for the second time in as many days. Then he reached over to where the ant, a shiny chestnut red and the size of a rice grain, was weaving drunkenly out of its suddenly rocky hideaway. He caught it up between thumb and forefinger, felt its squirming, crinkly shell against both, and began to squeeze. It stabbed at his thumb with hot little pincers, but he pinched its life out calmly, mashed it a while just to be sure, then flicked it away.

Thrusting his hands into his pockets to see what was what, he pulled out of one the chocolate éclair and from the other the diamond-labeled box of Wimco matches he'd used around the campfire. Both items seemed made to order. At the far end of the trek, sandwiches were probably being handed out, and paper cups of orange squash. Wondering if a head count would send a search party after him, he unwrapped the éclair and popped it in his mouth, then with his feet began to sweep into a pile the profusions of long dry leaves and husk on the ground, moving them into the flat space between the tree and the opening in the shrubbery through which he'd crawled. Once the heap was waist high and two or three yards at the base, he cleared a ring of bare ground around it, then stood over it and struck a match. It flared up, and he cupped his hand around the yellow, blue-centered flame and lowered it to the pile, holding it against the top leaves, one of which began to smolder and smoke. He lit more matches and held them in twos against the leaves, and when some began to crackle, held their flames against others near the base. Red tongues began to lick around the slopes of the bonfire. The éclair melting in his mouth to its liquid center, he rushed around his retreat gathering and breaking off twigs for kindling, ignoring the saw-edged scratch marks springing up on his skin, casting the twigs into the heap, then spinning away again beneath peripheral trees to search for small fallen branches. Arranging them against the fire or thrusting them in, he brought them to flaming life, felt the heat lap at his face, breathed the vapors in giddy transport.

At last when it was strong and crackling, gaining in density, he slowed to collect larger branches in his arms. Dropping the bunch by the fire, he fell to the ground himself and began to poke at his bustling creation and feed it. Its gauzy oranges and reds drew his eye hypnotically and his cross-legged attitude before it brought to mind the white-robed priests in the fire temple poking at small braziers of the holy fire, cloth masks shielding their mouths and noses from the smoke, chanting their mysterious prayers and the names of the dead in a dying language.

He had never understood a word of the prayers he learned by heart for his navjot ceremony in the pretyphoid days, only gloated—arrogantly, he felt, thinking back—over his sister, Soona, for the ease with which he'd mastered the lines. But now he began to hum the Kem na Mazda in a low tone and to rock a little to its lilting meters.

> Kem na Mazda
> mavaite payum dadat;
> hyat ma dregavao,
> didareshata aenanghe.
> Anyem Thwahmat Athrascha
> Manangashcha
> yayao shyaothanaish
> Ashem thraoshta Ahura!
>
> Ke verethrem
> ja thwa pol
> sengha yoi henti,
> chithra moi dam
> ahumbish ratum chizdi
> at hoi Vohu
> Sraosho jantu Manangha,
> Mazda ahmai
> yahmai
> vashi kahmaichit. . . .

It was eons before he caught himself, lifting his gaze with a conscious effort. Through the rising haze above the bonfire he could see the spiral opening in the shrubbery, and he looked to it for signs of the troop's return. After a minute or so, a quick breeze picked up about him, blowing the fire into a blaze, and dimly he began to hear laughter and voices.

They drifted in between the bushes, growing louder, until at their loudest he could hear across the opening Mr. Baptista say, ". . . but these Sausage Hill or Barometer Hill slopes are no good for planting crops. All jungle. Last camp, you remember the cultivated slopes we saw from Rajmichi Point . . . ?" And on and on.

Someone else remarked how close Duke's Nose had seemed from the top. Then the voices dwindled and died in the distance, the silence broken occasionally by the sounds of stragglers. The fire had slowed a little along with the breeze and begun to smoke. He held on still, unwilling to leave it, stirring it with a large limb, and presently heard a familiar, hated voice say, "Where's the smoke coming from?"

"See that hole in the bushes," responded the deep tones of Manohar Bhandari. Pesi heard them pushing closer through the brush, and some scrabbling sounds later a freckled, maturing choirboy's face appeared in the opening close to ground and was immediately transformed by a look of surprise and uncertain malice.

"What're you doing here, you freak?" Carl stopped in the tunnel, ignoring the shoves from behind, turning his head this way and that just past the opening to take in the solemn tableau: Pesi seated cross-legged behind a large fire, churning it with a stick like some pagan priest.

And Pesi felt in some way at an advantage over his old adversary, sensed that Carl felt it too. The memory of last night's reversal at the campfire was with both of them, and the new, equally vigorous blaze suggested a continuity, seemed to flare between them in protection of Pesi.

"I was here *long* before you," he said calmly. "What are *you* doing here?"

A curious Manohar had pushed up beside Carl, who seemed part infuriated and part daunted by Pesi's cool, perhaps sensing a loss of the domination he had long taken for granted.

"I meant, what is all this fire business, you mental case?" His voice was a snarl. "Does Mr. Baptista know?"

Pesi regarded his enemies across the fire and felt a crackling in his ears, as if the flames had caught there and his brain cells were burning up again. Putting down his poker and getting up, he reached toward the blaze, refusing the impulse to snatch his hand from the heat, fishing out a branch lapped half its length in sinuous reds and yellows. Coarse odors entered his nostrils. His end of the firebrand was hot enough to bring naggingly alive the ant bite on his thumb.

He sneered. "No. Mr. Baptista doesn't know." Then in a high, imitative, simpering voice: "Only speak to him, my love."

"Bloody runt," shouted Carl, wrenching forward but sticking at the shoulders and hips between a squirming Manohar and the bushes. "I saw you put your hand in the fire. Freak!"

"Ya," said Pesi, feeling his sneer go lopsided at the familiar taunt. Fighting his face muscles and the unexpected rush of bitterness, he passed his left hand deliberately through the torch's flame without flinching. The momentary heat surged through him like electricity. His hand stung all over, but he fought the urge to rub it. At least he couldn't feel the ant bite anymore. "Let's see *you* do it, talking so big."

Carl was out of the tunnel now and coming straight for him, setting off sharp twinges in Pesi's arms, reflexive memories of numerous twistings. But he stood where he was, raising the branch, offering its flaming end, waiting for an answer.

"I don't put my hand in fire!" said Carl, eyeing the firebrand and stopping short, but now just as close as Pesi to the larger blaze. Orange lights played on his freckles. A roasted shell of air encased them both, and for a second Pesi felt as if they were working out something together.

"Why?" he asked. "Scared?"

"Because I'm not *stupid* like you."

"Anything happened to me? You're *scared*," said Pesi, the static increasing in his ears. Manohar, having come up from the opening, was taking in the situation from the side.

"Scared!" said Carl, stepping up quickly. And he reached his hand out toward the burning limb.

But the nearer it came to the torch, the slower the hand moved, until it hovered in an absolute torment of confusion still inches from the flames. Its owner, Pesi saw clearly, was much better at administering pain than enduring it, and, his excitement ballooning, he watched a snarl rope Carl's face as the hand jerked backward in little snatches.

"Scared," said Pesi, his voice turned raw by the discovery, the crackling so loud now he could hardly hear himself. He lobbed the firebrand lightly toward Carl's retreating hand, which clutched and shoved reflexively at the flaming end in a violent spasm of horror.

Deflected, the branch twisted to the ground outside the swept ring and set the tinder leaves smoking. They ignited, and sparked others. Frightful screams came out of Carl, who held his hand by the wrist, as if to keep the pain from knifing up, and bent over and writhed in a manner that would have set Pesi laughing if not for Manohar's flabbergasted "Are you *mad* or *what*?"

The patch of fire around the fallen branch spread almost radially, a low wave of flame pushing for the surrounding shrubbery as if stalking it. Manohar bounded over and began to stamp it out. Pesi moved mechanically to join him but his eyes were still drawn to Carl, who had settled, no longer screaming, into a doubled-up position, his elbow between his thighs, whimpering to himself. Their heavy-soled shoes came down repeatedly in little whomps. When the wave was reduced to smoke and a few smoldering patches, Manohar stepped across to the bonfire and kicked it over. It spattered around the clearing and they went after the pieces, though Pesi's heart was not in it. The straw carpet caught again, portions flaring up with the shifting breeze, threatening the peripheral bushes, even gnawing at the roots of the tree, sending red ants scurrying up the bole while incinerating others, and it was a good five minutes of hard, sweaty work before they thought the fire dead enough, only wisps of smoke rising from charred remnants. Then they looked to the hapless Carl, who was still making puling noises that swelled as they guided him through the shrubbery tunnel, its branches catching and poking, and set off down the trail in search of cold water, the troop, and the first-aid kit.

That night after hot cocoa, unfolding his pajamas in the dimly lighted dormitory and changing into them, Pesi reviewed the consequences of his showdown with Carl. The catchment water, their first thought, proved many meters below their reach as they ran to the rim. They then slithered down past the abandoned railroad siding, holding Carl under his armpits, aiming for the lake by the shanties, but catching up, just before it, with the 43rd East Bombay still straggling along the bridge over the rails. The lake water plan was vetoed—unhygienic—by Mr. Baptista and Mr. Garewal, who decided to first of all take care of the situation, without getting too deeply into it. Carl's scorched palm was doused instead with water from water bottles and thermos flasks before he was whisked off in an autoriksha to the neighboring Lonavala Civil Hospital to have the burn professionally dressed, leaving behind some disappointed first-aid specialists.

When he returned to St. Mary's, his palm mummy-wrapped, the three boys were called into the scoutmasters' bedroom for an inquiry. Mr. Garewal looked grim, but Mr. Baptista was quite waggish about it all and did most of the questioning. To Pesi's utter surprise, a subdued, no longer ruddy-faced Carl, motivated either by the code against "sneaking" that had kept Pesi from complaining in the past or by a reluctance to let the truth be known among his peers, concocted a rambling, confused story that hinged on him, Carl, practicing to pass the scouts' fire-lighting test. He looked and sounded twelve years old. With demons of his own to fight, maybe fiery ones.

Manohar's eyes had gone down as the tale was stitched, and several times he lifted them and looked on the verge of bursting into speech. Pesi sat quietly, wondering if he was better off revealing the facts himself, deciding against it. Mr. Baptista casually tore holes in Carl's already netlike fabrication, then turned to the other two and with a series of pointed questions extracted something approaching reality. His expression then turned as grim as Mr. Garewal's, and his brawny right hand shot out and fell heavily across Pesi's face, cracking his calm. But when Pesi looked dizzily up from the slap, the side of his face numb, his eyes sought Carl's. And the blue eyes glanced away, devoid of gloating. . . .

By the time Pesi left the scoutmasters' room, he was under sentence to visit, in his parents' company, a still more daunting room above Campion's wide central stairway: the principal's office. In the six-year span of his reign, the raven-haired Father Coslo had established himself as a stern judge and merciless disciplinarian. The walls of his office, rumor said, were hung with the heads of students unwise enough to have crossed the law.

Shrugging off the future with no little effort and knotting his pajama drawstring simultaneously, Pesi kicked his slippers free and pulled the bedcover down. The other boys were mostly asleep or in little, mutedly boisterous groups on someone's bed. His left hand still stung from when he'd passed it through the flame, though he'd held it under a tap for quite a while. At any rate he saw no more arm twisting in store. Hopping up behind the cot's head rail, he turned to the barred window—and his breath caught at what it framed. Clear as a beacon, a long, red-gold ribbon of fire flickered wavily across the grille, cleaving the darkness.

A forest fire! It glowed and pulsed above a dim line of hills, and, knowing nothing at the time of the Khandala farmers' yearly routine, nor that the morning's Sausage Hills lay somewhere behind him as he looked toward Rajmichi, he knew as surely as his hand still stung from it that his fire had survived the afternoon's stomping out.

He could see now, as if there himself, how it had lain in the grass all evening, wounded, hanging on each puff of air, waiting for the breeze that would spring up by and by and set it stirring. He saw it line the edges of tinder leaves brightly, when at last the breeze came along, and creep under naked bushes. It flickered up a shrub, devouring shriveled brown bells, and reached over to neighboring plants. Repeating the move eagerly, it advanced, putting slithery little lizards to rout, until it had hemmed in the clearing. Then it pushed its way both outward and in.

At first it moved slowly, feeling its way over the hillside, still close to the ground, breathing deeply, gathering strength for what lay ahead. It was a shimmering wave that waxed and receded. It pulsed like firefly. But steadily it gained both size and momentum, its limbs reaching up into taller vegetation, feeding hungrily on the greens. It lapped at frail saplings, then tore at their hearts.

Now blustery and arrogant, encountering the very tree he'd sat under, it clawed angrily up, chasing squirrels into branches, catching up with them and setting their tails on fire, catching them again in panicked midleap and sending them up in small balls of flame like brain cells at 106 degrees Fahrenheit. It lit the tree like a filament and looked for others. It was grown enough now that the larger animals of the forest—chital, foxes, boar, rabbits, even the odd panther—sensed it in the air and ran before it, while the birds rose in their thousands and hovered on heated air currents. From the safety of height, they squalled their disapproval. Great cracklings like the snapping of flags in high wind came up to them on poisonous fumes. Dense with the color of anger at their escape, the fire rushed madly at things static around it as if to make them pay. Sweeping over bamboo groves, it played them like panpipes, mournfully, eerily, bringing whole clumps creaking to their knees in a fusillade of flames, flushing hares out of thicketed dreams into frenzied, bounding flight.

At its heart it reached unimaginable temperatures, the heat so searing large stones turned to ash. Nothing survived. But if human eyes could have looked into the center, the sense would have been not of death but life so intense that acres around were reduced to only color: bougainvillea reds, orchid blues and yellows, all rushing to fill the slightest void.

So it roared along, whooshing up trees and vaulting whole clearings in increasing knowledge of its might, rampaging across the hill as even the sun set in acknowledgment, until at last the fire spread, as Pesi saw it now, as it had long millenniums ago, across the entire skyline, lighting up the horizon, girdling the world.

And it filled his heart, just to look at it, with wonder and assurance, a sense that things were strangely as they ought to be, that there were powers on his side. Father Coslo, he knew, would plant cold eyes on him and on his parents, threaten dire things—pink cards, gray cards, expulsion. But the meeting would not go all Father Coslo's way. In Pesi's father the principal would find a stoic, unshakable calm, centuries old, and in his mother a formidable warrior. Something of both, he felt, must have passed into him. So he rested his chin on the head rail of his cot and sat there in the dark, at peace with his world, looking out on the night and a long wave of fire rolling redly over blackened hills.

Stray

———————

       "Hullo! And where do you belong?" The question carried easily in summer air, prompting homeward-bound apartment dwellers to stop and listen.

    But the speaker, a tallish, dark-haired young man, was only addressing a cat as it pattered across the glossy, links-perfect lawn toward him. So the listeners turned away. Pesi bent over to stroke the animal, his walnut-toned, smooth-skinned hand a floating pattern against silver-tipped gray. The fur felt sleek, excepting a clump or two. The cat pulled its head back at first but soon pressed up against his legs, thrusting its face into his hand. There was something seductive about its friendliness. Pesi dropped to a supple half-squat, weight supported on his right haunch, and inspected it.

"Trim and healthy," he informed the subject, grassy odors tickling his nose. The sun's heat reached into his chest. "But no collar. And quite clean, but look at these little scratch marks on your face—only place you can't reach with your tongue."

A stray, he concluded, lost or abandoned maybe not too long ago, but long enough to get into some trouble. It was a shame how some people moved out of the complex and left their pets—especially cats—behind to fend for themselves. That need not have been the case with this one, of course. So he straightened up to see if he could locate the owner.

Here and there, people just returned from work or college were pulling into parking spaces in front of rough-textured brown brick, two-story buildings. A young couple strolled along the edge of the field, holding hands, not so much as looking in his direction, making the most of summer days before winter came along. But they started to argue, and the woman snatched her hand away. She was good looking and blond like the Renee girl.

The sun was at forty-five degrees now, and its heat seemed to suddenly lessen. He got out his keys and opened the mailbox to discover some varicolored junk, but also the envelope with drab green-and-brown Indian stamps pasted so straight and the hand-written word AIRMAIL at left, a scraggly box drawn in blue ink around it. About time; why couldn't Mum write more often when she had hardly anything to do at home other than tell the cook what to make and the servants where to clean? And Dad must have written his usual two lines at the end. Not that he, Pesi, was any better than them—when had he last written? At least a month ago. Struggling for lines toward the two-pages-so-it-won't-look-like-it-was-a-chore goal, he'd had the strange feeling that he'd left them behind for good, would never come face to face with them again, connecting only through letters and hurried (because incredibly expensive), disembodied long-distance calls. Indian faces—comely, smiling, conspicuously bindied Hindu women in saris or salvar-kameez and their ethnically attired fam-ilies—were making their way onto telephone commercials and into the American consciousness by virtue of the sheer numbers in which they kept touch with their past. But Pesi found the process unsatisfying.

He slid the key into his front door. As he swung it open and stepped inside, he almost tripped over something that shot past into the poky living room. It was the cat, of course, and, entry accomplished, it padded around at leisure, inspecting the apartment, diving under tables and onto chairs, scratching its face against the sofa edges, ending up behind the couch with only its head sticking out, watching Pesi.

"So, what's the verdict?" he asked, laughing. "Is it okay? Are you hungry? I'll put out something for you to eat."

His pleasant, conversational tone drew a plaintive response from the cat. He wondered at the similarity between its vocal chords and those of human infants, then got the 2%-fat milk (funny concept, milk with different fat contents, yet how naturally sweet, the milk in this country!) out of the refrigerator and set down a bowl, calling to the cat. It didn't move but allowed him to pick it up around the furry portion between its front legs and belly, from where it hung limply until he set it down near the bowl. But it only nosed at the milk, showing no further interest.

"Hmm," he mused. "I thought cats like milk. Suit yourself. I've got to straighten up this joint before Shenaaz comes."

Bustle around the living room picking up shoes, damp smelly socks, and scattered clothing; throw them in the bedroom closet to join a general clutter of things; sort the bills (electricity almost due) and dump the cream-streaked can of New England Clam Chowder; stack textbooks and files in a more-or-less stable pile on the coffee table; hop across to the apartment next door and borrow Andy's vacuum cleaner; vacuum the wall-to-wall buff carpeting; skim the kitchen linoleum (look at the cat jump—mad fucking cat, getting all tangled in the extension cord now); mop up in the bathroom and do the bed; take off your sweaty shirt and sadra, put on a clean T-shirt, flop down on the sofa, flip on the table fan and the little thirteen-inch TV, open Mum's letter, put your feet up on the coffee table with one wobbly leg that you bought at an auction for next to nothing, and think, I would give anything to be able to bring the servants over from Bombay and just sit and watch them do all this shit.

But if it was hot here, it had to be like a sauna back there—that was some comfort.

The letter said the Madans had invited his parents to a dinner party, and everyone, even Mahrukh Madan's daughter, Aloo, had asked when Pesi would be back and did the family miss him? She'd grown up to be quite pretty, Aloo had; what did he think? His sister Soona's fiancé, Dorji, was such a sweet boy. Last week (which, of course, was last month by now—the letter had taken three weeks to reach), Buster the pug had eaten half the cook's lunch, left brainlessly on her small stool where he could reach it, before she rushed at him, flapping a dust cloth, and chased him onto the balcony. Then she'd threatened to walk out unless they paid her more—so hard to get good servants nowadays. (Such a wholesome, typical snapshot of Parsi existence in South Bombay, reflected Pesi.) Mum wondered if he missed Buster; maybe he should get a nice dog in the States. And Dad advised him in a P.S. to study hard and let them know if he needed anything.

Shenaaz opened the door and walked in, smiling. She wore her hair short and pert now, a jet-black frame around skin a shade or two lighter than his, a nose like a small eggplant, and a mouth pulled apart like an overripe mango by too-generous smiles.

"Hi, Nosey," she said, dropping onto the sofa next to him and snuggling up.

"Mm. Making fun again of my long but—unlike yours—aristocratic nose, I see," he deadpanned, folding the letter away, pausing for the expected giggle, which was not long in coming. Mock annoyance went over well with Shenaaz, as with most Indian girls. "And which village did you grow up in, by the way? Try knocking, next time you visit somebody."

"So cheerful." She stretched to kiss the tip of his nose. "And so charming also. What did I do to deserve such a—what was it—aristocratic Persian god? Hullo, and who is this?"

The cat had poked its head around the base of the kitchen counter to determine the source of this new, higher-pitched voice. Discovered, it sauntered casually into full view and suffered itself to be fallen upon by Shenaaz, who dropped to her knees beside it in an orgy of oh-mys and so-cutes.

"That's right," said Pesi. "Leave me for a bloody cat, hardly two minutes after walking in. Without knocking."

"Oh, Pesi." Turning to him quickly, she kissed him on the lips, left hand looping around to the nape of his neck. He ceased his fake grumbling. She turned again to pick the cat up, and it submitted to the indignity with a petulant wail. "Look, he has hazel eyes just like yours. Oh, see his face, all scratched up. Poor baby. Where did you find him?"

Pesi leaned forward curiously. "Just outside; came up to me on its own. Are you sure it's a he? Hmm, yes, it is." He smirked. "Very observant of you, Shenaaz."

"Hardly," she said, busying herself with the cat, smoothing a slightly ruffled area of gray fur.

He smiled but didn't press the issue. She hadn't changed that much. Outwardly, yes—gone the wavy, below-the-shoulders hair and the hipless frocks, those rounded hips now snugly held by designer jeans or shorts or clinging skirts. And yet, how many months had it taken to get her into bed with him? Stonewalling on the basis of outdated customs, deaf ears turned to his arguments, evenings ended in sullen stalemate. Then finally, accumulated and long-controlled passions spilling over like waters finding a chink in a neatly latticed barrage. Even now, she wouldn't come out from under the bedsheets or allow him to leave the lights on. And here she was, face red at having been caught deciphering the sex of a cat. It was very alluring, this virginal core, and he pulled her to him.

After a while she pulled away; they sat back on the sofa. The table fan whirred and clicked as it swirled, propelling packets of tepid air at them. The cat raised its head from cleaning its paw to regard them solemnly.

"Have you given him food, Pesi?"

"He's an abnormal billee and a fussy one—doesn't like milk."

"If he's not used to it, it might give him an upset stomach. Are you going to let him stay during the night?"

"I suppose so. Looks comfy enough." The cat had curled up in the armchair, eyes three-quarters shut.

"Then let's get some cat food, and also kitty litter so he can go to the bathroom."

After Acme, they went to Pizza Hut and split a large pizza with extra cheese and jalapeno peppers, the only item on the bland American smorgasbord approaching true Indian heat. Pesi was glad that at least he wouldn't have to cook something that night, on top of all the housework he'd done. His cooking was still just this side of edible. In his apartment again, once the cat had eaten its fill of Whiskas, they decided to give it a bath. But when they set the warm water running in the bathtub, the cat wrestled out of Pesi's grip and scrambled to the furthest corner of the living room, from where no amount of coaxing could extract it.

"So, Shenaaz, you gorgeous thing," he said, leering. "Looks like you and I will have to use up the bathtub."

"Pesi!" She was flushed again. "Be quiet now."

That night they were awakened by a scratching at the bedroom door, which they'd shut but not locked. A scrambling sound followed.

Shenaaz said sleepily, "The cat is trying to get inside."

"You can't push that door open," Pesi mumbled, his eyelids threatening to close again. "You have to turn the doorknob."

He started to get out of bed. But there was a thud against the door, then another. As he hesitated, there came a sound of the latch clicking, and, miraculously, the door swung open, squeaking a little. A small, furry object leaped lightly to the bed, clambered over their bodies, and inspected startled faces in the dark, breathing warm, slightly fetid, cat breath on them.

This cat could open doors.

The next morning was a Saturday morning. No college, so they could lie in bed late. The cat had other plans, though, and sat on Pesi's chest at the advanced hour of 6:30, when some light began to filter through the window in defiance of shut venetian blinds. Pesi dreamed he was floating face up in a pool of dirty gray, and a monstrous hand was pushing him under. He woke up to find his eyes held by a steady and impenetrable pair of hazel eyes. Except for their added tinge of green and the almond shape, it was like looking into his own. A low, throaty purr rumbled interminably from somewhere within the cat, as if from a holy sadhu seated serenely, the ancient Om–m–m–m swelling from deep inside him.

Putting such imaginings aside, Pesi grumbled aloud to Shenaaz, who came out of a shallow sleep. "This isn't fair. Obviously he thinks my chest is easier to rest on than yours. Not that I'm complaining about your chest—I like it a lot." Shenaaz's breasts were plump yet thrusting, gleamingly brown-aureoled, the very part of her that ought always to have been proudly naked.

"Mm," she said, automatically hiking the bedsheet up to her neck. "Listen to him; his motor is running."

"Mine too," he responded, turning to her warm smells and hilly contours, unseating the cat, who soon abandoned the bed altogether, voicing its displeasure at the seismic activity under way.

In the bathroom, afterwards, Pesi's Parsi nose gave abundant notice that the cat had used the litter box the previous night—evidence, presumably, that it had been someone's pet. They strolled over to the apartment office building, Shenaaz's hand in Pesi's, and pinned a "FOUND: GRAY CAT" note on the bulletin board, in case the cat's owner was still around. Then, getting in her wobble-wheeled blue Escort, Shenaaz left for her apartment on the east side of Harrison.

Pesi played with the cat for a while after returning, then got to work on an engineering mathematics reading assignment. The cat made a few passes over his lap and settled down for a snooze, obscuring the textbook. Pesi was somewhat surprised to detect a smug feeling creeping over him at the abandoned animal's obvious, growing devotion to him. He liked its heaviness across his lap, and the furry warmth. When he rewarded it with a tickle behind the ears, it preened upward, slitting its hazel eyes. On opening, they seemed to rest, as if in recognition, on the straw-colored, wood photo frame by the window. Dad looked back from the picture, face dark with bristle, a slashed-open coconut with a straw sticking out of it in his hand, while Mum, fair by contrast, her dress whipping about her, struggled to keep her arms around a yapping Buster. Sea spray splashed out toward Pesi, carrying the old salt smells to him. To the side you could see part of the coconut vendor's cart piled with green fruit, behind it the curving line of Worli seaface, people walking dogs, couples hand in hand. Maybe Mum was right about the pet thing; the apartment would seem more alive. And nice cats, he imagined, were just as good as nice dogs.

That afternoon, after a microwaved TV lunch for him and occasional dips into Whiskas and water in a double-cratered plastic bowl for the cat, he studied math while it padded around restlessly. Finally, it meowed twice or thrice, and when he raised his head, walked over to the front door and looked up at him.

"Want some fresh air?" He got up and opened the door. The cat stepped out gingerly, took a few paces, and settled down in a patch of sun on the walkway. Recognizing a good idea, Pesi pulled out a lawn chair and luxuriated too. A warm breeze played upon him and touched the tall, yellow-white, feathery fronds of nearby reed canary, swaying them gently. The cat licked its paws assiduously, passing them over its face once they were wet enough. The complex was hushed, no one was about, and Pesi had almost dozed off, when a car started up a few buildings away and revved its engine on the way out. The sound lay down slowly in the overheated afternoon air, and Pesi decided it was time to return to engineering mathematics.

"Come on, pal." He rose, bending over to urge the cat toward the door. "Let's go."

And the cat, hissing, grabbed at his outstretched hand with sharp front claws, sank pointed white teeth into it. Chalky scratch marks rose raggedly along the back of Pesi's hand. For a moment, he froze in midcrouch, uncertain, thinking the cat might be playing with him. Before he could move, it flipped, snarling, onto its back, brought its hind legs up. Using all four feet, it clawed and bit at his hand. This time he cursed and snatched his hand away, straightening up. Instantly, the cat was up and loping across the lawn in the direction of a distant copse of trees. Pesi stood there, startled by the turn of events, not knowing what to think. His arm hung like a flag on a still day. Not once did the cat turn its head, and he watched until it was a gray streak in the taller grass. Then, shaking his head, he turned to go inside.

Months passed, and Pesi and Shenaaz forgot about the cat, though once in a while they spotted it strolling languidly within the apartment grounds. Their time was filled by studies and by one another. The shared experience of living in a foreign land, a world away from the one they grew up in, had woven a closeness between them. Though they were enthralled by still new, still fascinating sights and sounds, there were times when the unfamiliarity of it all grew hard for them, and they gasped for the well known and the instantly comprehensible like beached whales for water. In their uncertainty, they felt different from all around them except each other. At such times they found the proximity to someone whose realities corresponded to their own a comfort, a buffer between them and a horde of insecurities that pressed in on all sides. Merely to hear one another speak was a relief, a validation of their hard-edged and flat pattern of speech, grown weary and stumbling in the continual presence of the smooth cadences and soft consonants of Americans around them. To plumb one another's minds was to tap a blessed store of images that threatened otherwise to blur and fall away with time— Bombay streets and parks, temples and monuments, restaurants and clubs grew in stature, quality, or beauty in proportion to their nostalgia. Sometimes, at the mention of some obscure shop in Colaba or Flora Fountain or Dadar T.T. Circle, Shenaaz threw her arms around Pesi as though she would never let him go.

Her dreams for the future, he knew well, still lay back in Bombay, to which she fully intended to return. It was her home, not to be supplanted by another. Often, her conversation still centered around her parents and sister and uncles and aunts and cousins, as if they still bustled around her rather than thousands of miles away in Dadar Parsi Colony. Pesi came to feel as if he almost knew them. It amused him to hear, for instance, that her Burzin Uncle had yelled at his poor daughter, Katy, until she cried, for failing first-year science at Jai Hind. Poor Katy (who, unfortunately, had inherited Burzin's hairy elephant ears) was now attending first-year *domestic* science at Nirmala Niketan. So Shenaaz's place in the family pantheon—the only girl so far to do postgraduate work—was safe for a while.

As time went by at Harrison, however, and Pesi grew more secure in his new surroundings, a slow, almost imperceptibly slow change began to come over him. He felt homesick less often, and when he did it was a more fleeting stab. The great malls outside Harrison, almost tiny, self-contained cities, full of the latest electronic gadgets, drew him every other weekend along crisscrossing, smooth, incredibly wide highways. Along them streamed hundreds of the dream machines—sleek Corvettes, Porsches, Camaros—that he'd only seen pictures of and drooled over back in Bombay. First thing on the agenda once he had his master's and a job was to upgrade from his Nova to a supple, growling Miata. All America seemed like a gigantic *The Price Is Right* to him and he'd just got the call to come on down. At the malls, his eyes couldn't help but light upon the golden, laughing, flirting American girls who seemed to cross his every path, throwing curious and not-indifferent glances at him out of eyes the color of ocean waters, in comparison to which Shenaaz's warm brown eyes, no matter how tenderly they looked at him, began to appear drab and commonplace. In bed, too, those brown, spreading aureoles that he'd once found so sexy now seemed less exciting than the mere idea of pink ones. Like the ones of the women in Andy's *Playboy* magazines, sold everywhere here in bookstores and convenience stores and even grocery stores. Pink was more naked than brown, somehow.

But Shenaaz was a sweetheart, no question, the kind of girl he'd dreamed of when growing up, a girl to spend the rest of one's life with. He was lucky to have her.

Autumn passed, and the leaves fell and formed a mosaic of vivid reds and deep maroons and drab browns across Harrison, and the wind grew sharp and icy and sent them slithering here and there, rearranging the patterns. The dew frosted over, early one morning, and people slipped and slid to their cars, little puffs of mist emerging from their mouths, and brought ice scrapers out of storage from glove compartments and trunks. One day, at Harrison College of Engineering, as Pesi sat at his desk in the room for research assistants, he looked out the window and saw, for the first time in his life, flakes of snow drifting by. Bombay didn't have so much as a winter to speak of, let alone snow. The flakes fell faster and thicker until they formed a white canvas that blanked out the world around, readying it to be painted over again.

The snow fell for an hour, and that evening when he drove cautiously home with the heater on full blast to compensate for having underdressed, the lawns slept under a soft white afghan. He pulled into a space and saw a small patch of gray moving over the white. It was the cat. It picked its way toward him, making sounds that plainly said, Well, and how much longer were you going to keep me waiting in this terrible weather?

He bent down uncertainly, starting to shiver uncontrollably as the chill cut through to his marrow, but the cat rubbed up against him as if against an old friend. He opened the door to the warmth inside and let it in. It shook its paws fastidiously to rid itself of any traces of snow, then made itself at home on the sofa, licking itself over. The next day, when he opened the front door to the frigid air, leaving it pointedly ajar, the cat sat where it was, looking lazily out of half-shut eyes at the open door and the snowed-over porch.

As the winter wore on, Pesi came to know his new cotenant well. He didn't give it a name, though Shenaaz often just called it billee.

They spent much of the winter together, curled up on the couch in front of the television set, laughing at the antics of the cat as it stalked little insect prey—sometimes real, sometimes imaginary—across the living room. If lucky enough to encounter ants or flies or even a fat little moth, it rendered them half-comatose with wicked swats from its paws, then toyed with them as they struggled around, now pinning them down, now releasing them, cocking its head in wide-eyed amazement at their erratic and progressively feeble movements. Or it raced around the apartment like a kitten, batting a little stuffed mouse in front of it. The mouse had a tiny bell on the tip of its tail when they bought it, but the sound drove them crazy so they took it off. The cat was quickly bored by the routine fare of dry cat food; they had to tempt it with the more expensive canned stuff—exotic, juicy mixes of chicken and liver, tuna and beef, pâté textured, strong smelling, so Pesi often said he'd like to put some on a Ritz for himself.

Even as they shared these comfortable times, however, he became slowly aware of the growing ambivalence in his feelings for Shenaaz. On her twenty-fourth birthday in January, while the cat jumped for the red-and-silver, heart-shaped balloon, she kissed him with less frivolity and more feeling than usual. Then, opening her badly wrapped present, she screamed and kissed him again for the box of Joy. And it only made him uncomfortable. Same thing when she whipped the bottle out and put some on right away, though maybe he'd have felt insulted if she hadn't. Her changed, sultry smell aroused him, though, and soon he had other things on his mind. A day or two later, the balloon drifted low enough above the sofa, and the cat made short, explosive work of it.

One Sunday afternoon, as the winter months drew to a close and the snow began to turn to slush, Pesi sat conversing with his next-door neighbor and friend. A ginger-haired business student, Andy Wood wore glasses to offset his boyishness and achieve the executive look, though he had no actual need for them. The lenses had zero optical power, Pesi had once discovered, idly putting them on while his friend washed up after a game of racquetball. When confronted with the evidence, Andy had amiably owned up.

"Don't go telling anyone, now," he said. "I have my image to maintain."

This Sunday he'd come over in an exuberant mood, whistling a new John Cougar Mellencamp number, "Wild Night," twirling a racket in his hand.

"Let's get over to the courts, buddy. I have a desire to get my ass kicked today."

By his own admission, it irked him a little that Pesi should win regularly at a game whose rules he'd learned from Andy himself. Afterward, somewhat deflated by another drubbing, he dropped into Pesi's armchair, took the useless glasses off, disclosing bright blue eyes, and dabbed at his ruddy face with a thick green hand towel.

"I don't know; it must be this vegetable game you played at your club in Bombay."

"Squash," Pesi supplied.

"Yeah, that one. On the other hand, if I can keep from getting sweat all over my glasses someday, so I can see through the fuckin' things . . ."

Pesi laughed. "Why don't you just take them off, at least when you play?"

"Yeah, yeah, yeah. I know. I'm just afraid someone might see me—one of my countless fans looking down from the gallery.

Tell you what, Pesi: women see me as the picture of a future red-hot business exec, and I don't want to blow it."

"Are you having enough fun or not?"

"Oh, couldn't be better—getting it regularly enough, happy to report. They don't seem to wonder I can see my way around them so well once I take the glasses off in bed."

"Anyone in particular?"

"Nah. Variety's the oregano of life, haven't you heard?"

"Hmm," responded Pesi. From where it lounged along the broad windowsill, the cat turned its head toward the door and half-lifted itself. But it settled back.

"How about you? How's it with Shenaaz, you lucky dog?"

"Quite good." His tone was unconvincing even to himself, and as Andy cocked an orange eyebrow, he hurried on. "No, she's a great girl, I mean it; but I've been feeling vaguely hassled nowadays."

"Yeah? I thought you were crazy about the gal."

"I was, that's for sure." He pulled his handkerchief out, wiped the sweat off his face, and leaned over to switch on the table fan for the first time in months. Picking up speed, it droned like an airplane readying for takeoff. The cat turned its head from the window, the picture outside less like one off a Christmas card now, and looked toward the fan. As the animal came languidly to its feet and headed for the couch, its hind foot caught the photo frame, tipping it over. The frame fell with a sharp report and lay facedown on the corner table. "I don't know what it is. Seems to have worn off a bit. Also, I don't want to think about wedding bells and all that stuff at this point."

Not that he hadn't thought about it before—dreamed about it actually. Those frustrating years without a proper girlfriend, first at home and then initially here, he'd imagined nothing could be better than to settle down with some sweet girl. And they didn't come much sweeter than Shenaaz. . . . So, what was his problem now?

"I take it she does." Had he imagined it, or was there a dry note to Andy's voice?

"Ya. Don't know where she got the idea. Listen to this. Last Friday night we went to the Bone. We had a beer, danced a couple of times, then they dimmed the lights and played a slow number and we slow-danced. Usual thing, every other Friday or Saturday. But you know what she said to me this time?"

"What?" The gunsmoke metal prop went back over blue eyes, dimming them, its aviator style sufficiently dashing while still projecting maturity and serious intent.

"She pressed up real close and said almost in time to the music, 'When we're fuddy-duddy old grandparents retired in Bombay, will you still hold me like this, Pesi?'"

"Heh." Andy smiled. "So what did you say?"

"Nothing. Made some sort of sound, or else there'd have been trouble. How do I know what I'll do or where I'll be when I'm a grandfather? What am I, Sydney Omarr or something? I hardly know what I'm going to do *now*, let alone half a century later."

"Yeah, I know what you mean. So she wants to go back after she gets her master's?"

"Yep. Maybe a work extension on the F-1 for a year, but that's all."

"Hmm. Well, Shenaaz is real cute, but have you run into that other chick lately? The blonde in 214 behind our building."

"Oh, the Renee girl. Not for a week or two, but guess what she said to me then."

"Something like, 'I want you, big boy, and I want you now,' I hope?"

"Close. She said, 'You know, I heard the other day that guys who have long noses usually have big . . .' and then she stopped and smiled. So I laughed and said, 'What?' and she laughed too and said, 'Feet. What else?'"

"Hey, hey—she really wants you, guy. Forget your dick, she'd probably get you to do it with your nose." A distant look came over his face. "Interesting idea. . . . And that is one hot-looking number."

"That she is," said Pesi, picturing the blonde too. Absentmindedly, he dropped his hand to caress the cat behind its ear as it fidgeted on the couch. And before the intrigued Andy's eyes, a snarl wrinkling its nose over pointed white teeth, the cat shot into its flip-claw-and-bite attack, sending up a cloud of animal heat. Its hazel eyes glinted, silvered hairs rustled up.

Recovering quickly from the surprise this time and snatching his hand away, Pesi grinned up at Andy, then walked over to the door, unlocked it, and swung it wide open. The cat righted itself and came down from the couch, pattered over to the doorway. It stepped across the threshold calmly, rocked its head back a moment to survey the melting world outside—not too cold for comfort anymore—then loped away across the pavement and was soon lost behind another building.

"What was that?" Andy raised tangerine eyebrows at his surprisingly composed friend sauntering back into the room.

"Oh, nothing. It did that once before. . . ." He shrugged. "Just wants to get out again."

And a thought startled him, dropping him back on the couch, uncertain.

Andy rose and got his racket. "Personally, I'd have slung the critter out on its ass."

"No," said Pesi, managing to speak but still stunned, rubbing at the long, whitening scratch marks on his arm. "It's all right— that cat's just smarter than I am."

"If you say so. Well, I'm off for a shower now, but next time I'll be an unstoppable machine. Ain't no vegetable game gonna help you then."

On his way out he was already whistling "Pink Houses."

Pesi turned to the phone, as the door clicked shut, and dialed Shenaaz's number. She picked up. Her voice registered with him as different, foreign in some way, even as he responded. Listening closer, in surprise, to his *own* voice, he had the same eerie, uncomfortable sense of hearing unfamiliar intonations.

"Hi, Shenaaz. . . . What're you up to . . . ? So I'll come over for a while; I want to talk about something. . . . Nothing; played some racquetball with Andy. . . . Billee left again. . . . Yes, he's gone. . . . Okay, see you soon."

He sat back and thought for a while. He could have done it on the phone. Insulting way to finish, though, and, like those echoing overseas talks with his parents, too unreal. He leaned over to where the photo frame around their picture still lay on its face, the pentagonal stand slanted across its back like a crooked necktie, and righted it.

No, just a phone call would not have gotten him out of it; she'd have come over immediately anyway. For a moment he could almost see her face once he told her—big eyed, pale, unbelieving, little eggplant nose reddening, wide mouth compressed for once. She'd probably scream at him when she saw he really meant it. Or cry. He felt suddenly nauseous and walked over to the window, where he leaned his forehead against the glass, disoriented to the point of vertigo. Maybe he shouldn't do it. What an asshole he was. What changes they'd been through together, managed together. And how could he blame her for assuming things? He'd had similar thoughts—hopes—himself, along the way, though he'd have to deny that to her. If they'd been back in Bombay, they wouldn't have gone this far without getting engaged at least. Her parents would have seen to that. She'd expected it to be no different here, and now. . . .

Cursing aloud, he snapped the sequence and slid the window up, then stuck his head out into the chilled air, breathing it in deeply. He felt better almost at once. He let his mind drift to less troubling things, to the waves at Worli seaface lapping incessantly below the parapet, to the bland taste of coconut water, to people walking their dogs along the side. But it was all too hazy. Glancing inward to the seaface photograph of his parents and Buster, he saw that a hairline crack in the glass now ran from beveled side to beveled side at an angle across the picture, as if on a No Entry sign. Something ominous about it jerked him around to the outdoors again. From the wooded area into which the cat had once disappeared came the sound, muffled by distance, of a branch cracking off and falling to the ground. His eyes scanned the clump mechanically for the branch, but he couldn't tell to which tree it had belonged.

It didn't matter. He focused instead on the drifts of snow still covering much of the lawn and opened himself to the frost. When at last he began to rehearse out loud, the words sounded foreign, as cold and as pointed as icicles.

Falling

As afternoon slipped into evening, the servant girl climbed out a window onto a ledge underneath. No more than a foot wide, it ran along the side of the drab yellow, reinforced-concrete staff quarters overlooking the Indian Scientific Institute's tennis courts. Veer Paintal and Abhinandan Ghosh were hitting balls to each other on the advanced courts for students, clay courts of a surprisingly odorless, dried cow-dung variety. It was their daily habit to get out and play after class. Veer saw the girl first, as the descending sun reached warmly around him to illuminate her. She had her back to them and was lowering herself from a third-story window onto the reinforced-concrete ledge several feet below. Her supple but short, toffee-brown arms grasped the windowsill, and bare, cracked feet groped the wall above the ledge, flaking off pieces of faded yellow plaster before touching down. Like heavy leaves, the larger chips fluttered almost thirty feet down and spattered against the flagstone pavement.

"Abhi, look at that!" Veer shouted, pointing with his racket.

By the time Abhinandan turned fully to look, the woman was inching left, hugging the wall, toward what appeared to be an upside-down, burn-stained frying pan lying half on the ledge and half on air, its handle pointed at her. Students on the other courts looked up too. The syncopated *fwop* sounds of racket strings on balls trailed off and a mild commotion went around—whistles, surprised laughter, encouragement, some lewd commentary. Veer relaxed as well and began to look on the whole thing as just welcome entertainment. Engineering college students, he'd found, tended to function along routine lines involving study, sports, friends, alcohol, and a smug contemplation of the future—his night dreams had vivid images of himself flying, stretched out in the air almost like Hanuman leaping mountains. Anything outside this pleasant but predictable formula was fodder for jaded senses. So when the woman reached the pan, bent over carefully to her left, and straightened with it in her hand, the tennis players cheered loudly. Several were moved to clap.

The sounds must have broken through her concentration, and she paused for a second to turn only her head and flash them a victorious smile. She was short and thick-waisted, her sari a dull olive with yellow bordering, her face round and plain, but Veer was struck by her blend of audacity and composure. He was afraid that it might distract her now that she knew she had an audience. But she retraced her steps carefully until she stood again beneath the center point of the window. Reaching up with the blackened pan, she tipped it over the windowsill so that it disappeared with a faraway clatter into, presumably, the kitchen. Only when she tried to pull herself up after the pan, nut-brown arms straining to inch scrabbling feet higher, did it become apparent that she had a problem.

To let herself down by her arms had been one thing, but, stretched out as they were just to reach the sill, she didn't have the strength to draw herself up. For a moment, as her feet found the ledge again, she seemed at a loss, and the tennis players quieted down to see what she would do. A warm wind blew up and ruffled the courts, sending up dust. As she looked tentatively around, a thick, cast-iron drainage pipe running vertically to the right of the window seemed to draw her eye. It was unpainted and rusty and the clamps attaching it to the building looked treacherously frail, but she moved to it and pulled at it. Gripping it in her right hand, her left holding on to the windowsill, she pressed her browned right foot up on a joint between sections of pipe, where her toes found some purchase. Then she raised her left foot barely off the ledge.

The pipe held, so she lifted herself entirely onto it and turned her face to the windowsill, now clearly attainable. Veer had begun to feel she could manage anything, when, leaning over to draw herself across with both hands, angled against the pipe like the short stick of a Y, she struggled with her balance, then lost it.

"Shit," he mouthed in the sudden, absolute silence, as she clutched and clawed and almost hung on to the ledge. Then she was falling, sluggishly, turning just a little in the air, but strangely horizontal—the way he saw himself flying in his dreams. Except that she was headed straight down. She fell without a murmur, her sari flapping, and he'd wonder later why she didn't scream to see the ground coming up at her. Still turning just a degree or two, she hit the pavement with a dull, gut-wrenching thud that jangled his senses and jerked him into a scramble for the gate.

Abhinandan was close behind him as he hurled it open to clang against the side rail. They dashed outside the tennis enclosure and around to the flagstone pathway encircling the staff quarters. She lay on her right side, her arm crunched to the ground—the blood around her head was startlingly bright against gray, pitted squares. Her sari's top folds had come off to reveal a shiny, dark-green blouse; her legs were splayed, stretching the sari just above her ankles. Dropping his racket, Veer kneeled almost into the luminous red liquid by her head—she wasn't moving. The only eye he could see was shut. The other side of her face, close to the ground, was sheeted in blood. Sweet, nauseous odors swirled around her.

"She must be dead," he said, nervously fingering his mustache, as Abhinandan crouched next to him. The rest of the tennis players had come out too and were crowding around, bending over to look, reporting back excitedly to those behind them. Not that they'd wished harm should come to her, but the servant girl was already more than a passing break in the monotony.

"Looks as if she's breathing," Abhinandan replied, pointing to an almost unnoticeable lift and fall of the dark blouse.

Almost as if to confirm, she twitched at the waist.

"Where is N. B. Dutt?" Veer asked, looking around for the physical training instructor in charge of the tennis courts, and soon the burly, heavily mustachioed PTI, breathing hard, shouldered his way through the players to where the girl lay.

"What is the situation, Paintal?" he asked over the chatter, noting the two nearest to her. Then, taking in the young woman's blood-spattered face: "Yes, yes. This is Mr. Pai's servant."

"She's alive, sir," Veer said. "But I don't know if it's safe to move her."

A decisive look came over N. B. Dutt's broad features, twitching the upcurled mustachios. "Okay, you stay there. Ghosh, you go get a riksha. I will go up to see if Pai is there, but don't move her until I come."

They rushed off. Veer, left kneeling by the girl, was now able to detect the shallow, irregular breathing. Her round, bloodied face contorted suddenly, and a guttural sound came out of her. Several of the tennis players made sympathetic clicking noises, but Veer felt encouraged. She's still there, he thought; maybe she'll be all right.

The sun, at a lower angle to the staff quarters now, lit the window. Soon two heads, N. B. Dutt's big one and a woman's, appeared and disappeared several times. The servant girl began to grunt frequently, her features contorting again. Slippery reds packed the front and side of her crow-black hair, pulled back into a knotted brown ribbon, and Veer wondered if he should lift her face from the puddle of blood so she couldn't inhale it. He decided not to.

N. B. Dutt came back first, huffing, his face ringed with sweat from climbing the stairs. "Pai is not there. Mrs. Pai says she does not know what to do with the girl—she is always making some trouble. What is happening here?"

"She's nearly awake, sir. I think she's in lots of pain." Making trouble? Sharp dislike kindled within Veer for the woman whose head, framed by the window, looked down expressionlessly at them. The palla of a white cotton sari pulled over her hair left only a band of black above pinched, middle-aged features. Veer wondered what other misadventures the servant girl had gotten into before she climbed out that window.

"Yes. My God!" N. B. Dutt said, as the groans grew louder. "Will you take her to the student hospital, Paintal? We will put her safely in the riksha by just keeping her in the same position—nothing else to do."

"Okay, sir," Veer said. Abhinandan came rattling back in a riksha, and they set about the transfer. Veer and N. B. Dutt slid their hands under her back, supporting her head with their arms, while Abhinandan and two others took hold of her trunk and legs. Though they lifted her simultaneously, keeping her horizontal, she cried out in frightening tones. The sound turned Veer's throat dry. Blood slicked his arms and then hands so he had to reach forward to get a better grip on her. They laid her flat on the torn black-plastic seat cover, her legs hanging over, and Veer and Abhinandan stepped up on either side as the riksha started off for Sarojini Naidu Hospital.

The rikshavala, a swarthy, rope-muscled fellow in a short, checked lungi, grimy vest, and apple red bandana, stood up on the pedals, his calf muscles knotting and unknotting beneath dark, sweat-sheened skin, for much of the kilometer along Scholars' Avenue. When he still couldn't move the riksha fast enough, they got off and ran by its side, Veer's hand against the servant girl's outer knee, his white canvas shoes flying over dusty gray macadam. Her utterances rose and fell with the slightest jouncing of the riksha as it whirred along. Though the evening was wearing on, the air was still like the inside of a tandoor, and soon they were sweating worse than the rikshavala. When they reached Naidu's whitewashed and window-pocked walls, they rushed on into an empty day clinic steeped in antiseptic odors, its yawning spaces testimony to the general good health of engineering students. They pulled the balding doctor on duty along to the foyer while still babbling the story out to him. He went straight to the side of the riksha where the girl's head lay and examined her. Her eyes were shut. Hoarse sounds came out of her as he gently turned her red-slicked face first to one side and then the other.

"This case is too serious," he said, looking up, slipping the stethoscope back around the collar of his white coat and pulling a white handkerchief from his pants' pocket. "You will have to take her to Railway Hospital."

They stood there, panting, staring at the egg-headed, light-skinned, bespectacled man. He was a doctor; what did he mean the case was too serious?

"Why can't you do something here only?" Veer's tone was curt: the railway hospital was off-campus, all the way over in town.

"No, no," the doctor said. "There is no equipment in Naidu for cases like this—this is only a student hospital." Sweat popped out on his bald head. "She will die on my hands! I will give you the ambulance to take her. And I will give her a pain-killing injection. That is all I can do."

"All right," Veer said, grudging any thanks but glad to have both offers.

They paid the rikshavala; he wasted no time on the usual bickering. When the spotless cream ambulance pulled around, they helped the driver get a stretcher out. The doctor gave the fallen girl her shot—she seemed oblivious to it. Then they lifted her onto thick, yellow-stained canvas and slid the stretcher through the rear doors onto its supports. Veer and Abhinandan got in with her, and the van rumbled off.

The painkiller worked well; apart from uneasy stirrings and small, plaintive noises as they bumped over railroad crossings, the girl lay quietly all the way into Dharampur. They sat over her on the partition housing, turning from time to time to the vibrating glass pane between them and the driver. Her blood had thickened around the black hair on Veer's arms, and he used the ocher upper border of her sari, now redraped across her shoulder, to wipe off as much as he could. He felt sticky. The small space was thick with odors—their sweat and her blood.

"Hope she'll be all right," Abhinandan said, his voice calm, ever the steady one in tight tennis matches.

"Hope so. You saw the way she fell?"

"Ya. She should have just left the vessel."

Veer wondered, as a matter of fact, what on earth the girl

might have been up to with a pan to let it drop outside a window. Shaking it clean?

"That Mrs. Pai didn't even come down to see how their servant was," he marveled. "Maybe the girl was scared that if she left it there they'd kick her out."

The servant girl shifted; a spasm ran through her body. They stopped talking, and ten minutes later the van rolled into the grounds of the Northeastern Railway Hospital, a group of connected brick buildings that managed to look a darker red than the individual bricks. When the ambulance stopped in the dirt courtyard, Veer and Abhinandan jumped out and ran up into a sick ward. A gust of disinfectant hit them as they entered. An ocean of steel cots stretched away in every direction they turned, upon each a gloom-filled patient laid low. A woman in a white sari, probably an attendant, came strutting along between the beds. Veer stepped up to her and said, "A girl had an accident. She is—"

"Go to Dr. Banerjee," the attendant said, pointing away from herself as she hurried along. The name, Veer noted, was a Bengali one.

Turning obediently, they navigated the sea of beds toward a slim man by the side of one, scribbling notes on a clipboard.

"Dr. Banerjee, we're from ISI," Veer said, ignoring the man's automatic hand motions, pen and all, toward the side.

The doctor looked up curiously. His mustache was neatly trimmed like Veer's, his face still young. Good signs, Veer felt.

"A woman fell down from a building. She's outside in the ISI ambulance."

The young doctor dropped the board with promising alacrity onto his seemingly comatose patient's bedsheet and strode out the door with them.

"She's a student?" he asked.

"No—a servant."

Something changed on the doctor's face. Heated, heavy air pressed around them again, as they tripped briskly down stone entrance steps onto the grounds. They climbed into the ambulance to crouch by the side of the stretcher.

The doctor was not long in examining the girl.

"We cannot admit her unless there's somebody to pay hospital fees," he said to Veer. Some of the blood on her face, neck, and hair had started to cake. "Lots of work to do on her. Where are her relations?"

"Don't know. But who will do it, then?" Veer asked, dismayed.

The doctor looked him up and down—the canvas shoes, white socks, and short pants, the black thatch of hair—and made up his mind.

"Take her to government hospital; they will admit her free of charge. Midnapur District Hospital is closest—thirty, forty kilometers."

"That much? What if on the way she dies?"

"No," the doctor said, shaking his head and getting up. "She will not die in that much time."

They kept pace with him as he strode back to his ward, eyes on the ground, shaking his head repeatedly in response to Veer's doubts and pleas.

"Abhi, tell him something in Bong," Veer said, tactless in his desperation, thinking the man might be swayed if the request were made in his mellifluous but sometimes, Veer privately felt, too-honeyed mother tongue.

Abhinandan said some quick words in Bengali but only earned another shake of the head and a terse reply. He tightened his lips and shrugged at Veer. Abhi, Veer knew, was not a garrulous man but—true to his nickname, which meant *now* in Hindi—a man of the moment, ready to leave the past behind and tackle what was at hand. As to the future, it would take care of itself.

The doctor picked up his clipboard. The patient in bed, just a sun-blackened, quilted face above a white sheet, seemed not to have so much as lifted his eyes. Looking around at the hundreds, or so it seemed, of other white-sheeted patients, Veer felt something like seasickness grab at his head.

In a rough voice he said, "You have writing paper?"

The doctor squeezed the board's clip to pull out a notepad and ballpoint pen, then turned back to his patient. Veer scribbled in peacock blue: "The girl is well enough to be driven to Midnapur District Hospital. We will not admit her at the Railway Hospital because there's nobody to pay hospital fees. She will not die on the way."

"Here—sign," he said to the doctor, thrusting the note at him.

The doctor looked wearily up, read the note, signed it without a word, and shoved it back. Veer folded it and put it in the side pocket of his tennis shorts. Then he turned and walked out. Abhinandan caught up with him striding back to the ambulance.

He went up to the driver's window. "Midnapur Hospital jaante ho?"

"Haan, sahab," the driver said, bobbing his head, and Veer was relieved that they didn't have to ask the doctor. For the first time, he looked closely at the driver: dark-skinned, local fellow—probably from town—in no semblance of a uniform. Cheerfully debonair in coffee bush shirt and powder blue pants. They climbed into the rear. The van set out once more, cutting through the frenetic railway-station bazaar and past the sleeping hovels of Old Dharampur. Through the quivering glass pane, Veer saw the driver turn to scan the huts near the street entrance, then yank the wheel barely in time to avoid a rikshavala bent on collision.

Just as the town's lime-washed and mildewed, single-story houses dropped behind, the girl began to whimper and bring her hands up to her face. Veer took hold of them and lowered them to her sides, but now they had blood on them. Chapped and small within his own hands, they'd felt warm. Not like the hands of someone who was dying. His all-white tennis clothes were already streaked with the browning red, so he wiped his hands carelessly on the shorts.

Clearly the painkiller was wearing off. Above the girl's whimpers, he said with a grimace, "Let's go back to Railway Hospital for one more injection."

"No point," Abhinandan said. "Better go fast to the government hospi."

The girl began to moan and throw her arms around. The movement clearly hurt her, so she lay still again, never opening her eyes. But the dirt track—hardly worth calling a road now—had become rough with dips and ruts, and as the van bounced over them, each jolt crossed her face and made her scream. The jagged sounds scraped at Veer's nerves. The stretcher began to slide and jump on its supports, so they leaned over and took hold of either end. It needed all their weight to keep it from moving, but every now and then they lost balance and it shifted.

She began to utter some words in Bengali and then to repeat a name. "Rana," she cried. "Rana!" Her voice was shrill above the tearing of her groans.

They looked at one another, embarrassed, wondering who the man was. Maybe she was married. But if there had once been the mark of sindur along the middle of the hair drawn back across her ears, it was lost now in the greater red of her wounds. The undamaged side of her face showed a spotty pallor, brown skin drained of blood. The air inside the van—their combined breath and sweat—stank like a dung heap.

His hands on the slippery stretcher rods, arms straining, Veer twisted around to look outside. The sun had dropped to the ground, a pink plastic beach ball, barely illuminating the passing flatland smothered in dust and the tops of runt trees furlongs apart. When the van finally wheeled, tires screeching, horn blaring for attention, into the grounds of a low, sprawling medical center—apparently a solitary outpost to serve the Midnapur rural district—Veer's arms were as stiff as the stretcher rods.

They clambered out and rushed into the squat, reinforced-concrete administration building, where they told their story once again. But this time, male attendants were promptly called and the stretcher taken down from the ambulance. Striding alongside through the gray, untouched-concrete maze of the main structure, they were once again surrounded by antiseptic odors. Veer kept a hand on the servant girl to stop her from tossing around. They reached the ICU—as still as a mausoleum—where she was transferred to one of two unoccupied beds and given a shot of painkiller. She lapsed into semiconsciousness again.

Veer was overjoyed to finally see a doctor looking after her— a short, curly-haired fellow—although he'd expected her to be rushed off to the operating room. Still, the doctor was testing her for blood type and giving quiet orders to a nurse, more business-like in dress, cap, and stockings this time. She bustled around to set up an IV for saline or glucose, while another nurse swabbed the head wound. Veer himself found he had little energy left, now that their work was done. It was Abhinandan who asked if the girl would live, and at the doctor's quick but reassuring nod, all the tension slipped out of Veer, leaving him limp.

Despite the coolness settling outside, he slumped in the front seat between the driver and Abhinandan on their way back to campus, staring along twin cones of dust-spattered light streaming from the headlamps. When the driver inquired respectfully in Hindi of the servant girl's status, they gave him the good news. The man laughed outright in celebration, a cracked, giddy sound that filled the small cabin, and all three began excitedly to recall the long evening's events as the van navigated the same ruts and dips in reverse order.

After a while, however, the driver's sharp chatter seemed to cross the line between a reasonable level of palliness and excessive familiarity. Veer felt something inside him shrink from it. So he fell quiet again. Abhi, of course, was hardly the man to keep conversation going longer than needed, and the driver's talkativeness subsided. For a while there was only the hum of the engine and the grinding of wheels over gravel. But now that all the urgency had leaked out of him, Veer began to feel quite proud of what they'd done.

"We must have saved her life," Abhinandan said, echoing Veer's thoughts.

"Ya," he replied. "I want to go after a few days and see how she is." She was partly their product now, and he felt a stockholder's interest in her health.

At Mussoorie Hall, they took the driver along to their wing, where they unlocked their rooms and gave him a ten-rupee note. All smiles, he said, "Salaam, sahab," to each of them before going off. Veer wondered again if the man lived on campus or in town. Given how he'd peered into Old Dharampur—presumably for women—when they'd cut past the locality, it was probably town. In which case he still had some driving ahead of him.

Veer stripped off and dumped the bloodied outfit, then stood under a tepid shower in an unlit corner stall for minutes, the stickiness and heat sliding off. Time slowed back to a crawl. The evening's excitement had undoubtedly been a break in the ISI routine. He had helped save a life—he ought to feel exhilarated. Like the ambulance driver. Yet, for some strange reason, he didn't. At dinner he and Abhinandan, in jeans and cotton bush shirts now, were ravenous, wolfing down hot dal and rice, but heads down and untalkative within the clamor of the mess. They walked out to the bicycle shed and, braced by cool breezes, rode under a carpet of stars toward N. B. Dutt's quarters in the C sector, whirring past uniform rows of drab yellow buildings whitened by moonlight.

"What happened?" the burly PTI asked, his chest bare, hairy like a jungle above cream trousers almost splitting at the seams, and they told him.

"Okay," he said, capping a series of interested grunts. Silent again for a moment, he deftly adjusted his genital sack, then twirled his mustachios with the same hand. "I will tell Mr. and Mrs. Pai. I kept your rackets."

He lumbered inside and got them.

Back at Mussoorie, Veer remembered to fish his blood-stained shorts from the dun canvas laundry bag to get the folded note out of his pants' pocket. Crisp brown blots splotched the script like a Rorschach test series. One reminded him of a tobacco pipe puffing forth other, smaller blots. He placed the sheet half under his table lamp, so the ceiling fan wouldn't blow it onto the floor. Then he dropped into a deep, dreamless sleep.

A week later, he and Abhinandan split the taxi fare and visited the girl at the district hospital spreading like an oasis in the scrubland. They were directed not to the ICU but to a sick ward. Again they found themselves in an absolute sea of white sheets and prone bodies. Veer almost felt the ground sway beneath him as they cut between beds. When they walked up to her cot, the girl was lying awake, covered to her neck. She turned her pillowed head placidly toward them, and Veer wondered if she knew who they were. He saw that the whole right side of her face was purple and misshapen.

"Kaisee ho?" he asked her. She nodded carefully to indicate she was okay. Abhinandan spoke to her in Bengali, and she made short replies in the clear, high voice that had cried, "Rana," but minus the agitation Veer remembered so well.

"Her relations know where she is now," Abhinandan translated. "They came here once." Once? Veer lifted his eyebrows.

Abhinandan spoke to her again. But she replied only in monosyllables.

"May be that it hurts her to talk," he said. "Look at her eye."

Veer had flinched at the sight of her right eye as soon as she'd faced them. A bright rose red eyeball blossomed across a shadowy iris, threads of darker red running like cracks across the whole. It stared almost demonically off at an angle to the left eye.

At Mussoorie again, their dhobi, Madanlal, brought the tennis shirt and shorts back with diluted brown stains still splashed across them. He was a thin, rat-featured fellow with a laconic but high-pitched way of talking, a sort of piped, weary drawl, and an aggravating habit of losing a vest or hanky, then insisting it had never been given him in the first place. Veer chucked the newly washed sports clothes into the fresh pile, to be washed again. In response to his accusation of laziness, Madanlal just shifted yellowed, ratty eyes and said, "As you like, sahab. But who did you kill to get so much blood on your clothes?"

When they saw the girl again the next weekend, the purplish bruising had faded to the toffee of her skin. But that side of her face still seemed out of shape, and the eye, no longer in bloom, stared blankly off in the wrong direction. She looked calmly at them out of the other, mud-brown eye and responded briefly to Abhinandan's queries.

"She says she'll be discharged soon," he told Veer, then puckered his generally undisturbed forehead. "I don't know what I should say to her; she doesn't like to talk, looks like."

And Veer himself did not know what they could talk about with a servant girl. It was doubtful she even knew all they'd done for her. And if she did, she ought to have thanked them properly, not acted as if she didn't even want to open her mouth.

"Will her relations come for her when she has to go home?" he asked, wondering if the Rana fellow was one of them. At least one family member ought to have been with her every day.

Abhinandan put the question to her, and she nodded in an off-hand way that left Veer still uncertain. Anyway, it was not their business to take her home, though if she'd requested it they could have given her the riksha fare.

"Okay," he said in Hindi, nodding at her. "We are going."

She nodded back, no change of expression, and they left. Veer felt deflated by the silence that had stood between them but said to himself it was basically quite natural. How many words had he ever said to the sweeper woman at home in Bombay, or she to him? It took a second to even remember her name—Maitri. Comely cleaner of bathrooms. She wore her deeply dyed indigo saris Maharashtrian-style with a long middle fold pulled through between her legs, up the cleft of her buttocks, and tucked in behind to get it out of her way while cleaning. When he'd reached puberty and she backed her washcloth across the floor on all fours toward him, that tightly defined rump in the air and waving, he'd had his first conscious erection. But Ma, craftily sensing what was going through her son's head those days, had spoken casually yet scornfully of a distant uncle who'd been such a billy goat as to carry on with even the servant girls. Well-brought-up boys, needless to say, didn't behave like billy goats.

Still, he remembered the bold smile the servant girl had flashed from the concrete ledge before she'd fallen, and felt that she was different now. In the gray rough-walled hospital corridor, they crossed her doctor on his way to the ward. Veer stopped him to ask about her.

"She will be okay," Dr. Basu said, smiling pleasantly out of a dark face below a mess of graying curls. "Only her one eye is gone. Her shoulder, also, will not function. Actually, because it took the impact in front of the head, she is living."

And Veer saw again in his mind how her falling body had been so nearly horizontal. And now he saw the shoulder hit first, with splintering force, then her head jerk forward and smash into the flagstone.

They thanked the doctor and walked back to the taxi. At Mussoorie, Madanlal brought the latest washload back—the tennis clothes were almost white again. That evening as Veer studied, he saw the scribbled, stained note under the lamp's amber glow and realized they didn't need it anymore. The large blotch now looked like a brontosaurus shitting smaller blotches. He crumpled the note, then dropped it in the rubbish bin.

Two months passed, baking summer months that gave way to cooler weather. Other matters, routine matters of study and sport—entropy and tennis—took over for Veer, though at times he'd remember his chivalrous rescue of the servant girl, as he saw it then, with satisfaction mostly and only a faint question mark. His conscious mind, given to single, often passionate focus, was more adept at serial processing than parallel, so midterm exams and intercollegiate tennis meets pushed images of falling women into back regions. For some reason, he found himself unusually nervous about the outcome of these familiar events, a general success in which he'd always taken for granted. This new and mysterious anxiety led him to study harder, and his exam results were actually better than usual. But the same anxiety tightened him up in match situations—where the college name was at stake—so though he sweated twice as much in practice, he lost more than he won.

His dreams, those nights, as he tossed on a thin-mattressed steel cot similar to those in the sick wards, were less sharp-edged than before. Blurred figures drifted across colorless landscapes. He thought of mentioning all this to Abhi, who was winning matches routinely and saw exams as only bothersome, but decided not to—why look womanish over vague tensions? So he put on his tennis shoes, instead, and got his friend to swat an extra quota of balls to his strangely tight forehand.

They were both still curious, however, about how the girl was getting on. Often, they looked up from the tennis courts to the staff-quarters window yet never spotted her. To actually climb up to Pai's flat and ask to see the servant would be too strange a thing to do. And, again, what would they say to her? So one evening before playing, they walked up to where N. B. Dutt was, on the concrete stepped seating along the side of the courts, and asked him instead. He'd played already, they could tell, from the stale vapors lifting abundantly off the broad planes of his body.

"Yes, yes," he said, leaning back heavily, arms folded, hairy blockbuster thighs pushing thickly apart below white shorts, black mustachios curling heavenward. "Pai was telling me they had to fire her."

"*Fire* her?" Veer said.

"Yes. No choice. She was always making trouble before, but now she was not even doing her work properly—not preparing food on time, always leaving the rooms dirty . . ."

"But, sir, she had become blind in one eye," Veer said, aghast, "and her shoulder was broken!"

"That is correct, Paintal, but what could they do? Pai says she was all the time crying about some fellow from town who was going to marry her. But he backed out because she had become so ugly. She was just crying and muttering all the time, or answering back rudely to Mrs. Pai. What to do? They gave her lots of chance, but she was very ungrateful. She even said we should have *left* her on the ground after she fell down."

Veer and Abhinandan looked at each other with open mouths. Left her on the ground. . . .

"Where is she now?" Abhi asked, palms turned outward, his voice enfeebled for the first time in Veer's memory.

N. B. Dutt looked slyly around, but there was no one close enough to hear. "Pai may be saying it just like that—how does he know?—but he says she has gone into Old Dharampur."

Veer went cold. Old Dharampur was the red-light area of town: just a side street lined with tin-roofed hovels in which the women accommodated townsmen and sometimes an ISI student. Dingy, windowless, low-walled rooms, he'd heard, a narrow wooden cot in each. A small group of the prostitutes usually sitting on a bare cot outside, chatting, waiting, dressed only in shabby petticoats and half-unhooked blouses, no saris, eyeing any comers and waiting to be picked. A side of Veer wanted desperately to disbelieve this, to feel, like N. B. Dutt, that Pai was just concocting something juicy. It was the side that, until recently, had flown in his dreams. But the engineering side of him saw a trend that was only too easy to extrapolate—from accident to injury to lover's betrayal to loss of livelihood to this. Maybe Pai did know. Maybe, to escape his miserable wife, he now went to Old Dharampur and screwed the servant girl whenever he felt like it. . . .

So this was the life they had saved her for.

N. B. Dutt sat there with a smug expression that dried up any response. They walked out onto the courts and played, but Veer didn't enjoy it. He even thought he could actually smell the cow dung, and didn't play again for several months. One day, he rode his bicycle into town and lingered outside Old Dharampur, flashes of sun bouncing harshly off the metal roofs into his eyes.

But he couldn't work up enough courage to enter the street. He winced at the thought that the girl might think he'd come as a customer or that she'd snigger if he tried to save her again. And how would he do that? What kind of hospital would he take her to, this time? So he finally turned the bicycle around and rode off. It was well into the next term before he ventured back on court.

His life had moved still further along expected lines by then—final-year projects, campus interviews, applications abroad, color snapshots of prospective brides in letters from his mother—and he'd put the girl out of his mind. Except that at night sometimes, before a sudden shortness of breath pulled him gasping out of sleep, he found himself dropping, tumbling unstoppably through shifting gray. Falling in his dreams.

Rabbit's Foot

It was a gun to take seriously—sleek, heavy, and oiled. Patently male. A gift from Veer's uncle Arun in Georgia, who was an avid hunter and collector of rifles. For an air pistol, its black-metal barrel was long, giving it a look of efficiency reinforced by the cylindrical pump-action piston case. Nor did it lack power. Pellets from the slim .22 bore above the casing tore through soup cans thirty feet away or slapped into brick wall behind the cans if Veer missed.

After he grew tired of shooting cans set against the back walls of First State Apartments, Veer began to cut through a field behind the old people's home to a patch of woods by the railway line. The small surviving thicket seemed vaguely anomalous, just its existence within even a tiny university town like Harrison. Nevertheless, there it was—a miniature forest full of rabbits, just a hop away from streets and buildings. Tim Heuertz had mentioned there were seasons, for hunting rabbit or bigger game, in the county. But growing up in concrete Bombay, Veer had never had the chance to go on shikar—deer, wild geese, boar, anything. And if he had, his mother would have been horrified. "No, baba, must not eat meat. Plus, poor antelope, what did it do to you?" So at twenty-two and on his own now in America, he gave no thought to whether it was season yet. He liked to walk with the gun in his hand, swinging at his side, a swaggering, stubble-faced antihero like Terence Hill in old Trinity Westerns. He'd seen every one of them, back in Bombay, when still an open-mouthed, short-pantsed boy in the cool, darkened, solipsism-inspiring back rows of New Excelsior or Sterling. Here, outside, it was bright and warm. But not so hot as to make him listless, the spring air still sharp enough to whet his appetite. Why wait for arbitrary seasons?

The first two days, he walked past the old people's home instead of cutting through the field. Through the spotless front glass, he could see them looking out from their card tables and armchairs and from around the piano. Was that worse than getting old and dying at home like Indian folk, or better? A "home" wasn't home, but even home could turn solitary, as his had for Dadima after his grandfather's accident. Despite his parents being there to console her. He could still feel her leathery hand tighten to almost a death grip on his as she glared down from the third-floor balcony at the stream of Fiats and Ambassadors rumbling by, muttering, "Government should pass a law, make everybody walk again." Now if he stayed on in the States after he got his master's, how would life on their own in Purnima Condominiums be for Ma and Pitaji when they grew old, or, worse, if one died leaving the other behind? Would they agree to leave their homeland—his too, but theirs for three-quarters of their life spans by then—and join him here? If he'd had problems assimilating, how much harder would it be at their age?

Well, he thought as the woods loomed, if he did get a rabbit, he'd make a wish for his parents' good health on its lucky foot. But no rabbit volunteered itself either that day or the next.

He could still smell the sapwood as he sauntered back home the second day, in no real mood to return to his thesis. "Stochastic Simulation of Blah Blah Blah"—utter tripe. Over by the old people's home, a dark-uniformed and helmeted motorcycle cop had pulled up. Smart-looking, not like the comic, half-pantsed traffic havaldars of Bombay. The policeman pushed a black, gleaming visor up, facing Veer. He looked back and nodded as a matter of course, then continued past the home. But only twenty feet along, he heard a man's voice raised from behind: "Stop right there!"

What? he thought, but halted. Trinity would have stopped too, wide-blue-eyed and good-naturedly astonished over the scruffy beard, a burp welling gently out.

"Drop the gun!" the voice said in smooth Delawarian accents.

Veer looked hurriedly around the side of the pavement and spotted a thick clump of grass. Carefully, he lobbed the air pistol to it.

"Turn around—slowly—with your hands in the air."

He turned slowly. The cop was now only a dozen yards away, feet planted firmly, arms raised, a heavy pistol in his hands leveled at Veer.

"Get facedown on the ground."

"Listen," Veer called, struggling by now for patience. The bad-Western plot had passed beyond fun into ridiculous. "That's just a—"

"Get down or I'll shoot!" The words were pitched higher, strung tightly in a row, and Veer heard the heightened tension in them. The dark gun barrel seemed almost to lengthen.

"Wait," he said, scared at last, scrambling down on his palms and knees, barely conscious of scraping them. He stretched his legs out behind him. The concrete, so near his black-stubbled face, was rough grained and powdery, its surface crossed by subtle variations in color. It felt cold and rough on his arms, smelled faintly of dog shit.

"Stretch your hands out in front of you," the cop said, still high-voiced, and when Veer complied, stepped carefully to the grass, still facing him, gun trained on him all the way.

One hand reached down to Veer's pistol within the cabbage-green sprouts. The cop picked it up, and sneaked a quick look at it.

Then another. Veer could see the slump of his shoulders and the gun hand dropping.

"It's only an air-pistol," Veer said, getting up cautiously and dusting off his corduroys. He saw now that they'd had an audience: behind glass, the old folks were intent. Must have been a switch for them, to watch someone his age come up against death.

The policeman, visibly embarrassed, less generically robotic once the helmet came off to show thinning brown hair, said there were so many trigger-happy crazies around he couldn't take any chances. They'd got a call from the old people's home that a guy with a gun in his hand was running around Harrison in broad daylight. Not to mention, Veer added mentally, the guy's brown-skinned and rough-bearded looks—couldn't have helped. Stupid of him not to have realized that the air gun would look like the real thing from a distance.

"Couple things," the cop said, as he filled out a report. "Don't carry the gun openly; it scares people. And when a cop tells you to do something, do it—I came an inch from shooting you back there, when you didn't get down. Count yourself lucky."

Lucky? thought Veer, suddenly outraged. Lucky you didn't *shoot* me for carrying an *air* pistol? That I'd already thrown away? The logic struck him as similar to that in the condescending, easy assumption by so many Americans (his acceptance of which was required) that he must thank his lucky stars nightly for the good fortune to be in America. And if not, well, why didn't he just go back? Why was he still here? Good question, he'd think in response—here, where he'd twice tried to donate his own blood and twice been turned down. Once because he'd come too recently from a "third-world country," and a second time because he'd had jaundice—hepatitis in American lingo— a dozen years back, when he was just a kid. (They'd made him feel like a villain too, after he'd waited half an hour in line outside the mall donation booth.) Here, where women, for the first time in his life, were turned off by his accent. (Aural creatures, women—you had to sound right even more than look right.) Here, where, again for the first time, he'd learned that his skin color was less than perfect. (Wop. Dago.) But he stayed his tongue, speaking only when the officer asked what he was doing with the pellet gun.

Target practice within the woods was well and good, the cop responded, clearly willing to accept Veer's half-truth and be done with it, but if he tried it outside of there he could be charged with something called "reckless endangerment."

So he cut across the field behind the home from then on, and wrapped the gun in a rag. He stuffed the rag in his pocket when he got to the woods, then pulled it out again when heading back.

For weeks the rabbits eluded him. He knew they were there—he'd seen them, flashes of gray brown blending with the shrubs. A sharp, zigzaggy bound or two and they were gone before he could even lift the gun. But Timmy Heuertz said it meant there must be plenty of them in there; rabbits were incredibly prolific. So Veer kept at it. The day he finally got his rabbit, an aging male caught out in the open, he forgot all about the rag and hurried back over the field and through the parking lot, with the gun in his hand and the rag still in his pocket. This time, though, no cops. He rapped on Tim's door, then rapped louder. Maybe the band was still at rehearsal.

"Tim," he called, hearing an edge to his voice. "It's Veer—you there?"

He looked down at the gun. The honeycomb stock sat heavily in his hand. Lifting his arm, he lined up the straight-cut U-notch with the front sight and, through one of the four glass panes in the corridor door, at the antenna of a white Buick. The tip of the sight described tiny, unsteady circles till he set his triceps so it moved only along the vertical of the antenna. Doug's old Ford was parked off to the right of the Buick, so Tim had to be back from rehearsal. He'd probably returned all sweaty from hours of maniacal drumming and crashed without so much as a bath.

"Tim! Wake up, damn it." Veer pounded on the door with his left hand.

The doorknob quivered to life and he looked into sleep-bleared, hazel green eyes over reddish stubble, noted the eyes for the first time, and was glad they weren't brown.

"Hey, man," said Tim, stifling a yawn. "What's up?"

"Listen, I shot a rabbit. In the woods."

"All right—you got your rabbit!" The hazel eyes lit up with good humor and the tone strengthened. "Where is it?"

"I left it there. I don't know if this is season or not, but I didn't want to just drag it back in the open. You know how to skin them?"

"You want to eat it?"

"Of course I want to eat it—why do you think I shot it in the first place?"

The words stood awkwardly between them, and the older of the two scratched his bare, scrawny chest. Sleep sweat still slicked its red brown hair into wet, pointed clumps.

"I can skin it. Here, take this with you." He went inside and returned with a large brown Acme paper bag nested into another. "It's a double. I'll get us Doug's Bowie."

Veer took the bag and set off. He stepped out past the Buick, twanging the antenna so it shivered like a tuning fork, and crossed over into the short grass. Far to the left stood the old people's home, its back to him. Beyond it ran Main Street, a stretch of it visible between the home and the laundromat. To his right the lone railroad track swept along on top of a gravel embankment, and power lines swung above the edge of the field. The field ended in the woods, though, and the lines and track went on. To where? He'd only seen occasional streams of flatcars, literally miles long, some loaded, some not, clunking painfully along for a good quarter of an hour each. Headed into Maryland and probably beyond, in a country thrice as vast as his own vast Bharat. What did he know of it? What had he seen of it, after all? Just glimpses, like he'd had of rabbits before today. Once his studies were finished, he'd take off for places like the Grand Canyon or the Everglades.

He stepped into shadow and pushed through the undergrowth. Strangely, it took only a minute before he came to the fringe of the tiny clearing. He'd remembered it being much farther in. The carcass was still there. Only the smells had changed, stronger, nauseous. A fly or two—uncommon in this air-conditioned country—were buzzing the head and the great chocolate eye. Coming up behind it, he laid the mouth of the brown paper bag above the head, put his right hand to the patchy gray flank and shoved the rabbit into the bag. The flies buzzed away in consternation. Bunching the top, he stood, felt the weight in his hands— seven or eight pounds—and started back.

The Bowie was quite a knife. Unsheathed, it gleamed with a life of its own—subtly curving, pointed, single-edged, razor-sharp—the blade leaping almost a foot long from dagger haft to rabbit's throat. It sliced through to bone, acquiring a smooth new sheath of red, then made four neat, circular cuts in the fur, just above each paw. Tim snapped the neck, and the head lolled and the eyes stared all over again. Blood splotched the kitchen counter. Then Tim took firm hold with his drummer's hands and in one continuous move ripped the fur down and off the pink flesh.

"You want to keep the skin?"

"No."

"Yeah, kind of a scruffy pelt. How about a paw for luck?"

"Okay." Impossible to turn down the legendary rabbit's foot. He'd heard of its powers in childhood but never thought he'd own one. His father had unearthed a twisted and rusting horseshoe from an old suitcase, once, and had given it to him. It had never struck him to ask what it was doing in there or how Pitaji had come by it, but he knocked two nails into the top jamb of the closed door between his bedroom and the kitchen, and the horseshoe hung from the nails like the U in *luck* till the day he flew for Harrison University. Barring rearrangements not mentioned in letters, it was probably still hanging there. The paw would be even better, completely his own.

The Bowie hacked off the whitish right foot, and Veer stepped around Tim to drop the skin, headfirst, back in the Acme bag. The paper began to stain. The knife bit deep into the chest of the skinless carcass and slid smoothly down through the stomach. An indefinable, bland odor rose faintly to Veer. Tim fished out squishy gray organs and entrails and dumped them in the bag.

"All right, then," he said, looking up with a smile that crinkled the ruddiness around his eyes, ever the laid-back Timmy who, with his flower-power buddies (several of them vegetarian), had taken Veer in like no other Americans had. "What're you gonna make?"

"I don't know—it doesn't matter. You want to help me eat it?"

"Yeah, sure. Tell you what: soak the meat in salt water overnight—takes the gamy taste out of it—and I'll come over for rabbit stew tomorrow."

Chop some onions, wipe your eyes, pour vegetable oil on the nonstick pot surface, fry the onions lightly, shake in coriander powder and cumin seeds. Go easy on the red chili powder (turn the whole thing red and Tim won't eat). Time for the meat (that's right, Dadima, rabbit; his luck ran out and you're as dead as he is). Sauté a bit (pink juice seeping from generously cut pieces; starting to smell . . . strange smell, sweet, sharp, sickening if breathed too deep). Add water, turn it up, chop a carrot and potatoes, throw them in, bring to a boil, slow boil; get the rice going, stab the meat with a fork, stab the potatoes. Time to thicken with corn starch. Too bland now—get out the Tabasco, lifesaver in this land of bland palates. Sprinkle garum masala and chopped mint leaves, cover and leave to simmer on low.

"Good job, man," said Tim when the stew, steaming spicily, was served.

But, up for water after only a minute on the couch: "It's kind of hot, though."

Veer would have liked it spicier, but he knew he should have cut down more on the chili powder; it was less a stew than a curry. Too late now. Still, it would've been good either way. He'd expected to find the meat muscled and chewy, but it was amazingly tender, instead, and the flavor was rich with juice. The smell was another story. Even through the masala, it nauseated him. What must Ma and Pitaji be eating at home? Nothing, he realized. They were fast asleep, almost a couple of hours before breakfast. Ramdas, the cook, would wake with the milkman's ring minutes from now and sleepwalk to the kitchen, sober for probably the only time in the day. Later, well fortified and smelling of rum, he'd fry potatoes and puris for breakfast. The smells would tickle Pitaji's palate as he sat on the sofa in the hall with the Indian Express rustling in his hands. Ma would hear the sounds shift to the dining room and emerge to sit at the polished black Jacobean table, calling to Dadima and Veer to come for breakfast. But Dadima was ten years dead now and Veer ten thousand miles across the world, digesting rabbit meat that he'd cooked himself. . . .

Tim went for seconds. "We won't get through it all, I don't think," he said, slopping around in the bowl with the serving spoon.

"That's okay; I'll finish it tomorrow."

When they were done, the plates rinsed lightly and left in the sink, Tim sank into the couch and rubbed his stomach.

"Let's take a look at the weapon that got us this food," he said, and when it was brought out, sat hefting it in his hands, turning it over, lifting it to peer down the sights, scratching his red brown stubble in approval.

"You skinned that rabbit like you could do it in your sleep," Veer said.

"Yeah, I've done a few rabbits in my time. Mostly, though, my brother and I shot quail with our father's twelve-gauge—great-tasting bird, incidentally, other than a little heartburn. Howie's a good shot."

"Your brother." Tim's habit of inserting asides made Veer work to follow him sometimes.

"Uh-huh. Still better'n I am by miles."

"What does he hunt now?"

"Duck, mostly. Goes fishing too."

"Ya, I noticed Americans are crazy about fishing. The only time I had the chance was off the side of a houseboat in Kashmir when I was a kid on holiday. Just a length of twine with small lumps of dough pressed around the hook. Little fish like silver earrings came up and nibbled away at the dough without getting hooked until it was all gone, and I'd pull the twine up and wrap some more dough on."

"Kashmir, huh? Did you catch any?"

"Some other small, flat kind of fish—I don't know what it was, but the Kashmiri manager of the houseboat took it off the hook and cooked it for me while my parents were on land, sight-seeing in Srinagar. I almost vomited from the taste. When my folks came back, they got the fish smell and called in the housekeeper—who was a Muslim—to tell him he ought to have known we were strict vegetarians, and that we'd leave the house-boat if he didn't keep his cooking smells in the kitchen. I was really surprised to see my mother so stressed out. The poor fellow just said sorry to them, closed his kitchen doors tightly, and kept quiet about my part in it. But the weirdest part of it happened after we got back to Bombay, half a month later.

"We'd left my dadima—that's paternal grandmother—alone at home. She never used any kind of transport after my grandfather died in a car accident—just walked if she had to go somewhere—so she refused to fly to Kashmir. My grandfather's name, Amar, by the way, means *immortal,* and she was sure, when I was born a year after he died, that he'd reincarnated."

"As *you?*"

"Ya. Anyway, when we got back from Kashmir, she came creakily down to my level to hug me. But when she let me go, something had changed on her face. I knew somehow she had sensed my . . . what to her pukka Brahmin soul was a serious sin. Just like the Kashmiri, she said nothing in front of my parents, but the next day, when they went off to the club and I sat with her in the hall, reading while she embroidered a sari for my mother in these really bright reds and golds, she said without so much as looking up, 'First time I saw your grandfather's face, beta, was the same day we became married. Forty-one years we were together after that, but he did not even eat omelet. Still, beta, what he ate some days when he was a little boy, I never asked him. So now in the morning when I see you eating Ramdas's puri bhaji, I feel happy that God sent me my Amar to take care of this time when he is growing up.'

"And she got on with her embroidery. What a sweetheart she was, Tim. I missed her like crazy after she died. . . . Anyway, that's my fish story. You like to fish, I take it."

"'Fraid so." Tim smiled. "I like getting out with Howie when I visit. Lazy days . . . Cast your line and let the world go. Listen to the stream and the birds. Wait for the keeper, he bites, you fight him, you reel him in; if he doesn't show or he gets away, you've still had a good time. That is the life."

"Not for me, pal." And, before he could catch it, there was unwanted vehemence in Veer's voice. "I can't even stand the smell, let alone the taste."

Which earned him a close look. Stupid of him to expect an American, even Tim, to understand. What was he doing in this country, surrounded by people he didn't understand, who, in turn, couldn't understand him? The kitchen odors increased in pungence, and a silence settled, light as a hunting falcon, on their shoulders.

There was light filtering through in streams and patches, falling on leaves as they shivered, turning them green and dark, dark and green. Some were dappled with yellow or threaded by thin yellow veins; they smelled of freshly exuded sap. He moved between thick, catching branches as quietly as he could, his sneakers looking for softness underfoot, sidestepping dry fallen leaves. But he was at best a muted crunch in a damp, heavy stillness. When twigs broke too loudly he froze and listened, and there were little rustles in the brush around him, little scurries in the deepest thicket. Twice he heard a bird call—a clear warble followed immediately by a deep, startlingly metallic *krrr-krrr*. The second time, it was so close he peered in its direction until he saw the bird. Young raven? Entirely black, but with such a sheen where the light caught it that it seemed midnight blue. It called again, flaps low in the throat vibrating visibly to sound the rattle, and he thought, Jackdaw? Not in the States. He moved on.

The trees opened out into a small, sunlit clearing, and he saw the rabbit. It was a gray cottontail, partly side-on, sitting in the short grass near the opposite edge of the clearing, head raised, stock still. So close he could tell each silver-tipped hair from the next, could see behind the gray the velvety shadings of brown, the muscled gathering of the haunch. He froze, laying his left heel back quietly down, stopped breathing. Then slowly he brought the gun up and lined the sights with the rabbit's head.

It still hadn't moved a muscle. Why? They were in full view of each other; it had to know he was there. Why didn't it bolt? Did it think he couldn't see it? Or that he'd go away if it was patient enough? He brought his left hand carefully up for support, and the head stayed right behind the sights, eyes to the front, not even a whisker waving. Did it think if it just stayed the way it was, everything else would come to a stop too? Or was he in some way expected? Whatever the reason, whatever its thoughts—did they think?—it just sat there, waiting.

Somewhere behind him, the American jackdaw sounded its warble, and he squeezed the trigger on the first count of *krrr*. He didn't hear the second—the gun huffed, recoiling just a little with a jerk of his heart as the rabbit leapt wildly, almost straight up in the air, its body twisting. On landing it just flung itself back up again, higher each time, no attempt at flight, just contorted, agonized, monstrous leaps that sent it here and there.

The gun wasn't powerful enough!

What a fool to have thought an air pistol could kill a rabbit on the spot. . . . He fumbled to reload, dropping a pellet, fished another—tiny and gray—from his shirt pocket and worked the piston. But there was no way to aim. Look at it jump—as if on springs. Fully a minute now and not a chance to put it out. If it only stood still for an instant. . . . He waited for the moment, and still it flung about like a demon.

But finally it was tiring; the leaps grew feeble, more sidelong than high, and he pushed his frozen legs to stay with it. At last it lay on its side, flank heaving. He came up to it gingerly, taking in the unexpectedly ragged gray and the notched ears, the long, waving whiskers and the heated, rising smell. It was bigger and heavier than a dachshund when he stood at its head.

The upper eye was open wide, huge . . . deep brown, almost black, and it stared unwaveringly, not quite at him—through him, if anything, uncomplaining. He put the gun barrel to the short-haired area between the visible and the hidden eye, probing queasily for a spot. Then he pulled the trigger. The head jerked with the impact and the heaving lessened, but the great brown eye still stared quietly past him. So he reloaded and shot it again, and the rabbit shuddered, then lay still. And the eye grew glassy and vacant.

"Tim."

The smell of stew was dense in the room. Tim, too, seemed dulled into a trance by Indian spices.

"Hmm?"

"That rabbit jumped around like crazy. . . ."

"Yeah? I did think maybe even a pellet gun like this one wouldn't put it right out."

Veer nodded. "It kept going almost two minutes."

Tim considered the threadbare carpet as if debating its reason for being there, then said, "One thing you could've done, if you couldn't get a bead on it, was club it with the gunstock. But it's hard to think of if you haven't been there, and harder to do.

"Look at it this way," he added, after a pause. "No rabbit, no stew. Right?"

"Right," said Veer. The stew was undeniably tasty.

He looked over to the kitchen counter at the paw floating vertically, turning just a little in a large, clear pickle jar filled with white vinegar. A couple of gray hairs had separated from the foot and were drifting.

Flora Fountain

I know all the buildings around Flora Fountain by heart, the banks, the spectacle shops, the commerce colleges. Every week, I see the crimson fist of the Thums Up signboard on top of the massive old Jehangir Wadia building, the Chippendale entrance, the tawdry streetside stalls and the stream of pedestrians. I catch glimpses behind of the great stone winged-and-bearded Persian bull-men who guard the Parsi fire temple but couldn't lend wings to the *Emperor Ashoka* when the plane dove into the Arabian Sea, taking my parents down with it. High above the opticians there's the Globe Detective Agency, which handles fire alarms as well as investigation. Behind me the Fountain restaurant, whose red-lettered sizzlers I don't feel like trying at two o'clock on already sizzling Saturdays. And finally Flora herself, the centerpiece—everything revolves around her. I give them all a look only when there's a gap in the traffic coming at me along D.N. Road. That way I won't miss the woman in the slate-colored Fiat if she comes through again, and it gives my eyes a rest. The survival of the Banajis depends on keeping them sharp.

Hardly one year back I could stare all day, if I wanted, at the cars dodging toward me, then read the smallest letters on a signboard right at the top of a building. But now if I twist around in the front seat of my Fiat and look past the martyrs' statues and the Akbarally Island parking lot to the building near the back gully, my annually expanding stomach scrapes against the steering wheel, and some parts of the Titan ad seem written in small blobs. Beautiful watches, Titans, but I don't like what they measure, the stealth with which it stalks you. Relentlessly. Ten years ago I could run all the way from Nariman Point past Chowpatti Beach, up Malabar Hill, and back. Now, I start coughing every two minutes at home because of the dust, until Cawas Uncle tells me I have asthma and should go to the doctor. He knows it irritates me when he of all people says that, the way he coughs constantly himself, dribbling snot from his vulture's beak into his charcoal-drawing beard. But he also knows I won't say a word.

His own son talks back to the old man all the time, but I have too much respect for Roshan Aunty to act like Sammy. I vaguely remember hanging on to my mother's hand, shopping in Akbarally's not long before the air crash, but my clearer thoughts of Fountain go back only to meals of Parsi dhansak, a heavy mash of lentils and vegetables over brown rice, with Roshan Aunty and my cousins at Pyrkes. She took us there for lunch on days when Cawas Uncle had lunch appointments with clients. She seemed more light hearted than usual outside the house, smiling at Sammy's antics, leaning over to fuss with Nazneen's frock, squeezing halves of lime over my plate in a circular motion, her bare arms already hanging extra flesh outside a sari blouse. I think she had the idea that I would starve myself if she didn't make everything tasty enough to tempt me out of my misery. In those early years she never mentioned it, worried I'd drop into the long spells of silence that frightened her so much, but later she often told me I had her brother's face (roughly oxlike, but in her eyes handsome).

"You have no idea how much you remind me of your daddy, Noshir darling. But you're such a quiet boy next to him." She'd speak softly herself; to raise her voice would be to disrespect the dead.

"He wasn't quiet?"

"Oh my, he was always jumping around at your age."

"Like me," Sammy would say, proud as a peacock.

"Yes, darling, like you."

When Nazneen grew out of her cotton frocks and big enough to need to visit the bra shops in Colaba with Roshan Aunty, Sammy filched a flesh-pink specimen from her cupboard to inspect and handle and practice unhooking. Something squeamish in me stopped me from touching it. Sammy spent lots of time at the keyhole of the door between Nazneen's room and ours, those days. But whenever he beckoned frantically to me and I put my eye to the cold brass, there was a narrow, cut-off view of the side of her cupboard next to a strip of a Tom Jones pin-up, in front of which I saw brown flashes of Nazneen's arms screening flickers of more interesting parts as she crossed in and out of view. Then Sammy would push me aside and take up watch again.

Whether Nazneen actually caught on or not I don't know, but one day she rounded up Cawas Uncle and the two of us to help her rearrange her furniture.

"Daddy, see," she said, halfway through, "I want to move my cupboard here."

And she pointed to the connecting door.

Cawas Uncle swaggered his rangy but powerful six-foot-two frame over to the steel cupboard, put a shoulder against its side, found too much resistance. He stepped back, blew down into his beard (more black than gray at the time, crisply trimmed and jutting), and said, "Empty it out first, Naz; what is this? My hernia will start bothering me again."

"No, Daddy, everything is so nice inside." She pouted at him, then said sweetly, "Sammy, Noshir, go help Daddy, please."

So we left the table and bed and went to help, looking at each other. Sammy's face was a study. The cupboard left scrape marks as it screeched across the floor tiles, but, when we finished, Nazneen's breasts were behind solid steel.

At my weekly vigil for the woman in the slate Fiat, I see that two of the nymphs seated around the base of Flora's statue are naked above the waist and their white marble breasts would probably need a large size in bras. Flora herself, erect at the top of the tapering structure, is more modestly draped, but the wind shapes the folds of cloth to her body, and her right breast is exposed. She has her hands held out low to her sides, offering fruit, and her hair is wreathed in flowers, so I used to think of her as the spirit of plenty. At dinner one Saturday night a year ago, soon after I saw the slate Fiat, I asked Roshan Aunty if that was correct. She looked blank and turned to Cawas Uncle.

"Flora?" he said, guffawing as usual about nothing. "Why? You like her, Noshir? Ask her out; she can't say no and you aren't too old for her."

I kept quiet, knowing I'd made a mistake in asking while the old man was there. I thought for a second I could literally smell his contempt, but it was only the fried fish.

"Or you don't have the guts even for that?" he continued.

"Cawas, what is this?" Roshan Aunty said, coming to my defense. It's wrong to say I never had the guts to ask girls out when I was younger. Nothing came of it when I did, that's all, so I didn't try very often.

"The fellow was born without balls, Roshan," Cawas Uncle rasped, spitting out some bones from the fish into his side plate. One, thornlike, caught in his beard and stayed there, glistening. A straggly, unkempt, grizzled beard, it had become; all his vaunted manhood couldn't keep back time.

I started to get up and walk out, but Roshan Aunty caught hold of my arm and pulled me down. *Her* arm, by then, was much heavier than when it had passed lime over my dhansak at Pyrkes.

"Don't say such things about my Noshir," she said to Cawas Uncle. She rarely used such a sharp tone with him in the old days, but I've heard it more and more in the years since Telco transferred Sammy to Poona. Nazneen was already with her husband and kids in Calcutta, so that left only the three of us in the flat, except when Sammy and family drove into Bombay.

Even though Roshan Aunty takes my side against Cawas Uncle and has always made me feel wanted, I know she too would have liked it if I'd gotten married. Somehow, she seems to have more fondness for the family name that used to be hers than for Gobhai, her married name, and she doesn't want the Banaji line to die out with me. Add to that her fear that Parsis as a whole are a dying community. We've been inbreeding for centuries to preserve the supposed purity of our Persian blood, and now statistical trends are giving elders like Roshan Aunty ulcers about posterity. Our community—our tiny, highly literate community, which pioneered the industrial revolution and is famous for its charities—has a death rate that overshadows its births like the wings of vultures shroud corpses in the Towers of Silence. Both women and men are marrying later and later, some never, some outside the community. The highly educated, mostly working women get around to it in their late twenties on average and the men wait until they're well established and in their thirties. Hardly any couples have more than two children and many stop at one, so they don't so much as replace themselves.

I've never seen Flora actually function as a fountain, though she must have at some point. Quite dry now. The inscription on the metal plate at her base says she was constructed in 1869 by the Esplanade Fee Fund Committee at a total cost of Rs. 47,000, almost half borne by Seth Cursetjee Furdoonji Parekh, a prominent Parsi gentleman of the time. He must have known who Flora was. Roshan Aunty didn't, but Cawas Uncle did.

One evening just one or two years ago, not so long before I saw the slate Fiat, I drove Roshan Aunty to the Colaba agiary to attend her friend Aloo Pavri's daughter's wedding; Cawas Uncle didn't want to come. The ceremony was long and boring as usual, the priests in their white robes droning on and on, throwing raw rice—a symbol of fertility—from time to time at the seated couple on the flower-festooned center stage. But Goolestan, the bride, looked prettier than usual in her white lace sari worn the Gujarati way and flopped over the top of her head. (One especially clear memory I have of my parents, before the *Emperor*

Ashoka took them down into inky waters, is my mother telling me how the grains of rice kept spattering noisily against my father's shiny black wedding phenta, a sort of brimless top hat shaped like a pharaoh's headdress, making her giggle during the prayers. The fluffily white-bearded chief dasturji glared at her—so she put it—even as he droned on, which only made her giggle again. My father, apparently, just sat through the whole ceremony without blinking.) The dinner was, as always, the evening's highlight, gastronomic extravagance, all ten courses of it, heavy with spices and the redolence of meat, scorching my fingers as I shoveled it up off plantain leaves. I had to loosen my belt two holes. We had managed to get into the very first sitting (I'd gone ahead and turned up two chairs facing the harbor lights—merchant ships lined up along the horizon—as soon as the caterer coughed into the mike and said the magic words, while Roshan Aunty came waddling along, taking her own sweet time, a shimmering round vision in her beaded and sequined sari, clutching her silver lamé purse). So afterward we relaxed for a while in the salty sea air and listened to Nelly's band playing banal but cheerful pop hits, high-heeled Nelly herself pumping the accordion for all she was worth, rocking on those heels, big smile fixed on her face.

"How sweet Goolestan was looking, Noshir," Roshan Aunty said, and I agreed with her.

"So then why didn't you ask her out, those two–three times you met her?"

"She wasn't interested in me, Roshan Aunty; I could make out." Best not to mention I wasn't very interested myself. Or that asking women out didn't come easily to me—something she already knew.

"Yes." She fetched a sigh from the core of her rotundity. "Her mother, Aloo, told me the same thing when I asked her, except she said she was generally not yet keen to get married. And now look . . ."

"I'm too old for her in any case," I said, touched for the nth time by her concern. As much as Cawas Uncle had thought me an unwanted stepchild, she had always treated me as her own.

"No, no, what nonsense—not like that for men. So many get married in their thirties or forties; only for women it's a problem.

How happy Eruch and your dear mummy would have been if it was you on that stage—you know how they first met, Noshir?"

"No. How?"

"Your daddy was just walking along happily one day on D.N. Road when he saw Amy buying something from one of the hawkers—who sell foreign goods?"

I nodded.

"He liked her right away, so he stayed a little bit back and followed along to see where she was going. Amy was always walking instead of taking the car; she went through the Flora Fountain area, past Jehangir Art Gallery and Elphinstone College, past Regal cinema and the gateway and the Taj hotel along the bay (so nice and open but so dirty, the water), then turned onto their lane and went into her building. You remember your grandpa-granny's building we used to go to?"

I nodded again.

"Eruch waited for the lift to come down; then he gave the lift-man one rupee—in those days it was lots—and asked him your mummy's name and surname and which floor she stayed. When he came home for lunch by taxi, he told us what had happened. First thing my mummy—God rest her soul—first thing she asked was, 'Is she Parsi or no?' To which Eruch, very impatient, said, 'Yes, yes—her name is Amy Nullaseth.' Mummy—your bapaiji—was quite happy at first, but then she said, 'How do you know all this, Eruch? You went up to her and spoke to her just like that?'

"So then he told her about the liftman and the third floor of the Cooverji building, and she said she would find out more. It turned out that her Goola Masi knew one old couple who lived on the ground floor. They said, Of course, Amy was a very nice girl, and they would ask her parents if she would like to meet Eruch. So Amy's parents invited us all for dinner and then she and Eruch just hit it off like that."

She snapped her fingers to show how they'd hit it off, then pulled out her embroidered pink handkerchief and put it to her eyes, so I knew she was thinking of the Air India crash right alongside the picture of my parents hitting it off. The jumbo *Emperor Ashoka*, such a huge, heavy thing it must have known it was never really supposed to fly, had taken off from Santa Cruz for Dubai and London on a New Year's Eve, but instead of banking over the Arabian Sea and climbing, had dived into the water, taking down with it every single person, crew and passenger, two hundred and thirteen in all. There was talk about the artificial horizon malfunctioning and the usual rumors of the pilot having had one too many before the flight, but the black box probably ended up in a shark's stomach and the truth with it. My mother and father became one more statistic of a Parsi couple marrying late, dawdling at the gates of parenthood, and producing only one child in the end (though in general the deaths were at a later age and often heart related: high rates of heart disease, mental illness, suicide, side by side with a high literacy rate and income per capita). Besides them, there were a number of Parsis on board, and the dispirited community wondered how Ahura Mazda could have allowed it.

All of which is a good indication of our self-absorption, since for every Parsi who went under, there must have been a dozen non-Parsis: Hindus, Muslims, Sikhs, Christians. . . . On the other hand, one out of twelve would be eight percent, while the entire community, at eighty-five thousand and dwindling, was hardly one-hundredth of a percent of the national hundreds of millions (breeding, some Parsis felt, like rabbits all around us). So, there were grounds for considering the tragedy especially hard on the endangered species. And within a smaller group on board, just the cabin crew, the numbers were no less than depressing. As many as six of the twelve hostesses on the *Emperor Ashoka* were Parsis—not one of them older than twenty-five—and two of the eight pursers. Air India 855 was a New Year's Eve flight, so the Christian hostesses scheduled to fly had asked for replacements, and the Parsis had stepped in. People like to say that the Gods of all religions are just the same one God, but this time it was startlingly obvious that the Christian God had pulled strings at *our* cost.

Most of this I gleaned years later, from back copies of the *Times of India* and the *Indian Express*, the *Jam-e-Jamshed* and the *Parsiana*, when at sixteen I was suddenly consumed by the need for detail. I found the newspapers at the Bombay Public Library, bound unfolded into gigantic books between cardboard covers. Sitting at a reference desk under an inverted bathtub dome, leafing through them, I was depressed to the point of vomiting, not by the either laconic or melodramatic accounts of the crash, but by the way the paper had yellowed and begun to crack at the edges. A Xerox copy of Air India's *Magic Carpet*, mailed to me on request, was smudged in spots but had a different effect. The newsletter had run pictures of the hostesses and pursers in memoriam, and the girls looked so vibrant, so attractive even in black and white, so smilingly inviting, I felt in my sixteen-year-old heart crazily drawn to them, then instantly ghoulish at the recollection that those bright, sweet faces were long dead.

At the time of the crash, though, not even Cawas Uncle spoke about it in front of me. The murkiness of detail matched the underwater images that sloshed around in my head, and I was too disoriented to want to know more than the one relevant item: my parents, on their way to tour Europe and America for a month and a half, from where they'd promised to send me two picture postcards a week, would never arrive and would never return.

Give any romance, or as a matter of fact anything, enough time and it all comes to nothing. I'd learned that quicker than most people.

"What about you, Roshan Aunty?" I asked, changing the subject, or at least its direction. "You and Cawas Uncle?"

"Oh my, your Cawas Uncle was a big show-off, Noshir." She put the hanky away in her purse. "You know what he used to do when he was courting me?"

I shook my head.

"Remember the old Frigidaire we had before we got a bigger one? It was at my daddy's home those days. When Cawas came to see me and we went to pull out a drink, he used to lean over and put his orangutan arms around to the back edges of the fridge and hug it and make eyes at me. Then he would say, 'Take a bet, Roshan, I can pick up this fridge.' I told him not to do such things, but he would just laugh and rock backward, and the whole fridge, all full of things, would just come up off the floor. Those days I was more worried that something would break when he put it down, and your bapaiji would shout at me instead of Cawas. But now look—he has such a bad time with his hernia. . . ."

I smiled.

She sighed. "So stubborn, your uncle."

Her eyes roved, while she talked, over the crowd of long-nosed Parsis in their glittery saris and dark suits—not too many men in daghlis and phentas anymore—and now she lifted her little finger subtly in the direction of one of the seated families. "Noshir, just look casually over there. What do you think of that girl?"

I looked without making it obvious and saw a girl with a pretty moon-face in a russet-colored, lacy sari wrapped tightly around her, chatting away to an older couple.

"Good looking, no question," I said. "But she must be hardly twenty-two, twenty-three."

"Good, otherwise she would be hooked up already. As it is she might be, but at least there is no boy with her. I wonder if Aloo can—oh, see, they're getting up to go. Noshir, go after them and see what you can do."

"What can I do?" I said, getting up hesitantly.

"Just go," she said. "Something might happen."

So I strolled obediently along behind the girl and her parents, my hands in the pockets of my navy blue suit pants, still too tight after dinner, toward the gate with the flower torans hanging in a big vee above it and the gully where the cars were parked. Someone I'd seen among the groom's family came up to the threesome just inside the gate and started to shake hands and thank them for coming, so I kept going in case I could overhear names as I passed. But none were mentioned. The girl's voice was a very young trill. I went out to our Fiat and opened the passenger-side door, away from the wall, then flipped open the glove compartment as if searching for something. The odor of countless urinations came wafting off the base of the wall. After two or three minutes, I heard the purr of their car and looked up. A boxy Ambassador, and as it went past I saw the girl's round, pleasant face look vaguely out from the back seat.

No impact. At either end. At mine just a neutral emptiness, even a sense of something stagnant. . . .

When I got back to my chair, Roshan Aunty opened her eyes wide at me, so I gave her an account.

"Boy's side," she said, sounding disappointed. "Still, I'll ask Aloo; she might know. What, Noshir! You should have done something when you were next to them—dropped your handkerchief and asked her is this yours, or anything. Useless, you are."

It was said in a fond tone, a teacher shaking her head at her favorite pupil, but maybe, like Cawas Uncle, she was thinking I had no balls.

"What will happen to the Banaji name?" she asked, lines forming over silvery eyebrows.

If not for the Parsi-Parsi thing, how she and other elders see marriages outside the community as so many steps toward its extinction, I could have told her about one of the times (and there had been others) I showed just as much balls as my father but it did me no good.

I was a youngster then—none of this flab on me—driving back from classes at H.R. College one evening. Just before I turned into our gully, I saw a tremendously pretty girl at the B.E.S.T. bus stop near the corner. So I parked and sat in the car for a minute, trying to think of something smart to say to her. Sammy would have had seven or eight different lines, but only things about the buses kept popping into my head. Finally, I got out and skirted spots of oil and rubbish to the flurry of the main road. The girl was still at the bus stop along with other people, none of them bothering to queue, so I went over and stood casually a yard from her. She had on jeans; her hair shone with a brownish sheen at about my nose-level and she smelled of talcum powder. Yellow cotton top, sweet-nineteen features. My heart going like Alla Rakha on the tabla.

Clearly one can be too young. Small consolation—not as bad as being too old. But would I react today to that face in the jaded way I reacted to the girl at Goolestan Pavri's wedding? Probably not; I still remember an exciting newness to it I didn't find in the wedding guest. Something about its appeal spoke to my blood in a way the moon-faced Parsi girl's didn't.

After a minute of looking out on the road as if waiting for a bus, a minute of rehearsing my line, I said to the girl in jeans, "Has 70 or 133 come recently?"

She turned her face just a little to see if I was speaking to her, then nodded and said, "70 went hardly two or three minutes ago."

Nice English-school accent. Bright black eyes that quickly weighed me as she spoke and seemed to like what they saw. Then she looked in front again.

"But not 133," I persisted.

"No," she said briefly but pleasantly; nothing abrupt about it, considering how superfluous the question was.

A nice girl. Even an intelligent girl, I felt.

So I let a second or two go and said, "You stay here somewhere?"

I could see her eyes open slightly, but she nodded without saying where.

"Me too." I pointed to our lane, wishing it looked cleaner. "I live in Meghdoot, third floor."

She smiled a bit, hesitated, but finally came out with it: "We're in Nizam Court."

"I've seen it," I said, nodding; we were meant to meet: "Only three lanes away. My name is Noshir, Noshir Banaji."

That told her I was Parsi, of course. She nodded too, and said, "Noor Aziz."

Ah, Muslim. Dangerously sweet, these Hindu and Muslim girls.

I was about to ask which college she went to, when she pointed to a cherry red mass of metal and noise thundering down the road. As it drew close enough to read the number slot, I did some unusually rapid thinking.

"There comes 133," she said.

"Are you taking it, too?" I asked, discovering the logical question only the split-second before I put it to her.

"No," she replied, hitting answer (b) but adding something that had me redrawing the flow chart. "I'm just waiting here for a friend."

"Oh," I said, as the double-decker screeched dead in front of us and people began to pile in. The choice was still simple: I could either come up with a confession or make an unwanted bus ride to Opera House. "Actually, I don't need to take it either."

She looked at me sideways from under long black eyelashes, without the look of surprise I'd expected.

"I saw you from my car when I got back from college," I said, breaking into a smile, confidence surging as the bus shuddered off. "I just wanted to talk to you, so I came out here."

Still sideways, she smiled back at me, setting my inner tabla off on intricate patterns, but again there was little surprise in the smile. I had an idea all along, it seemed to say.

Whatever the case, she was smiling. I had basically told her I was trying to ask her out, and she hadn't snubbed me. *Au contraire.* The rubbish along the footpath flashed all sorts of green, car horns honked, streetside hawkers grinned toothily. The monsoon sky had just a hint of passing rain. It felt as cool as January mornings.

I was as ready to take the next step as I've ever been, even readier than on Saturdays now at Flora Fountain, when she said, "Oh, there's my friend," and I looked out on the road to see a shiny green Fiat go just past the bus stop and pull over to the side. A Muslim-looking fellow, a little older than me, put his head out and looked back at us. She waved to him.

"Okay," she said to me, nodding and smiling. "Bye."

"Bye," I said. I watched her walk over to the car and get in. The fellow looked like a local, his well-oiled hair swept up in a puff and the top button of his shirt opened to show his curly black chest hair. . . .

Still, thinking about it later, I felt less discouraged. I was almost a neighbor, and I knew her name and her building. If she could go out with that fellow, why not with me? Because of our Iranian origin, people sometimes thought Parsis were a type of Muslim sect—maybe she'd feel the same way. She'd been friendly, no question, not like the Hindu girl in my accounting class (80 percent of the girls were Hindu, first of all, maybe a dozen Muslims, a sprinkling of Christians, not a single Parsi) who'd snubbed me when I asked if she wanted to have lunch and from then on walked past with her nose in the air as if *I* had insulted *her.*

That Saturday, Sammy went to the movies with one of his St. Xavier's girlfriends and Nazneen was sitting in the hall in her lemon stretch pants, waiting for the operator to connect a trunk call to Mehernosh (their wedding was still a month off) while Tom Jones sang "Delilah" on the scratchy old gramophone. I went downstairs two–three steps at a time, hammering out a nice galloping rhythm, then put my hands in my pockets and strolled along the back roads till I came to the Muslim girl's lane. Turning onto it, I saw the locality was more run down and cramped than in the memory I had of rushing through it as a kid, trying to either catch Sammy or get away from him, failing at both. Nizam Court, when I came to it, was only a two-story house, its plastering streaked with dirty black stains from the monsoons.

There was no name board near the entrance, so I checked the brass nameplates on the ground-floor doors, then wound my way up the wooden stairs to the first-floor landing. Parts of the steps were darkened and damp from a morning wash. The door on the right, closer than the other, said Muhammad Aziz. I stood there at first, planning what to say if her parents opened it. Then, seeing no bell, I knocked. I thought I heard life behind the wall: people talking, kitchen utensils clanging, pressure cookers boiling, whistling, sighing. But after a bit, no question, someone coming to the door. It opened a foot or so, and the girl's face looked out. As soon as she saw me, her eyes went big.

"Hullo," I said, smiling not only to see her—to feel again that sense of freshness signaling at the level of my blood—but at the recognition in those eyes.

"Oh God!" she said in a muffled voice, looking quickly behind her. There was disbelief in her tone, and shock. "What are you doing here?"

I was taken aback. "I just thought—"

"Please," she said, stepping out into the landing with me and pulling the door almost shut behind her. She had on a dress this time, in white and brown; it fell to her calves. The sweet, strong smell of attar seemed to issue from her dark eyes. "You can't come here. Go quickly now before somebody comes to see what I'm doing."

"But why—?" I started, absolutely bewildered but beginning to realize I'd done something stupid.

"*Please. Please,*" she said, and there was more urgency in her voice than I'd ever heard, as she began to push me toward the stairs. In all the strangeness, I was instantly aware of her hands on my body. "Just go. My father will kill you if he comes out to see!"

My mind whirled with garbled responses and questions, but my tongue froze on the whole mess. So I turned and started back down the stairs, feet plodding heavily against the wood. At the mezzanine level I looked up, but she'd gone inside.

Thinking about it now, more of that serious little comedy makes sense than it did back then. I was too insulted and discouraged afterward, and disgusted with my own bad instincts, to recognize that the girl was literally terrified of her father. She'd seemed too modern to belong to a very orthodox family—definitely no question of her being in purdah since she'd not only answered the door without a burkha over her face but was out in the open without one at the bus stop, not to mention wearing jeans—but there had been at least one indication of a strict household. Even though her friend was probably Muslim like her, she still had to meet up with him half a kilometer from her home and had probably gone through the prearranged pretense of standing at a bus stop in case someone she knew saw her waiting. . . .

But there was no point telling Roshan Aunty all this old stuff, so I drove her home quietly from the wedding. Instead of just thinking I was useless—nothing new—she would have unnecessarily been upset to learn I was that interested in a non-Parsi girl. That it was almost twenty years ago wouldn't matter. She'd still be disturbed. And not just her, the whole world would have minded our business if anything had happened between the Muslim girl and me. I more or less stopped thinking about non-Parsi girls after a while, basically because it bothered me more and more how people would react.

Roshan Aunty would have no problem with the girl in the slate Fiat. The one I look for now. At Flora Fountain.

I don't need to have her name to know that. The minute I saw her, the minute she looked at me, so composed and steady, I felt a recognition pass between us, different from the kind I'd seen in the Muslim girl's eyes: minus the sense of newness. An ancestral kind, I realize now, that went back beyond the moment my father first saw my mother on the very road the Fiat was traveling. Beyond when their parents' parents' parents moved from Navsari and Udvada to make a better living in Bombay. Beyond the time their forefathers built the first sacred fire on Indian soil at the Anjuman fire temple in Udvada. Beyond the day—more than a thousand years ago—the first Parsis fleeing Iran in wooden dhows landed on the shores of Sanjan and the Gujarati king Jadav Rana took them in but stipulated that Parsis must not convert others and that Parsi marriages must be held after sunset. Beyond the defeat of Yazdegird III, king of all Persia, by Muhammadan forces that converted Iran to an Islamic empire at the point of their communal sword. Even beyond the days when Zarathustra breathed the word of Ahura Mazda into the hearts of every man and woman in the land. Beyond *all* of that through to ancient times, when white-haired Zal, father of the warrior-king Rustum, was first enthralled by the charms of Rudabeh and she by his valor.

The weight of all those millenniums, I can see now, brought me along M.G. Road a little before two that Saturday exactly a year ago, past Bombay Gym and the communications tower to the red traffic light at Flora Fountain, precisely when the slate Fiat's driver stopped at the light merging D.N. Road with M.G. Her intelligent, angular, almost familiar Parsi profile was set against the background of the fountain and the statues of freedom fighters in the parking lot, exactly along my line of vision. Then she felt the weight too, and turned to face me. A second for that look of peace and gene-deep acceptance to pass between us, enough for me to retain the impression permanently, but not long enough to recognize the importance of what I was seeing. Then her light was green and a taxi in the right lane pushed up between us. The stream of cars grumbled across in front of me, and the slate Fiat went ahead of them.

I should have started up too and gone after it, red light or no. That is what Zal would have done on first sight of Rudabeh, what my father or Cawas Uncle would have done, definitely what Sammy would have done, even what I would have done just seven or eight years ago. But I sat there and thought, instead, foot halfway between brake and accelerator. I thought of the look on her face, wondered who she might be, why I felt I knew her, and where she was going. Flora's untroubled face told me nothing. . . .

Flora is not the spirit of plenty. Not, at least, in the proper sense. I found that out on the night I asked Roshan Aunty about it and Cawas Uncle put in his ten paisas' worth.

After she scolded him for it, he kept quiet for a while and ate the yellow lentils and rice left over from lunch. Then he blew his nose loudly on a napkin, brushed the fish bone from his beard into the plate, drank some water, and said, "Flora was a Roman goddess, Noshir."

"Of what?" I asked, none too keen on talking to him but too curious not to.

"Of spring, flowers—all those things. Best part was once a year in spring the Romans had a big festival for her. Great fun they had. What do you think they did at Flora's festival?"

He looked at me with an expectant light in his eye, dirty old swine, and I had a good idea of what was coming. I shrugged.

"No, what do you know about those things? Nice big orgies they had," he said with immense satisfaction, as Roshan Aunty glared at him and I smiled a grim smile. "Big fat orgies to cheer life starting off in spring."

He broke out into guffaws again, till he had a coughing fit and had to drink a glass of water while Roshan Aunty went around and patted him on the back. Romances don't inevitably come to nothing, after all—theirs will continue in Nazneen's and Sammy's and *their* children's. The Gobhai line is in good shape.

Goddess of renewal, then, goddess of fertility. Of life generating life.

So I go to Flora on Saturdays to ask for a second chance. There is no way to tell if she notices. On one visit, I take a creaky, shaky old wood-paneled lift up to the Globe Detective Agency and ask if they can locate a slate-colored Fiat driven by a Parsi woman in her early thirties. But the man smiles, honest fellow, and says there must be thousands of grey Fiats in the city, impossible to track down. It's true—our own Fiat is a pigeon color. One night, when I'm too restless in bed, I dress and go quietly out of the flat down the stairs in the dark, get in our car, and drive off to Flora Fountain. I have some vague romantic idea, picked up from movies, that the woman in my thoughts will be drawn to the spot at the very same time. The area is deserted and soundless in the night's humidity, and only the glow of streetlamps lights Flora as she looks out over me into space, still holding out the promise of fruit.

I go so far as to step over the enclosure in the eerie silence, cross the dry basin, and climb to the base of the statue where a nymph is seated, her bare knees now at my eye level. It takes the cold smoothness of marble against my hand to wake me to the strangeness of the situation. I feel as queer as when, decades ago, I was drawn to the pictures of the air hostesses who went down with the *Emperor Ashoka.* So I stick to Saturday afternoons from then on. Today is the fifty-second. I pull out my lunch (meaty, tempting smells and grease stains on the wrapping paper tell me Roshan Aunty has made mutton cutlets), put away the week's ledgers, lock up, and drive here to give Flora another try.

Many things have changed around the fountain since the days when Roshan Aunty took us to Pyrkes for lunch—Pyrkes itself is gone and a bank has taken its place; the entrance to the Akbarally lane is blocked off for cars and has become a thoroughfare for pedestrians; the entire traffic arrangement was redesigned years ago and half a million commuters cursed the traffic commissioner till they got used to it. But Flora's expression stays the same. The thought gnaws at me that I may have had my only chance at spring and let it drive away. That I've put finis to the Banaji line. Yes, I was given my chance, but it was snatched away in a flash. I know I'm stupid to think that some day the woman in the slate Fiat might come along again—I haven't seen the Noor girl, maybe still my neighbor, in nearly two decades—and that this time I'll be able to follow it and learn where she lives.

But if it's meant to happen at all, being here just in case is the only part that's in my power. The rest is in Flora's hands. I feel that Zal and Rudabeh, the mighty Rustum, Zarathustra himself, all the brave Parsis who sailed into darkness to keep the sacred fire burning, and the entire line of Banajis down to my parents must think less badly of me when they see I'm still trying. It's a line that has held off the titan time. So far.

Holy Cow

Tehmi Pavri, who firmly believed her family was the best in the world, was all bustle and nerves that particular afternoon in the neat suburb of Birmingham. Maybe a third of Detroit's Parsi population was due to land up at her modest stucco three-bedroom, two-bath for the monthly religious meeting, to give the next generation a sense of belonging and a grounding in the Zoroastrian faith. Not that the entire population couldn't fit inside. Even including (as often) the Camas and Shroffs from Flint and Windsor, there were hardly a dozen Parsi families all told. But it was the Pavris' turn this month to host the meeting, and Tehmi meant to see the house was shipshape, so neither Naju Golvala nor Piloo Olia could secretly note a fine silver gray buildup of dust on a side table or an overlooked curl of black hair along the inside of the commode (which she was quite sure they'd ask to visit for no other reason than to inspect it; good thing she'd bought the lavender-scented deodorizer).

As she rushed about in her long frock (she was still in the habit of saying "frock" after all these years), Tehmi called to her husband, Adi, to adjust the feroher hung on the short wall of the living room. When she got back from the bathroom, the bearded angel done in gold-plated, raised metal on a black wooden plaque was nicely aligned, his hands folded benignly and protectively over the Pavri household.

"Thank you, sweetie-pie," she said, still on the move, and listened for Adi's voice, the slightly nasal but well-loved tones.

"Welcome, Tehmi."

Hmm. Preoccupied. Maybe even a bit nervous about emceeing the meeting.

Thinking back to when she'd bought the plaque so many years ago on Princess Street in Bombay, she smiled to herself and kept moving. What a good, reliable man her angel Adi was, had always been. How many husbands, on a weekend after a long grind at the plant, could be expected to help out around the house without the slightest bit of fuss? And that too with all the frustrations he'd been feeling for so long now about not moving up. Poor love felt each missed promotion as sharply as if it were a *de*motion. All the reassurance and back-stroking she'd given him hadn't kept him from feeling slighted.

"You have to be part of their buddy system or you can forget it, Tehmi," he'd fumed so often. And it hadn't helped when Boman Olia flaunted his promotions in Adi's face. "Of course," her husband would say then, suddenly loud, a bitter twist to his normally gentle mouth. "If you're ready to butter them up like that ass-kisser Boman, of course they'll promote you."

With all that, there he went now, Windex spray in one hand and paper towels in the other, doing his best to clean the showcase glass into nonexistence. She went over to help with the curios. Globular-cheeked and sumo-bellied, the hand-painted porcelain Laughing Buddha on the top shelf smiled out at them with wine-splashed lips that matched the color of his nipples. Tehmi had always thought the flabby breasts were as big as a woman's, and the bald, gleaming white pate was still irresistibly pattable. Below him on the middle shelf—the tallest of three levels—the wise old man of China curved pliantly up from the base of his carved elephant-tusk gown, the point of his ivory beard pouring into the flask of myrrh in his hand. How scared she'd been when they'd brought the serene but lead-heavy old fellow over from India in one of their suitcases. Adi, quite rightly, had scoffed at her timidity and insisted that family heirlooms didn't fall under the strict new ivory laws. He'd never been short of confidence, those days.

But now he felt like a failure—she could tell. It showed in his hesitance: his often tentative voice, his flip-flopping over choices, the time he took over trivial decisions. . . . And in his irritability at those closest to him. He'd been impatient with the youngsters and snappy even at her. She understood what was really going on, of course, but it was only putting Ruby and Vispi's back up, turning them more toward their American friends. Just when it was most important to hold them fast to the community as they approached marriageable age. Well, the lord Khodaiji would help Adi build up that old confidence again. In a burst of fancy, Tehmi imagined the gold-bearded feroher unfurl his great, gold-feathered wings, float free of the wall plaque, and flap across to hover protectively above her husband.

As if Khodaiji had heard her prayers, Adi straightened up from the bottom shelf and with that sudden, subtle twitch of a smile that went deep into his slightly bulging brown eyes, brought himself eyeball to eyeball with her just as she gave in and patted the Laughing Buddha on his head.

"Next function we throw, Tehmi, will be our silver anniversary. Can you imagine?"

She smiled shyly back, he had brought his nose so close to hers. It was making her cross-eyed. "That's true, Adi. Unless," she added, "Ruby gets engaged before that."

"In the next seven months?" And his mouth twitched again. But he pushed his lips at hers, as she knew he'd planned to do, before heading off into the garage for something.

Speaking of Ruby, where was she? Really, that girl! Going off to Greek Village with her friends for lunch, when she knew her family was getting ready for company. Vispi one could understand; no one expected boys to clean house. But if Ruby got into lazy habits *now*, what would she do when she got married? If, that was, they could find a nice . . .

Tehmi half-groaned before she knew the sound had come out of her. She coughed quickly so Adi wouldn't wonder, and switched the oranges with the pears in the fruit bowl on the dining table. Ruby, approaching her midtwenties not yet engaged, let alone married, was a cause of tremendous anxiety to both Tehmi and Adi. The problem was simple to spot but hard to fix: up to a few months ago there had not been a single Parsi boy of Ruby's age group in Detroit. When the Pavris first came to Detroit in the early seventies, the only Parsis already there were Jal Pastakia and the Kapadias, part of the general Indian medical guard that arrived in the States before the engineering contingent. And, of course, Faram and Roshan Kapadia had to go have the two girls. As for Dr. Pastakia, he had stayed single but was past fifty now. (The standing joke around the community was that being a gynecologist he got to see more than enough of naked women anyway, and maybe, as Piloo Olia had once bawdily remarked, laughing heartily at her own joke afterward, he'd come to prefer colored hairs.) Then at steady intervals the other couples had landed in town, and a number of Parsi boys were born to the community. But they were all years after Ruby (after both Homai and Hilla Kapadia, for that matter, so the Kapadias had been in the same boat—still were, where their younger daughter, Hilla, was concerned). None of the boys was much more than a teenager even now.

So last January, when the third wave of Indians, the computer people, brought to Chrysler one solitary Parsi, a nice young Commissariat boy, four or five inches taller than Ruby (a good five-six herself) and quite good looking with his Magnum P.I. mustache, he'd seemed to the Pavris like a gift from Khodaiji. Ruby clearly liked him—she appeared more inclined to flirt with him than with the American boys in her group of friends, which was at least a temporary relief. God forbid that one's daughter should be excommunicated and one's grandchildren barred from becoming Parsis.

The meeting began with a joint recitation of the Jasa-Me Avanghé Mazda in the original Avestan. A translation into English was also on the printed sheets that Adi handed around. As host, he was automatically the master of ceremonies for the day, and Tehmi looked on fondly when he took the center space in their wood-paneled living room, slightly hunched over his copy, almost as black haired as the day she first saw him, but permanent bags under his eyes now and his mustache either thinner or smaller, she wasn't sure. Or maybe his face had gotten squarer. Or his lips fuller. She sank into the thick fawn carpeting with her legs tucked under her, leaving the sofas and chairs for the others, noting happily that they'd shown up in even better numbers than last month at the Golvalas'. The chorus of high and low voices ballooned outward from the hall up the staircase, and she modulated her own to blend better.

Come unto my aid, O Mazda. Come unto my aid, O Mazda. Come unto my aid, O Mazda. I am a worshipper of Mazda, and as a Zoroastrian, declare myself an ardent believer of his faith.

Tehmi looked around at the gathering as they chanted, in case there was something she, the host, ought to be doing. In a moment of paranoia, she suddenly thought she'd left one of the bathroom doors open—something reeked sweetly, though she'd forgotten to spray the air freshener around. She almost dashed off to check but settled back again. She could tell even ten feet from the sofa, that it was only the imitation Chanel No. 5 that Piloo Olia, intently following Adi's recitation, must have dunked herself in.

I solemnly dedicate myself to good thoughts well-conceived, good words well-spoken, and good deeds well-performed. I confess myself dedicated to the pure and good Mazdayasnan religion, which disarms, ends all strife, teaches self-sacrifice, and leads to righteousness.

On one side of the couch, Boman Olia—his black-and-white beard bobbing in time—and his best friend, Shapoor Pundol, each had their hands clasped earnestly. The Golvalas had taken the other side, their teenaged son, Naval, perched on the well-padded arm. Almost half the loveseat was occupied by Soona Pundol in a lovely mauve georgette sari. Soona was wheezing in and out of her nose even at rest, she had become such a baby elephant. Her children, Shavak and Jean, were jostling for room on the other half and trying to read the prayer at the same time. The elder Olia boy, Darab, his navjot ceremony many years behind him, was looking bored on one of Tehmi's tall-backed wedding chairs—such a blessing that the lilac-and-blue tapestry had kept its shine over all the years, helped by her washcloth—while that nice Zubin Commissariat, on the matching chair, had his brooding black brows cocked at the facing translation as the prayer unfolded.

Hilla Kapadia, Tehmi noted, had strategically brought a chair in from the dining room and set it up close to the young man. Being nearby was always a help, no doubt, but, where looks were concerned, Hilla was not quite in the league of her elder sister, Oh-My (which was how Americans liked to say Homai's name; the Parsis of Detroit had all picked up on it just to tease her). Homai had married a Chicago Parsi, Homi Parakh. So they were the perfect couple, Oh-me and Oh-my. From all reports, Oh-My was very happy, and Chicago not too far for the Kapadias to visit even on a weekend. Maybe Tehmi and Adi could look at boys in Chicago for Ruby.

But in the meantime—who knew?—Ruby and the Zubin boy might hit it off. She was certainly better looking than Hilla, even if Hilla was fairer. Tehmi supposed she ought to be glad that Ruby had actually made it home from Greek Village for the meeting, let alone ask that she find a spot near the only eligible Parsi bachelor in town. She and the elder Pundol girl, Perin, their backs against the corner wall, were gooss-goossing about something instead of reciting the prayer. Tehmi tried to frown across the room at them, but they were oblivious. Perin Pundol, Tehmi knew, was seeing an American boy against her parents' wishes and had already declared she intended to eventually marry him (she was only nineteen yet and prettier than a Chinese vase). Poor Shapoor and Soona Pundol—such staunch Zarthustis that they even drove a red Mazda! Thank God, Ruby had been sensible about not dating so far, though at twenty-three and a half she was getting impatient by the day. As for Vispi, who was still not home, Tehmi was sure he was dating someone on the sly. But at least in his case she knew that even if he married an outsider, both he and his children would remain Parsis. . . .

> Of all the religions that exist or that shall be, the greatest,
>   the best,
> and the noblest is the religion of Ahura, revealed by
>   Zarathustra.

It was the Detroit Parsis' custom to begin each such meeting with one of their many prayers, and Tehmi had always felt a sense of communion as they all chanted together, had found peace and a certain comfort in the lilting rhythms of the ancient Avestan. But the sight and sound of this line in the translation threw her, all of a sudden, into such a turmoil that her voice completely fell off, quite unnoticed by anyone, before the gathering intoned the final words. It reminded her of the so many times she'd encountered and resented the Christian assertion in a Christian country that Christianity was the only road to God and all other roads led to hell.

Just within their circle, the somewhat lesser assertion in the Jasa-Me Avenghé was all right, she supposed, to help the children with their self-worth and their faith, so surrounded were they by messages to the contrary. No different from how the regular picnic outings in summer or, once everything turned gray and freezing outside, the indoor volleyball they improvised in racquetball courts helped the Detroit Parsis maintain a sense of community. But had there been a time, she wondered, when the Persian Empire had publicly proclaimed her religion the greatest and noblest, for Jews, Hindus, and Confucians to hear and resent? And where was that empire now? The religion, of course, was barely surviving, its handful of followers struggling to pass it on and keep it alive.

> All good cometh from Ahura Mazda. Such is the solemn
> dedication of the Mazdayasnan religion.

The chorus ceased. Her husband, Adi, announced something to the gathering, and, shaking off a mild headache, Tehmi tuned her ears again to his voice. The two younger of the three Olia children stepped up and began their scheduled presentation on the importance of the navjot ceremony, how it initiated a child into the faith, accepted him as a true Zarthusti. Boman Olia and Shapoor Pundol were having a little chat in undertones—even so, a bit rude of them, particularly since Boman's own children were addressing the group. Little Jeroo Olia was reading aloud very seriously from her handout, while her brother Cyrus fidgeted and waited his turn to read.

"During the nahn ritual," she read, "the initiate rubs a few drops of nirang over all his body three times, and then milk and rose petals are—"

"Wait, please." Podgy young Shavak Pundol raised his hand from the loveseat where his sister had managed to squeeze him right into the corner. "I want to know what nirang is, first."

"It's a sacred potion, Shavak," interjected Adi the M.C. from the front wall by the television set, to where he'd retired once the presentation started. "One that has been prayed over by the priests."

"Also," announced Cyrus Olia (employing an officious manner he must have learned, at just seven years of age, from his father, Boman) in his high-pitched voice, reading from further down his sheet, defeating Adi's careful wording without intending to, "it is made from bull's urine."

"Eeuw!" said several of the children in disgust. Such a strange Americanism.

"And we have to bathe in it?" squeaked Shavak, quite panicked at the thought.

"Don't they also have to *drink* it?" Perin Pundol called out with wicked satisfaction, always so rebellious, from her corner with Ruby.

"Yes," confirmed young Cyrus from the sheet. "At the end, the initiate sips nirang to purify himself."

"Aaagh!" gagged Shavak, slumping off the loveseat, while the other children flinched visibly and Darab Olia made an exaggerated bitter-taste face, probably more at the mere thought of what he must have once swallowed than at any real memory of it. Tehmi's thoughts took her back to the second time in her life she'd had the bath ritual, on the morning of her wedding day. (As had Adi. Separately from her, of course—just imagine if they'd done it together! How scandalized both families and all the priests would have been at just the thought.) The sensual tingling of the natural body rub came back to her, and the light, cool feel of milk, the soft plasticity of petals. She almost felt young again.

"That's enough, Shavak," said the gagging youngster's mother, Soona, stirring her gelatinous bulk to yank him back onto the cushions, the gauzy mauve of her sari once again catching Tehmi's eye. "Adi Uncle just now told you that it's a very holy thing."

"Yes," said Adi, a wry look on his face. "It's how they say: Holy cow!"

A titter ran around the room at that, and Tehmi felt her heart lurch with love for him. How he could surprise her every now and then with that sudden irreverence, like how he shocked her in bed at times with the things he'd want to do right out of the blue. She'd managed to surprise him too, once in a while, or so he'd told her. He was always so sweet afterward. Even though she was hardly the classic beauty—jutting chin, straggly eyebrows. And even now, when she could easily be a grandmother.

Zubin Commissariat, all seriousness just a minute ago, was laughing the loudest, she noticed. Looking over her shoulder, she saw that the young man's spontaneous merriment had drawn Ruby's eyes to him in what seemed to Tehmi a quizzical then thoughtful look. She was glad to see that the girl had changed out of her faded jeans into a nice skirt and top. And taken some pains with her hair and make-up. How sweet she looked with her new haircut; it didn't hide her nice, symmetrical features the way the last style had, sweeping over half her face like a black silk curtain. Now you could clearly see a softened young feminine version of Adi, at least, thank God, around the chin and eyebrows.

The doorbell pealed through the mist of Tehmi's conjectures. She boosted herself off the floor and ran for it, getting there just as someone started to pound on the door, opening it to let in a dazzle of sunlight and their oldest friends in Detroit, Dr. Faram and Roshan Kapadia, such wonderful, wonderful people, bluff and boisterous but with 24-karat hearts—how they had helped when Adi and she first landed in Detroit so long ago, naive and confused, hardly two suitcases to their names.

"How are the rhyming Pavris?" boomed Faram, wrapping her

up in an almighty hug. That was his favorite joke about them: he insisted that they'd planned their marriage and naming of children so they could be Adi, Tehmi, Ruby, and Vispi Pavri.

"Fine, fine," she said, laughing, and gave Roshan a hug as well, something that needed all her arm length. "So nice to see you—Hilla is inside already."

She led them in and got Zubin Commissariat to help her bring two more dining chairs to the living room entrance and seat them next to their daughter Hilla, just as dusky little Jean Pundol was wailing, "But why can't they pray over something *else* instead and make *that* holy?"

"What? What?" shouted Faram, never slow to make his presence felt in company. His whispers were conducted at normal speaking levels, and as Tehmi lowered herself to the floor she thought she saw Zubin Commissariat flinch from the sheer volume up close. "Pray over *what*, Jeanie?"

Everyone chimed in at once to fill him in, and Faram sat back in the chair, thick black eyebrows lifted like accents over French syllables, hamming it up: "You mean you sissies are worried about some harmless bull's piss?"

"Faram, please." Soona Pundol was all jiggling remonstration, a great mauve shimmy. "Think of what you're saying in front of our children at least."

"All right, everyone," said Adi the master of ceremonies quickly, pursing his full lips, clearly uneasy as Faram seemed ready to respond in still less than genteel fashion, his wife Roshan squaring her broad and capable shoulders as well. "I think we've wasted enough time on this. Let's let Jeroo and Cyrus continue with their presentation, please."

And they all settled down for a bit. But no sooner had poor little Jeroo Olia in her daisy yellow frock timidly begun, "Then milk with rose petals in it is poured all over the body," than she was interrupted once again, this time by Perin Pundol, the rebel in the corner, not about to let the meeting slip back into boring routine.

"Adi Uncle, can't we spend some time on adult things too?" she cried, from her vantage point of nineteen years. "Some of us would rather hear about the wedding ceremony than the navjot."

Adi, looking a bit harassed by now, cast a quick glance at Perin's mother, Soona, who shrugged her shoulders—setting off a flesh wave or two—and looked noncommittal.

"Yes, okay, Perin," he said, a trifle more nasal than before. "We can do that. But it would be better if we scheduled a *presentation* on the lagan ceremony so somebody can prepare material about it."

"That's fine," persisted Perin, who, everyone knew, had an ulterior motive for asking. "But we can just talk about it without material this time, can't we? Like I want to know why we're not allowed to marry Americans!"

Adi looked worriedly over again at Soona and then Shapoor Pundol, but they were maintaining slab faces, so he sighed. "That is not what we are saying, Perin. Only thing is, our Parsi community is already very small, and we don't want to make it smaller."

Perin was relentless. "But aren't Parsi *boys* allowed to have non-Parsi wives and still be Parsis and still have Parsi children, but only Parsi *girls* can't marry outside and still be Parsis?"

Tehmi saw her husband hesitate, uncertainty on his face.

"That is true, Perin." She spoke up from her spot on the carpet just as he finally started to say something. Even so, better than to leave him struggling out there. "That is what the priests say, and maybe it is said somewhere in the Avesta. What to do? But even for the boys, we don't want them to ignore Parsi girls and go get married somewhere else.

"What does Zubin think?" she continued, thinking she ought to move the mike away from Perin if possible. For some reason she felt comfortable in turning to the quiet young man, even though he was still so new to the Detroit community. "Don't you think Parsi boys should try to marry Parsi girls?"

A fleetingly quick shield passed over the generously mustached young fellow's dark eyes and was gone before Tehmi was sure she had seen it. But he responded with a strong enough, "Yes. Of course," in his pleasant baritone, without elaborating. Adi, she remembered, had not particularly taken to him and his South Bombay Parsi accent at first, pointing to his inability to speak much Gujarati. A sure sign of snootiness. But the boy had always gone out of his way to be nice, and ultimately Adi had conceded that for a South Bombay type he was all right (almost all the Detroit Parsis were from Dadar Parsi Colony or the various baags).

"But why is there that difference in the rules for the men and the *women*?" This time it was Tehmi's own daughter, Ruby, sounding quite aggravated, siding with her friend Perin. Understandable, of course, but Tehmi wished she'd kept quiet.

And sure enough, Boman Olia, whose asides with Perin's father, Shapoor, had been interrupted by the new controversy, now slid his smooth tones into the momentary pause produced by the blunt query.

"Ours not to question the teachings of Zarthust saheb, Ruby. He knew best." The emphasis of Boman's voice capitalized the pronoun.

Casting a sidelong glance at Adi, Tehmi saw from his tightening face that in this rebuke of Ruby he read a rebuke of himself, both as her father *and* as host and manager of the meeting. There was little love lost between the two men. Boman, also an engineer when he first arrived in the States, had done his MBA part-time at Ann Arbor, taking the path Adi had hesitated over when the kids came along. Afterward, while Boman moved into administrative positions at Pontiac and grew a salted beard to suit, Adi had stagnated in the design ranks. In typically pompous fashion, Boman hadn't hesitated a bit to advise Adi to follow his example, which had only made her husband less willing. When Adi had finally changed companies, she'd seen his hopes swing up for a year, then settle back when little else changed. And he was left to mutter about old boys' clubs. . . .

As to the whole problem of marrying outside the community, of course Boman, with two *sons*, and little Jeroo not even at her navjot stage, didn't care about the difference between rules for men and women. Maybe when his daughter grew older and there were still hardly any Parsi boys around, he'd change his mind.

Ruby certainly looked incensed by his reproof, and Tehmi noted the engaging color that had flooded her daughter's face.

"There seem to be plenty of other Parsis asking about this, Boman Uncle, if you read the letters to the editor in *Parsiana*," the girl said, evidently unimpressed by her adversary's years. "Some of the letters even said the rule isn't part of Zarathustra's teachings—it was added later by the priests. Whatever *their* reason was, I don't think it's a coincidence they're all men!"

"Now, Ruby," Adi warned their daughter, clearly embarrassed and disturbed at the turn his prayer meeting had taken and the part his own family was playing in the debacle. Tehmi could read, as if off a thought-cloud above his head, the concerns running through his mind as he glanced around at the younger children, all quite confused by the raised voices, by what was happening to the adults. Nothing like this had taken place when Cawas Golvala emceed last month—the meeting had gone like clockwork.

"It's true, Adi Uncle," cried Perin the rebel, climbing back into the ring. "That rule is so ridiculously chauvinist! Even if it was written in the Avesta, that was all *thousands* of years ago!"

"All these Western ideas in your head," said her mother, Soona, finally opening her cupid mouth, pink without the help of lipstick. "If you had grown up in Bombay, instead. . . . See this young boy, how sensible he is."

Spread out like a grand mauve vision across the love seat, she waved her regal arm, sagging triceps and all, at the heavily mustached Zubin Commissariat, who promptly looked uncomfortable.

"Soona Aunty," said Ruby in exasperation. "He was just being polite! Mom put him on the spot, that's why."

Tehmi wondered if that was what she'd done, manipulated the young man into the response she wanted out of him.

"Zubin—" Ruby turned smartly to him now, flushed in unconscious exertion of her femininity, her voice changing pitch. The young, brash smell of Charlie marched to join imitation Chanel No. 5 at the center of the room. "—Don't you think it's unfair? Don't you feel we should *all* have the right to marry *whomever* we want?"

He looked back at her for a moment, clearly on the spot once again. Beneath the lush black mustache Tehmi saw a wry half-smile come on. Indication, it seemed, of a good-natured willingness to respond to Ruby's plea, even if it meant contradicting his own last words.

"Sure," he said then, nodding at Ruby, barely having missed a second before coming out with it. "We should, no doubt."

"There!" She flashed him a dazzling red-and-white smile that set Tehmi's heart a-flutter with hope, before her daughter turned back to Soona Pundol, laughing and breathless at Zubin's turn-around and her triumph over both of them. "See?"

But Soona just looked away, miffed, and Adi the M.C. cleared his throat to bring the afternoon's program back on line.

He was not in time to foil Boman Olia.

"Please try to stick to the program, folks," said that prominent citizen, his mouth hardly seeming to move within the light-and-shade brush of hairs. "My children have been preparing their presentation for over a week."

This from the man who'd been chatting away to Shapoor Pundol when the presentation started.

Once again Tehmi saw the harassed look, the sense of being publicly chided, cloud Adi's eyes. And her heart full for her husband in his distress, she stepped in on his behalf.

"Boman, we all—" she began, meaning to say that they all wanted to hear what little Jeroo and Cyrus had prepared, but she got no further.

"SILENCE, WOMAN!"

Tehmi froze. It was not Boman Olia who'd spoken—the bellowing voice was her normally contained *husband's*, his forehead scrunched, his face suffused with frustration. And as its echoes died, it sent the whole room deep into the silence it demanded of her.

She knew almost at once that his lashing out was blind, that she had stepped unwittingly into the line of pent-up fire, that his rage, uncontrollably released, was directed at his own ineffectiveness even more than at Boman, who was now sitting back smugly and watching the show. But knowing this did not change what had been done to her, nor take away the shock that was paralyzing her now, cramping her stomach, petrifying her facial muscles into stone. In front of *everyone*! In her own home, with her daughter and closest friends looking on. . . . The polished wooden paneling around her swirled, then seemed to turn darker, suffocatingly close. What was she to do now? Where could she show her face after this?

Out of the hush, a voice finally emerged. She couldn't move her head or even shift her eyes to look, but it was a calm baritone and she recognized it from her daze as young Zubin Commissariat's.

"Boy!" it said, light yet clear. "Adi is really going to get it after we're gone. . . ."

No one was likely to believe that, Tehmi knew. But so matter-of-factly was it said that it released them all to laugh nervously, released the bearlike Faram to gruffly joke about Adi's fate, released Boman's wife, the ribald Piloo Olia, to add sexual innuendo. It even released Adi to force a smile at their jokes, the bags under his eyes suddenly more pronounced.

And it released Tehmi finally, her neck muscles unloosening a fraction, to swivel her eyes and twitch her lips in a grateful look at Zubin. But so calmly did she find his eyes still resting on her that she had to look away again. Her stomach was continuing to cramp. No, Adi was not going to "get it" from her once the meeting was over. More likely, she knew, she'd stay locked inside her shell, unable to emerge for weeks. He'd try hard to make it up to her, day after day, but something numb inside of her would stop her from responding. And what if that made him angry again, caused the whole thing to snowball . . . ? Still, time was the only possible antidote. She saw that clearly, as she heard his strained voice get the presentation rolling yet again. The remaining tension would slowly loosen its hold on her, and her shields would eventually come down. They'd have to.

Adi's voice stumbled to a stop, and young Cyrus Olia's high-pitched one took over self-importantly. Unable to follow a word, her mind clogged and whirling at the same time, Tehmi eased her neck cautiously, hearing it creak, and darted a glance over to her daughter's corner. Ruby's head was turned down toward her lap, fingers picking at the folds of her skirt. A nice new amber skirt. What must she be thinking? Of her father's words? Her mother's silence? Maybe, with some luck, of the way young Zubin Commissariat had spoken up for her mother. At least this much Tehmi now knew: one day she would look on as her daughter got married. Boys would line up in the dozens for her, if they had any sense.

So Tehmi still, with a mother's eye, saw Ruby in a white lace wedding sari draped Gujarati style. Seated in Tehmi's own wedding chair on a flower-laden stage. Under the gold-winged and black-bearded protection of an enormous feroher woven in silky, sweet-smelling jasmine and marigold. (Come to think of it, why no female angels?) But when Tehmi tried to bring the fuzzy figure on the matching tall chair into focus, or even tell whether he was dressed in a daghli or a suit or—dear Khodaiji—a tuxedo, she was quite unable to, and finally had to stop trying. Her head hurt too hard.

Matters
of
Balance

We were a brilliant and a competitive bunch at the Indian Scientific Institute; the legend above our college walls labeled us the cream of the nation. Every year, tens of thousands of oil-shiny brown youngsters just out of school in Madras, Bombay, Calcutta, Bangalore, Surat, Delhi, Mysore, Kanpur, any city that deserves to be called one, sat at wooden desks in school or college centers to write an entrance exam, all chrysalid scientists and engineers. Only three hundred made it in. Draupadi, fresh out of school, supposedly gang-raped and all, got in on her first try. It took me two. Sudhir Malhotra made it in one, but there was more than brainpower involved.

He still had a year to go when I finished at Cathedral and John

Connon in Bombay and first tried for ISI. Those early, free-as-a-bird months out of school, I actually attended Aggrawal's coaching classes, study crutch for the aspiring ISIte, but—naturally—goofed off, ruined the opening physics paper, and didn't bother to return for chemistry and math. Some hypocrites in the St. Xavier's School courtyards were shaking their heads over missing one out of the twenty problems—I'd only finished eleven. So I pulled out and went to Elphinstone College for a year of idling. But I kept Aggrawal's notes and sample questions, stashed them in a drawer for another day. Sudhir finished school, and we wrestled samples together, tested each other, opted for the same center, then dropped off our applications simultaneously at the Sachivalay post office. Not surprisingly, our seat numbers at St. Xavier's, when they came back in the mail, were consecutive.

"Means joint placement, son, either lateral or vertical," said Sudhir, which deciphered meant our desks would be either side by side or front to back. I've known him all my life—our family flats are in vertical placement, and I spent more time up in his room than in mine as a schoolboy—but I freely admit he's what we called a pseud. Which means what it sounds like. "Hope it's lateral."

Off we went on the first morning of the tests, and were not intimidated by the appearance of St. Xavier's, a gloomy, stale structure of gray stone blocks, but disappointed to find that in fact my desk was behind his. This reduced the scope for collaboration, we felt. In any case, all the mugging paid off: this time in the courtyard I was able to report seventeen out of twenty on the physics, Sudhir eighteen, and the language section after break, to quote him, went like watermelon in May. But he was not as cocky on the morning of math, leaning sluggishly against me as we caught the bus, preferring to sit on the first level than climb to the top. En route, he mumbled things I could barely hear above the bus.

". . . all night, son . . . oof, orgasmic chemistry . . . popped couple of dexis . . . try later, desperately, sleep . . . took calmpos, three–four, drop off . . ." And here he clutched at my arm and grew still more garbled. "Remember orgasmic . . . easy . . . okay . . . life depend on you . . . math . . . got to, son."

All of which meant the multivalent world of organic chemistry was an open book to him and duplicating it as simple as carbon copying. Especially since he'd have his wits back by then. But math was only minutes away, and his mind in no shape to deal with the convolutions of ratio and proportion, algebra, geometry, or trig.

We were ready with a plan at the hour. Had his seat been behind mine, I would have only needed to lift my answer sheet from time to time. But it was the other way around—what isn't?—and two invigilators per room watching. Sixty minutes for a hundred complicated multiple-choices. Not easy even normally, so it's strange that I never considered just letting him handle it by himself. Now, at times, I think I should have. Everything might have been different then—no ISI together, maybe even no Bhuppy, no Draupadi, nothing.

But in the thirty-six seconds available for each item, I calculated, chose, looked for the schoolmasters, picked a moment, dropped my head and said "D." Or "A," whichever it was, keeping my voice within the distracted and disbelieving square of desks around ours. No skipping questions—how would he know? If I was stumped, I guessed, risking the quarter-point penalty for errors, ticked the box, spoke, and moved on. Painful, fearful seconds crept by when the invigilators loitered too close to risk the syllable, and my blood boiled at the thought I was probably destroying my own chances. At hour's end we stood at number eighty-three.

My nerves were still shot and my blood high when a recovering and optimistic Sudhir thanked me profusely at the break.

"Forget it," I said. Fellows around us in the courtyard were moaning about getting a problem or two wrong. "We can both say bye to ISI." For the second time, in my case.

"No, no, no," said the erstwhile mumbler. "We're both going to get in; I'm sure of it."

Even when he turned out to be right (which says something about the courtyard loudmouths, since we never saw them at ISI), I had a lingering, testy feeling of imbalance. It was more than just his rank turning out higher than mine. He'd had nothing to lose, I plenty; his gain was tremendous, mine nonexistent.

Out east at ISI, two nights across the breadth of the country by train, we went to the same hostel, of course, roomed next to each other, chose the mechanical department. Staying ahead of the game in the Indian Scientific Institute, we found, was easier than becoming players had been. Between exams, we woke at leisure, climbed the enclosure walls of the swimming pool to float on our backs in tepid water until lunch, played records at pussy-plumbing volume in the common room, visited town on our bicycles, and cut or attended classes as we felt like.

When we attended, there was no need to take notes: Sudhir's good friend and later mine, Bhupinder Chawla, was already there, scribbling away. The week before exams each term, we got together in Bhuppy's room to go over his notes. On exam nights he held forth on each subject to an audience of two, his block face suddenly mobile the way animated clay figures are, saying it helped solidify his own fundas. Good fellow, though at first I held off from getting friendly—something inside me felt he was trespassing. Sudhir owed me exclusive rights to his friendship, I thought. During our study sessions, that worthy lounged in a bent steel chair, looking too chiseled and elegant for his own good. The usual female response to a picture of him and me—both tall and not too dark, brothers brown, he only an inch or two taller—is, "Oh, who's your handsome friend?" I took a break every three hours to stretch out on Bhuppy's steel cot and shut my eyes, instructing them to wake me in ten minutes but resisting consciousness for at least five after they tried.

We won through those exam days by means of our God-given intelligence and our set squares. Sudhir said he invented the scheme, though I think it was an ISI tradition orally handed down from batch to batch. In any case, I got it from him. On the night before first-year statistics, my brain was already crammed with now unneeded mechanics formulas, and I was panicked by the impossibility of packing in a bunch of volatile cryptograms from Piskunov, a Russian mathematician, with the first syllable of whose name we'd had some fun in class.

"Not to worry, son," said Sudhir. "Let me show you the statistical function of set squares."

And picking up a pencil, he demonstrated what he meant.

So I arrived at the exam room, a pair of set squares protruding from my bag. After scanning the question paper, I pulled out the 45-degree isosceles and laid it on the desk. Bright white lettering at the center of transparent hard-plastic said RAGHAV'S GEOMETRY INSTRUMENTS. Making sure Shivdasani, the literature prof and our invigilator for the morning, was far enough, I slid it onto the answer sheet as if to draw a line across the paper. Against the white background it was subtly transformed: the trademark turned indistinct, but around it swarmed lightly penciled figures, their slate gray showing up clearly. It's hard to remember that the moment-generating function of a binomial distribution is $M(t) = [(1 - p) + pe^t]^n$. Hearing Shivdasani's sandals tramp up the rows, I pushed the triangle back over the wood brown. The formulas vanished. He passed close enough to leave a whiff of pomfret, but I didn't bother to look up.

A degree of balance was thus restored between Sudhir and myself, but not parity. Any risk he took when employing the scheme was for himself, not me. And my modest gains within our new domain hardly compared with his entry into it. . . .

Holidays between semesters we spent back in Bombay. They were our release time, rutting periods. We were like Krag, the bighorn mountain ram in my childhood *Classics Illustrated* comic book, ready to butt heads with other rams, glorying in our full-blown strength, conscious to the extent of narcissism of our demonic beauty, of secret and open looks from women, of breeding, wealth, and limitless prospects, of the honed edge of intelligence and the power it cast over the world in our fists. It was all too intoxicating. Our haunts were many: my old and familiar Samovar across the road from Elphinstone for one. Elphie chicks still streamed into Sam's in all their lipsticked, pert-breasted, nude-naveled, full-buttocked nubility to dawdle over cold espressos or sweet lassis, looking less away from us now we were no longer dime-a-dozen Elphinstonians but rare-bird ISItes on our way to techno stardom. From Sam's to three-course lunch at the club, lunch to Ra-worshipping by poolside umbrellas. Then night lights at Studio 29 or Talk of the Town, and after a day's ride like that, one in five girls was ready to ride.

At the pool, the long swimming hours in ISI paid off in terms of streamlined musculature, now much admired and stroked. Lounging in a chair meant to lounge in for a change, his head pulled back by playful, manicured fingers enmeshed in his longish, seal-sleeked hair, Sudhir was given to say, "Good kismat, son; our kismat is very good."

"Oh," the owner of the fingers once said, teasing his hair. She was daring, for those days, in a jade bikini streaked with black. "Do I enter into your kismat at all?"

"All of today, darling," he answered with a smile, earning a petulant tweak. "Tonight I'll enter yours."

"That's what *you* think," she said, pleasurably titillated but drawing herself up and flouncing off into the water.

"Went too far this time, son," I said to him, as my companion, more conservative in a one-piece, patted me on the arm and followed.

"No, no, no," he responded, unperturbed. "She liked it. Ten to one I'll plumb her before the week is finished."

And he did.

He knew them better, already, than I did. Knew himself better, too. My sense of myself was a swirl of confused and contrary impulses. At any rate there was parity in plunder—he plumbed, I plumbed. And those we plumbed were all of a likeness, even once or twice the same. Draupadi and the jealousy she brought in her wake were as yet concealed in our kismat.

Dharampur was less copious in its offerings, what with the lone women's hostel on campus, the relatively studious leanings of Jhansi Hall's residents, and the medieval nine o'clock curfew they lived by, not to mention our competition in numbers (if not caliber) and in intensity of need from a thousand frustrated male ISItes. Old Dharampur's prostitutes were a vent for some— Bhuppy went regularly—but most made their only physical contact with womanhood once annually on Holi, the festival of color. Preferring hand-applied powdered colors to the remote liquid spray gun, male packs ranged the campus grounds in search of females, wasting only a couple of perfunctory alibi powder scuffles on each other, smearing the women's faces red and green, receiving love pats on their own. And if their hands slipped at times to pat illegal subneck territory, it was an accident, of course.

Sudhir and I usually avoided the desperate scene altogether, or at any rate absconded to our rooms once the Holi morning bhang was had. One fine March in our fourth and final year at ISI, however, Bhuppy hauled us along with him. There was a fresher from Calcutta in Jhansi Hall that year on whom he had an eye. He was not alone. She was made on buxom, Sridevi lines, and the grapevine said the permanent sullen look on her face was the result of having been raped as a teenager, some said gang-raped. In a strange way, that made her more exciting, certainly more than the unversed virgins who populated Jhansi for the most part, though it hardly followed that rape made an experienced woman of a girl.

That morning the three of us trooped down to the mess for special breakfast, the special part being an aluminum mug filled to the brim with a thick, greenish, liquid bhang concoction: dried and crushed hemp leaves and seeds mixed with a milk, banana, and saffron mash to help it go down. The taste, nevertheless, was chalky. The effect was two-phased. Bhuppy blew out of the hostel on Holi mornings a tiger, all fired up and dashing around campus with his colors. By late afternoon, he trudged back in a listless daze, looking like the cow-trap grille had been built for him. Once he hit his cot, he was out until dinnertime, though one afternoon he tried to read instead and came running out of his room yelling, "Look at this page; what's happening? All the letters are moving around—I can't read anymore!" On the Holi morning of our final year, he wangled an extra mug, talked us into coming, drained it while we bought powder packs from the fruit stall, and spun us out onto the road.

The destination was Jhansi Hall. On the way we encountered and anointed some campus BHMBs (Badi Hoke Maal Banegi: will grow up to be hot stuff) on their young, shy faces, then dropped in on professors' quarters to sample trays of sweetmeats laced with bhang offered smilingly by the profs' wives. Under their watchful husbands' eyes, we played Holi and innocent with them. By this time, we'd acquired anonymity under masks of an orangish blend of caking colors, and it was onward ho for Jhansi.

Inside the compound, a group of Jhansians had brought out chairs and were seated in a circle, wrongly assuming safety in the open and in numbers. A bunch of male ISItes were milling around with colors on the inside of the circle, and we joined them. Sudhir led. As we made the round and I bartered make-up and banter with Jhansians across from me, my peripheral vision showed, further along, the Calcutta fresher of violation fame in a prim brown dress and equally starched smile.

When Sudhir came to her, I looked less at the simpering giggler in front of me than at the two of them. He liked her even through her thickening mask, I could see, and despite her lank hair and broad shoulders. Though her dress was the worst she could have chosen for Holi other than a plain white (most of the other girls were sensibly in old T-shirts and jeans), it was still, apart from sprinklings of powder that had sifted down, relatively bare of extraneous color, and I noticed he left it so. Rotating past the giggler to the fresher, I added my ministrations to his, saw troubled black eyes between the green I applied. Her touch on my face was hurried and light. We had hardly moved on when I heard a scream, and turning, saw her look down, aghast, at her breasts, as the fellows around her stepped hastily back. Finger marks of red and blue had flowered around both her substantial mounds, purplish palm prints smack across their centers.

Bhuppy, who'd been making the rounds behind us, was suddenly between Sudhir and me. Looking for all the world like a cornered animal herself, the fresher lifted her head and shouted, to everyone at large, "Animals! You animals! You call yourselves human beings? What's wrong with you? Have you gone *mad*, all of you?"

A general hubbub was her reply. We hit the road, on Bhuppy's quiet urging, before matters got out of hand, but I was taken by the drama in the fresher's voice and the desperation on her face. The rape rumor was probably true for her to have reacted so strongly.

Our crass friend was openly exuberant once we'd trailed back onto Scholars' Avenue. "Wow, you buggers, I had those tits right in my hands—solid size, I tell you."

"Yes, son." Sudhir yawned; we were both slipping into the second phase of the bhang cycle. "You were quite a hero."

"Don't sneer at me, big shot. Where were you fellows, with all your boasts about Bombay chicks—just playing patty-cake with her face."

"Quite right, Bhuppy," I said, measuring our performances as I was accustomed to do, and coming away none the worse for it. "Can't compare us to a Don Juan like you."

He was still so wound up when we reached Darjeeling Hall that he got on his cycle and shot off to Old Dharampur in a heated blur that boded energetic times for his regular girl. We climbed the stairs slowly and crashed in our rooms. By the time we awoke, he was long returned and not wakeable for mess.

A week or two later, he was waddling painfully bowlegged around the corridor and missing classes—a situation neither Sudhir nor I could afford with midterms not far away. In his excitement, Bhuppy had forgotten to ingest the customary tablets of pentid sulphide before visiting Old D., and now that he thought of it, there had been an unusual odor about his girl. So we walked him out to a riksha and in to a doctor at Naidu Hospital. One solid shot of penicillin and we had our notetaker installed in class again.

No real question of balance there (though Bhuppy saw it as friendly return for past assistance, and there was, as a matter of fact, some of that). Just one of mutual necessity.

But the need for the fresher of the fingerprinted breasts (let's call her Draupadi; unlike Bhuppy, I'll leave our victim her anonymity—and me mine) developed into a mutually exclusive one for Sudhir and me. "Draupadi," then, may not be an appropriate appropriation. Unlike the fraternally generous Pandava five of the Mahabharata, the two brothers drawn to her by fate (and, possibly, by the need to go where a third brother had been) found they had no inclination to share her. (Bhuppy himself had lost interest altogether. Weak-mindedly believing himself to have been visited by heavenly retribution and sweatily relieved to be off the hook, he kept himself far removed and in a state of temporary celibacy, resorting to copious application of, ironically, his offending and infamous palm. Poetic justice, one might say.) The difference this time from our joint plumbing ventures, of which we'd had a few, may well have been Draupadi's steady refusal, despite month-long attentions paid and received at Jhansi Hall, to be plumbed by either one of us.

Which is not to say she didn't like us or wasn't flattered by the attention from seniors. Sudhir's charm, turned up high, almost eased the sullenness off her face, had her wriggling and flapping hands like a coy seal. Seductive movements, given her near-voluptuous dimensions. She'd gone to one of the top convent schools in Cal. Hence, both, her fairly high rank in the ISI entrance exam and her blend of prim sensuality. Teasing her about hypothetical past affairs prompted only mysterious smiles. She was not going to be drawn into provocative revelations, let alone admissions of gang rape.

So she remained an enigma to us, and our imaginations worked overtime to fill in the blanks.

In turn, she didn't know how to decipher me—how could she when I couldn't yet?—and as a result seemed ambivalent, disturbed yet drawn. She liked us together better than separately, however. Complementary flavors, maybe, the way cocktail ingredients gain something in combination. And I've no doubt she (rightly) anticipated less plumbing overtures in tandem, though we weren't by nature averse to such a thing. In her case an unspoken competitiveness had begun to consume us, and sharp prickings assaulted me in sight of her responsiveness to Sudhir or at the thought of him alone with her, inveigling himself toward bull's eye. So I weighed down his shaft while advancing mine.

"Remember what happened to you at Holi?" I asked her—purely rhetorical question—one afternoon while he was off at a meeting with his final-year project advisor.

We were seated on a cracked wooden bench outside Kaku's cigarettes-and-snacks stall a hundred meters from the gym, easing his potato patties down our food pipes with tea. The cup and saucer tinkled in her hand at recollection of her encounter with the masked ISIte. Her midriff, hourglassed between blouse and petticoat, shuddered apprehensively, rocking the misused mounds.

"I was there," I continued, and her other hand flew to her mouth. "I saw what that crude bastard, whoever he was, had done to you. I wanted to find out who, after we realized what had happened, but . . . " Lengthy pause from me; expectant, troubled look from her. "But the friend I was with thought we'd all get in trouble if we stayed—all the Holi players in the circle—and pulled me away with him. I still wanted, afterward, to find out who and bring the swine to you by his neck . . ."

She was impressed and cautiously curious. "Did you manage . . . ?"

I admitted the trail was slimy with red herrings: too many frust ISItes balloted for, campuswide, as culpable.

"Who was the one with you?" she asked in predictable sequence, a dash of anxiety seasoning the question.

I counted to three and rubbed at my chin before saying, "Actually, you know the fellow, Draupadi. So if you don't mind . . ."

"Oh," she said, and a twitchiness worried her features as she edged toward me. The palla of her sari brushed my arm. An unexpected wave of tenderness swamped me at this renewed proof of her vulnerability. I wanted very much to kiss her, and a week later she allowed me. But the North Pole would have proved warmer territory than she did to Sudhir from then on. So he retired the expedition.

"Three's a crowd, son, and so on and so forth," he said wryly, removing the bone from my kebab, which, however, remained provocatively beyond fork's end for a while longer and grew more expensive than I realized at the time or thought the menu had said. The dish's reluctance to be consumed, it became eventually apparent, could only be overcome by assuring her that the proper conventions would be observed. If she was to be my dish, in other words, then I must become her catch. Her parents back in Calcutta were progressive enough, it transpired, to permit a "love match," and orthodox enough to still see marriage and motherhood as their daughter's ultimate vocation, forget about electrical engineering. Nine months along (our only pregnancy to now), just half a year after I graduated from ISI, Draupadi and I were tied at the waist, circling ceremonial fires in Bombay.

Occupied though I was at the celebrations with family—mine as well as hers, down from Cal—I felt an incidental shift in balance between my competitive friends and myself. A shift that took me past simple parity. In Sudhir's thought-burdened face at the function, I saw his recognition of that. Bhuppy came too, on leave from Steel Authority's Rourkela plant, all smiles and, later, drunk (with the help of a hip flask in his suit pocket; no alcohol served in the wedding hall, thanks to my father). Draupadi's parents, her father balding and hook-nosed, her mother bejeweled and round, were transparently proud of their daughter's brilliant ISI catch. The wedding dais felt like a winner's podium.

My confidence that the prize was worth the price stayed strong that night as I slipped through snowy garlands curtaining our wedding bed where she sat bathed in the fragrance of jasmine, improved when I parted the shorter, velvety petal strings veiling our faces to confirm the suppleness of her darkened, still-sullen mouth, grew as I undraped her (her glittering red wedding sari coming completely away, not the original Draupadi's endless unfurling at the lusty hands of Dushasana) to place my own palm prints, finally, on her unexpectedly oblong, heavy-hanging breasts, mounted to certainty at the point I pulled down her underwear, ruffled her thriving bush, and, spreading her compliantly open, impaled her at last, but fell off strangely when, encountering unexpected impedance to my prong, I learned the unequivocal way that the accounts of her rape had been as much campus folklore as the ubiquitous legend of the institute director's daughter. (In desperate sexual heat, so the story went on ISI, BITS, and IIT campuses across the country, the diro's daughter had sought relief from their pet, an Alsatian. The canine angle of penetration happening to differ from the human, the natural course of detumescence and uncoupling failed to follow the conclusion of the act, and the mixed-species pair found themselves stuck with one another. The diro's daughter had been obliged, despite her state of unusual and excessive immodesty, to call in her parents, who, after prolonged tug-of-warlike efforts failed, had no recourse but to summon a doctor. The whole messy business was finally resolved, in one version, by the sawing off of the hapless house pet's prick—a case for the SPCA, if ever.) Strangled cries from Draupadi upon my pushing home, and a blotchy red staining of brand-new bedsheets (a news item that would drift through the household next morning, eliciting quiet nods from servants and family alike), confirmed my analysis.

I felt, in a peculiar way, cheated.

Doesn't make sense, except that the rumor, such a bizarre part of her initial allure, had also become part, in my head, of the woman I was marrying.

I kept this, of course, from Sudhir—to divulge shortcomings in the prize we'd contested was to cede my edge. We each had letters after our names now, and trainee titles with plum Bombay concerns (ironic, considering our indispensable notetaker Bhuppy got stuck in Rourkela; we made better interviewees). But nobody I'd wanted had changed her name to his.

Draupadi had dropped out of ISI, naturally, a price to pay of her own (though I doubt she knew how steep, at nineteen), to become trainee home manager under my mother, who was a delicate woman with increasingly hennaed hair. Mum had not appreciated the denial of her prerogative to pick my wife and maintained a cold politeness toward her charge that by its constancy over the years seemed somehow to gain in bite even as they brought more red to her hair. Draupadi's demonstrations of daughterly devotion inevitably progressed from eager to desperate to subdued to nonexistent. She talked more to her own mother two thousand miles away in Calcutta than to mine. We went out for dinner more and more often as she grew less and less involved with meal preparations in the kitchen and began instead to frequent meetings of a women's book club. Mum was outraged, in her contained but recognizable fashion, at this straying of her ward, but I backed Draupadi up.

Maybe I shouldn't have. She was my wife, not an extra cook—I wanted that clear. And she appreciated it, looked almost tenderly on me for a while. But had she stayed under Mum's thumb, it's possible that things would not have eventually come to such a mess.

I got on no better than she had, with my "superiors" at work, common types who resented my inherited status and comforts as also my brains and lack of servility—all a revelation to me. Sudhir, his hair cut to size now, reported similar smallnesses in his higher-ups: he was quizzed as to his need to work at all. One of my bosses, carless and tired of train crush, tested me unsubtly each time he hitched a ride in my air-conditioned Contessa after work, hinting at an invitation home only to turn it down when made (the one time he came he was uneasy before my parents and saucer-eyed at Draupadi). Sudhir was cornered into poolside entertaining at the club, and, complying, generated more envy than benevolence. So all was level—his roadblocks were my roadblocks, and we gave a joint shit.

But bosses and ladders was not the only game played on company premises. He rarely hesitated to honk his own horn to me, and the tune often spoke of secretaries and receptionists sounded.

A member of the second tribe, if Sudhir was to be believed (which he usually was), once rose at his early arrival to bolt shut all entry to the reception room and offer herself on top of her desk, saying, "Five minutes before I have to let people in." They were at it for ten. My legal bondage, already cause for twinges when encountering women of any charm, grew irksome after repeated endurance of his news items and intolerable when we foursomed to dinner with a succession of his young-and-delectables, each of whom rendered my still-attractive but permanent consort tedious in different ways. And on returning to bed afterward, I felt the lie given to, ironically, an old motto of ours: a hole is a hole is a hole is a hole.

So I found some others in time, and redress in the bargain.

Draupadi came to know in ways mostly intuitive though occasionally circumstantial. I was too slick for more, my forays too numerous at last for less. My mother caught the same vibrations and acquired an aura of smugness: how predictable the fate of these so-called love marriages (not that I'd ever used the term). She passed her suspicions on to my father, who sent dour looks down the dining table at his wayward son. My sisters heard rumors emanating from Sudhir's family (which got the drift earlier for reasons to follow), quarreled and broke up with their boyfriends, then submitted one by one to our mother's choice of groom.

And it was necessary for the purpose of equilibrium that Sudhir hear my accounts in rejoinder to his.

Still better satisfaction was to be had through employing *his* bedroom. The risk (of doing it only three floor-slabs above Draupadi—a situational aphrodisiac) was all mine once again, but so was the gain this time. And he was the helper. I reestablished a random pattern from childhood days of spending odd evenings up with him, closeted off from the rest of the Malhotra flat, entering directly through the corridor connection, leaving the same way. Often now we talked about politics and the state of the country under Congress. Both of us approved the party's return to power after the Janata Dal fiasco, but Sudhir felt we'd been better off under I-Gans despite her literally castrative policies, while I was glad to have her son, Rajiv, in charge, even if she had more hair, streaked or otherwise, than he did.

On most days we sat across Sudhir's draughts board as we talked, zigzagging over it in long diagonal skips, devouring the other's pieces, building kings, jousting wildly for conquest when only the flying double-deckers were left. On some days, a friend of his dropped in through the inner door and I out the outer. On some the friend was mine but coached to ask at the front door for Sudhir. He'd tease her a little, then be on his way through the corridor and into the lift with no one the wiser. Dinner foursome with Draupadi, in either case, was now a more interesting affair. There was a keen sense, around the table, of things contained, and an awareness of double entendres and self-generating ironies.

One night at the Shamiana, Sudhir looked to the fourth— an elfin face with a nose diamond and a floppy, exaggerated Princess Di cut, lissome as a plant in bed—and remarked, with a smile to indicate the spirit, "What a nice-looking orifice you have, Farzana."

"Oh, you like it?" she asked, quite unperturbed, clearly appreciative of his attentions, still tingling, I would think, from mine.

"How bad you are, Sudhir," said Draupadi, sipping her rose-essenced falooda. My wife's hand holding the glass, I noticed (not for the first time), was tastefully manicured, the nails a muted burgundy, the fingers long and elegant. Floral perfumes, her favorite, wafted about our table. She'd lost some weight since Dharampur days, a self-possessed woman now. It worried me. I, too, had a better sense of who I was, by then.

"Why?" I threw in. "Nothing wrong with the idea of rating orifices, diamond studded or otherwise. And who better a judge than Sudhir, since most of us explore only one, no matter how good?" The last with an acknowledging nod at Draupadi. It was true. An intensely passionate (or passionately intense) side to her had taken a while either for me to discover or for her to show. I could better recognize it now that I had immediate comparisons. Notable, too, that she continued to let it show.

"Oh, you explore so many, Sudhir?" inquired the recently studded elf without batting an eyelid at my claim.

"Can't help it," he replied, sawing modestly at his chicken-in-a-basket. "So much demand, only one me."

"No one like Draupadi to tempt you into extended study?" she persisted, but drew only a smile and a shrug.

"I think he wants you to try," I said.

"I don't know," she said, with a cool smile of her own. "I like exploring too. And don't forget, if orifices can be rated, so can their studs."

"Nothing wrong with that, either," I said.

"In fact," she said, looking slyly around the table, "it's a shame none of us can give ranks, first and second place, amongst ourselves."

"Ya, what a shame," said Sudhir.

"Easy to correct," I said. "Why don't we find out tonight, all of us together?"

"Draupadi would really like that," the black-haired Princess Diana pointed out, looking to my wife with an odd expression. Draupadi was bland enough in response, but those black eyes told me something was working within her. I knew them so well by then, the movement in their depths. Condensation beaded her tall, rose-pink falooda glass as if her thoughts were crystallizing.

"What do you say, Draupadi?" asked Sudhir, winking at her.

"You three go ahead," she replied, "and Farzana will let me know your ranks later."

"No, no," said Farzana. "It's all four or not at all—orgy is fine, gang bang avoidable."

"Subtle difference," I said, and the talk moved to other matters.

In our bedroom that night, Draupadi was dressed to conceal in a neck-high blue nightgown that hung like a box from wide shoulders, redeemed from sexlessness only by perfunctory lace trimmings. Her perfume too had worn off, and despite my recent libidinal satiation courtesy of Princess Farzana (though there was now something about her that would keep me from another tryst), it galled me to see my wife like that.

"You wouldn't have gotten very high rankings to start with, if you'd worn that to the orgy," I said from under a bedsheet to take care of the light December nip, hands crossed behind my head. Just peevishness—it was true about the nightgown, but all in all, Draupadi would have won hands down over Farzana on my scorecard. Something to do with that intensity. Also, paradoxically, with the five years we'd had, five more than I'd known with any other woman. My old motto was proving untrue in unexpected ways.

"I'd have worn something else if there *was* an orgy," she replied.

"Oh, big talk *now*," I said. "A bit late, sorry."

"Yes," she said. "A bit late."

And switching off the fluorescent lamp, she slipped under the top sheet, facing away to settle for the night.

But I'd had enough of her sullenness.

"I didn't need the orgy in any case—to give ranks. . . ."

The room grew still; the green-and-black HMT wall clock was suddenly audible. She'd bought it from Benzer four years ago when redecorating after the marriage, the first quartz clock in our family flat, and now it tocked in the dark as if about to shatter. When at last she spoke, her words slipped in between the beats. "Neither did I."

I was stunned for a moment, no question about it. Then as I lay there and thought, I saw two possibilities.

"You're making that up to get back at me," I said, hearing the rough edge on my voice.

She made a sound, probably a sniff. Even in the dark, I knew she looked her most attractive when sniffy, those full, pouty lips curling. "Where do you think he went, when you stayed upstairs with your prostitutes?"

Where, indeed?

"Oh, my prostitutes, is it?" I said. But it had come painfully to me that the second choice held. At some point between her first knowledge of my affairs and now, Draupadi had begun to cuckold me in *my* den on the very occasions I'd cheated on her in Sudhir's.

I could almost understand: looking for balance with Sudhir, I'd created an imbalance for her she'd felt compelled to correct. I should have foreseen that. The main complication, of course, sprang from her choice of *Sudhir* to correct it with! I hadn't slept with *her* best friend. . . . How hard must they have laughed to themselves at dinner? How differently, now, I read his wink at her. And that passionately intense side of hers—discovered with him, not me? That placed me only too deep in the minus vis-à-vis both.

She was silent.

"Do you still remember Holi at Dharampur?" I asked, for the second time in our lives, looking for level ground.

"Yes," she said. "And I know very well Sudhir didn't pull you away."

"That's okay," I said, though her quick defense of him clawed at my stomach. "I lied about something else. I *knew* who'd done it." I skipped two or three tocks from the time machine to let it sink in, then thrust beneath her guard. "In fact, he was very much a guest at our wedding. . . ."

Tock.

"Bhupinder Chawla," she said, in a strange voice. And if I'd needed signs of how intimate the connection between my wife and best friend, her knowledge of Bhuppy and his secret spoke volumes. "I wondered so often what he was like . . . to look at, to talk to, what he thought . . . long before I knew his name. For months after it happened, every time I felt his fingers on my breasts I saw flashes of him . . . in his war paint . . . just wondered and wondered who was behind it."

I thought about that in the pause that followed. Bhuppy, increasingly forgotten old friend—more or less incidental to my life and narrative, someone I'd paid little attention to except when he lectured us on exam nights. Who was he, in the end? A good fellow, a crude fellow. A friend who shared notes with his lazier pals, if with the open motive of consolidating his own basics. A frustrated sower of seed who, in the grips of hemp given freely by authority with the license to play, was led by his penis to molest instead. Wild enough to be proud of it when still in heat, weak enough to repent under threat of divine gelding.

"I can tell you," I said. "I'll show you the man behind the mask, the mind that worked the fingers. I can even introduce you. I'll invite him to Bombay."

But again she was ahead of me.

"No. No, thanks—I don't want to know any longer. I could have asked Sudhir if I wanted, but I was scared to once I learned that man was his *friend* . . . and yours." Sudhir first . . . I sensed her half-turn to me in the night, could smell her warm odors. Unexpectedly, I had the urge to bring her still closer, kiss her hard. Five years of more or less unconscious bonding, I suppose, cropping up at the wrong time.

"I might have found he had Sudhir's charm . . . ," she continued. "Or your intelligence . . . Or . . . I don't know—that he was funny . . . Something that would keep me from completely despising him." She'd turned so close now I could hear the breathiness of her voice. "I could never stand that—it's bad enough not being able to despise the two of you thoroughly."

With that, she turned over again and burrowed into her pillow, a signal that our talk was finished.

"He's *very* likable," I insisted, deeply unwilling to leave it like that. 'Despising' me, fine, but not this tired damned neutrality. It was a protective casing that shut me out. "You would like him very much."

But she would not take the bait. I tried desperately to turn her to face me again, but she was dead weight. An experimental hand along her arm she pushed off. So a second of utter frustration, then rage sprouting like a fairy-tale beanstalk. And suddenly I understood the only act that could establish once and for all between *us*—not her and Sudhir, not her and Bhuppy—the peak of intensity. Then she'd really have the violated past I'd believed in!

The thought excited me. Primal instincts—the animal kind, to use her word. As if something infinitesimal but omnipotent inside me, which so often had said to Sudhir and myself in lascivious, imperative tones, "Pass me on. Pass me on with your seed, and I'll reward you with sensual pleasure," was now expanding its message. "If you meet resistance," it added slyly, "*overcome it*, and I'll increase the excitement!" That's who Bhuppy is: Dawkins's lumbering survival machine driven by his selfish gene; still, at the core, neolithic within a civilized shell, resentful of the shell's confines and prohibitions even while equating himself with it; bursting through at times to rut like any dog, confused and guilt ridden at other times over his supposed aberrations. Of course we're animals—which fool says we aren't? Primal man was hardly required to wait for women's permission. It was simply plumb them or let your cells die.

It's not just chance that a few years back almost every popular Hindi movie had to have a rape scene in it, part of the hit formula. I remember a fantasy recounted by one of the frust brethren in our ISI class, a studious topper who dreamed, we'd thought, only of thermodynamics: Once God saw fit to send him a girlfriend, he said, he'd take a walk with her in the jungle. When they were in far enough to be quite alone, she'd run screaming from him, thorny branches catching and ripping at her clothes as he chased her down. Ah, we said, nodding knowingly, if a little surprised to hear this from him. All only in pretense, he amended hastily; she'd *let* him catch up with her and strip her naked there in the woods. His eyes and near-drooling mouth told the rest. Ah, yes, we said again. . . .

Just one recollection kept me from turning Draupadi over and taking her. The thought of an Elphie chick, back in joint hunting days when I was still forming. She lived out by the Bandra seaface, and the day we came across her, Sudhir and I dropped her home from Studio 29 in my Contessa, all three of us in front, she in between. The road had no streetlights I can recall; the lights of oncoming cars skated across our faces. Playing an old game, I pulled the wheel hard on turns, so she swung into either one of us. She giggled sportingly at the contact but taunted, "Cheap thrills!" after going especially hard into him. "Ya?" he retorted. "Let's see who's cheap—stop the car, son." Amid alternating, scornful "You don't have the guts!" from her and an increasingly stung, "Stop the car!" from him, I drifted into the ditch by the side. And her cries changed to "Wait, wait—I was just joking."

"Okay—who's cheap?" I asked, cutting the engine. We'd both turned upon her, and I heard waves coming in, pushing salt through the window. A headlight lit her face by degrees. "No one, no one," she said, her voice roughening, catching, cajoling. "Please don't, you two." Then turning swiftly to me, "Start the car, please." The approaching light was bright enough, now, that I could see her eyes, and it was a shock, somehow, to catch the naked fear in them. The game had clearly turned too serious in her mind. Inside me something was bemusedly responding to her pleas. . . . So I made her recite a long, babyish apology—which she did with disturbing eagerness—before I switched the engine on. Then, against Sudhir's protests at letting her off so easily, I pulled out toward her home. And now, so many years later, the memory of that unnamed something within me was making me hesitate. I had the sense it had survived only tenuously and would vanish forever, unlit even by intermittent headlights, if I raped Draupadi.

But lying there in the blanketing darkness with her, listening to the clock and the evening pattern of her breath, I knew that if I didn't, she'd have beaten me. I'd forgotten all along—a dangerous lapse—that I was dealing with another ISIte, not to mention someone who'd passed the entrance exam, unaided, in one shot. As I've said before, we're a brilliant lot. Which is fine, but I couldn't afford to let my wife think she wore the pants or by some trick of words could more than nullify what she'd done with my best friend! Her credit account with Bhuppy was not by any good logic to be applied to her debit account with me, nor the two fused in some hypothetical general account with men. I was out of patience with all the back and forth.

Fully in mind again of the naked offering she'd made of herself—how many times? how many times?—to Sudhir, I felt a mushrooming rage at her denial of my prerogative, sensed an immediate corresponding inflation between my legs. No sooner had that picture of her nakedness blossomed in the gloom than I put rough hands to the back of her thighs, ripe and spreading under the light cotton material, felt her start and twist around as I bunched the nightgown about her waist. Then, to the tune of her stifled cry, I yanked her pants down in the dark. She clutched and slapped at me furiously, gasping like a pressure cooker. Spurred by the sting on my neck, climbing over it all and eventually between her clenched thighs, I tore the closed throat of her gown down to those breasts, which spilled into my hands like springy water balloons. My prong's passage into her was constricted, almost as it had been on our wedding night! But I pushed through once again. Then I plumbed her mercilessly as she clawed and struggled beneath me. . . .

It must have been her kismat all along.

There was no display of histrionics afterward—she has grown up since the Holi incident. I heard this on STAR TV's CNN channel, once: an actor on an American soap opera had his female fan mail *skyrocket* after an episode in which his character raped one of the women on the show. Men are not the only closet neolithics, no matter how women throw words like *loathe* and *despise* around. At any rate, there was no cursing and screaming and throwing of dishes like you see in foreign films—that's not the way with Indian marriages. No question of divorce or any public sordidness—just a trip to Calcutta for her to spend some time with her parents, then calm acceptance and a sensible carrying on. Our families won't be shamed by Draupadi.

As for Sudhir, he'll be married too some day.

Hamid
Gets
His
Hair
Cut

"Hamlet?" asks my haircutter, turning a sweet, snaggle-toothed smile on me, quickly eliminating two other guys waiting in the WonderCuts lobby. We're shamefacedly reading old *Cosmopolitans* or *Glamours* off the table, though I do like the pouty-lipped, shiny-haired models in them. Cool, air-conditioned, plastic smells all over the place—the wall's stacked a mile high with white plastic shampoos and hairsprays for that supernova shine. Neither of the other guys, of course, looks foreign enough to match the unpronounceable name on the ticket between the haircutter's blue-varnished fingernails. I don't either, not particularly anyway, but my darker looks are her clue.

"Yeah, right," I say, getting up, used to people having either a hard time or a good time with my name. My friends at Mandarin High just call me Ham, which is fine, but my mom and dad never shorten it. Mom says I should be proud of my Muslim heritage. I am; I really don't see how preferring a nickname means I'm ashamed of where my folks are from. It's like saying Mom's ashamed of it herself because she doesn't cover her face with a burkha anymore to protect her from the gaze of men other than Dad. There's a part of me that's American and a part that's Indian. I'm clear about that and comfortable with it, except that sometimes people want me to be just the one or the other, depending on who *they* are. Indians who came over from the motherland have an acronym for my generation: ABCDs. Stands for American-Born Confused Desis. I could tell some stories about *them*, like how they can think fair skinned equates with beautiful yet still make a big deal about color prejudice in America. But if it makes them feel better to call *me* confused, that's fine.

The name tag on the haircutter's chest, compact but curvy in a black-and-green knitted top, spells "Clara." She introduces herself and shakes my hand (awesome how alive and sweet a woman's hand feels in yours), then gets me to pronounce my name. Humeed. I follow her to the chair. She asks how I want it; I say just a trim. Famous last words. And I don't mean how haircutters never listen to directions anyway (or do, only so they can cut it differently—think they're artists who know best, or something).

She pulls the sheet over me, ties it at the neck, comes around the side of the chair. Then she leans toward my forehead with her scissors. And before I know what's what, she has her *crotch* pressed right up hard against my hand where it sits covered on the head of the armrest. The exact same hand she shook, a minute ago. The scissors are going *tsik-tsik*, snipped black hair sifting down to almost disappear into the deep blue of the sheet, a couple landing ticklishly just off the side of my nose. So, head held still, I flick my eyes up and right (my mom says never trust mirror images or photographs). Crooked, sure (the teeth), but not that much—like a cute vampire. Midtwenties. Thin, oval face; plenty of eye-black. Gray eyes—bright. Brown hair streaked like the grains of the mother lode and untidy! Probably cut it herself.

So after a moment of What is going on here, I don't know whether to be glad or worried. Maybe she has to stand right where she is, the way these chairs are, to snip that particular area of my very black, very thick hair (way too long for Mom's liking), and maybe I ought to move my hand away. And if I don't, soon, maybe I'll be forevermore a lecherous asshole in her mind and— given all the cross talk between haircutters (makes you wonder how much of their attention's on the job)—in the minds of the other women in the shop. I'll never be able to show my face in WonderCuts again.

Problem is there's no way I can move that hand unobtrusively—it's almost clamped between her crotch and the armrest. And second, I'm about to tent the sheet over my lap. My buddies say I'll be able to go hours when I have sex because my folks had me circumcised when I was born. Still, I'm not sure I want that for my son (when I have one). Plenty of time to decide; other things on my mind right now. Like the base of my nose wants desperately to be scratched. Actually, I don't even want to think too much about how it feels against the back of my hand with her crotch pressed around it. Kind of squishy and shifting and— woof! No question she looked hot when I followed her to the chair, nice ass swinging under a long, chocolate skirt in some kind of cheesecloth. If you think about it, why didn't I drop my hands on my legs when she pulled the sheet over? Maybe I had a wish. And what if she wants me? It'll hurt her feelings if I yank the hand.

She finds some *more* hair to cut from right where she is. She's into it, then—livening up her workday. Unbelievable. My bangs are piling into crisscrossed little fuzzy black heaps on the sheet, and I'm starting to worry I might lose my long-haired look. But my tongue's frozen with the rest of me.

"Is it still real hot out there?" she asks. Like that's what's on her mind. Don't know how she can sound so chatty and unconcerned, but she does. Sounds sweet, actually.

My tongue's still frozen, and I just go "Mm-hm" like a cow or something. I'm well past stupid distinctions between image and reality now, so I bulge my eyes at the mirror and catch the yellow glint of a ring. Hmm. Unfulfilled in marriage, wants to have fun? Or maybe she has no idea my hand's there, really, just a pimpled plastic armrest rubbed down over the years to where it got surprisingly and pleasantly knobby. May work better if I'm clueless too. I slump a little, just to look casual.

But another haircutter sashays behind us, yelling to the receptionist, and I'm so tense my head jerks left, so "Clara" has to stop the scissors and wait. My *hand* tugs involuntarily too! It stays lodged, but now for sure she knows there's something live between her thighs. . . .

"Sorry," I say, turning stiffly back. "Sorry."

In the mirror I'm as red as a communist.

"Oh, it's okay," she coos, cadence on the okay, in *no* hurry to shift her crotch from my hand. Gives a little wiggle there, in fact, coolly finishing up in front before moving off at last to go behind me. Feels suddenly like I don't have a hand anymore—gone, amputated, though actually I don't think hands get cut off at the wrist (except maybe those of Iranian thieves, back when the Ayatollah Khomeini was big there). Then she tilts my head back just right, lifts some hair in her comb, and goes *tsik-tsik* again. . . .

Mom likes my short hair when I get home—she ruffles it after I shower and says I'm her sweet boy. Irritating, but that's Mom. And at Mandarin High the next day, my buddies can't wait to try that branch of WonderCuts themselves. They think it's cool I was sort of seduced by this older woman. Even if I was a wuss and didn't make the most of it. They take to calling me Sam.

For Samson.

Ticket
to
Minto

The first time we rode a Patna city bus, from the railway station to Minto Hostel, we paid for our tickets, as one might expect. More correctly, our team captain paid. I wonder now how the bus conductor reacted when asked for tickets to Minto. Jyotish, our captain, mentioned nothing to us, at any rate, and we were too busy sponging up the smells and sounds of a new place, river breeze from the Ganga drifting through it all.

I was a dozen years younger then, just out of my teens and not at all tired from our overnight train journey into Bihar. Still, after the dirt and boiling heat of our second-class compartment, I felt right through my skin the leafy, cooling presence of the ashok trees around the hostel and the slim palms lifting from inside its courtyard to twice its height—two stories with high ceilings under a sun-baked double-tier of terra-cotta tiles. Outside its walls, a khaki-colored dog, skin like parchment, lifted scrawny hindquarters and slunk away from us to where the shadows had shifted.

Nothing whatsoever about the large, red-brick, U-shaped building we were to stay in for the length of the tournament told me I'd still be puzzling over its inhabitants' nature—or my own, for that matter—a dozen years later. Newspaper reports about violent people and even violence among our youngsters, our future, are common enough. I remember old stories about some students in Osmania University slamming knives into their wooden exam desks to warn off invigilators, then calmly opening textbooks and copying out of them onto their answer sheets. But my mental picture of such people, as I bicycled to classes at the Indian Scientific Institute in the daytime and to its badminton courts in the evening, was of unshaven ruffians—goondas only masquerading as students.

Firoz, too, must have slept well on the train; he talked nonstop both to me and the two college seniors on our team in his boyishly exuberant manner. But they'd been abrupt with us all the way from Dharampur—we were too new on the team for that type of familiarity. We trudged after them across the grassy courtyard to a staircase at the base of the U, and soon they were busy talking to the senior Minto residents who came out to receive us. The latter, an all-male, unusually polite group of students, presumably Biharis, spoke to us in the most beautiful, high-flown Hindi I'd come across outside literature textbooks. With courteous inclinations of their heads they delivered extravagant welcomes: their home was ours; it was an honor to have as their guests sportsmen from so famous a college as ISI; we *must* inform them of anything they could do—it was their sole desire that we should experience no discomfort.

We were slightly overwhelmed by all of this, but also impressed. Firoz is Muslim, but from Bombay like me, so the Hindi we speak is not the pure type spoken by North Indians. Ours is quite casual—in fact, some of my South Indian elders see Hindi as an imposition and refuse to speak it at all. So I was not inclined to shame our group by uttering more than the necessary thanks, and even the normally talkative Firoz was happy to let our seniors (both Calcuttans, themselves more accustomed to conversing in Bengali) speak for him.

Graciously acknowledging our gratitude, the Minto residents ushered us up to the second floor, where Firoz and I were shown into an empty, lime-washed room, roughly twelve by fifteen, at the base of the U, and the two seniors were led off to a room in the left wing.

"Wow, what deadly Hindi those buggers use!" Firoz said when we were by ourselves. The room was bare except for two steel cots, clean white sheets already spread across the mattresses. Each of us slung his bag onto one.

"I swear. Maha polite," I agreed. "I don't feel like even opening my mouth: all the time aap this and aap that, and aaiye and padhariye."

"No point chalaoing our Bombay Hindi," he said. "But quite nice fellows. They asked when our matches are—looks like they want to come and watch."

We stripped off our smelly shirts and travel jeans and uncomfortably clinging old underwear—no need for modesty among sportsmen, too used to changing rooms. Then we wrapped bath towels at the waist, stepped into rubber slippers, and went looking for the bathrooms. There were toilets around both corners, but no bath cubicles. Strange. Firoz remembered he'd noticed something on our way in, glanced over the balcony into the open courtyard, and called me to take a look. In the center were half a dozen adjoining concrete stalls, open at the top and front, a waist-level water tap piped into each. Not the best arrangement, but, as students and, furthermore, guests, our attitude was, When in Minto . . .

"Come on, come on," Firoz said, starting off toward the staircase as I hesitated and waving me along. So we went down with plastic mugs in our hands, soap dishes rattling in the mugs, and took up neighboring stalls under a warm blue sky. My very pores were panting for water.

The side walls on which we hung our towels came up only to our chests, so we could look over them and talk. But we'd hardly opened the taps and begun to pour mugfuls of lukewarm yet refreshing water over our heads when we heard loud whistles and whoops from the wing behind us!

We looked around quickly, but behind a series of brick archways only anonymous windowpanes stared back. I turned to Firoz and saw doubt spread across his face even as it must have across mine. Then, putting an end to all doubts, the whistles were followed by loud, amorous comments in Hindi definitely aimed at us.

"What a bottom you have, beloved!" one said.

"How beautiful," another followed. "And how fair!"

"What the hell is this?" Firoz was obviously not flattered.

"Come on, hurry up," I said, the air suddenly cooler around my backside.

We soaped lightly, washed off in milliseconds, and put on our towels without bothering to dry ourselves. Dripping water, we strode quickly back to the stairs, relentlessly followed by the admiring voices and wolf whistles.

"Oh, don't go!"

"Ah, what a pleasant gait!"

Up at our room, we sloshed in across the concrete floor slab and shut the door. Turning red face to red face, we caught sight of each other's irritation. More at ourselves than at the faceless cat-callers. Ignorance and stupidity on our part: if some unknown fellows had visited our Diga Hall in Dharampur and brainlessly stripped to have a bath right out in the open, God only knew what *we* would have yelled at them. On the other hand, we'd both heard of the tendency for homogiri assigned so generally to Bihari characters in campus jokes and rumors back at Dharampur. I'd dismissed it as just part of all the regional mudslinging and backbiting, but was there some truth to it after all?

"*Your* fat, bloody arse they were after," Firoz shouted.

"Balls," I retorted. "*You*, Fi-Rosy, because you're so fair and so chikna." He had hardly any hair on either his face or his body.

"Must be washing their clothes there," he concluded, sidestepping the issue of his natural beauty. And we started to laugh at the whole thing.

We didn't feel much like laughing when we walked over to Jyotish and Kaushal's room in the left wing to get our practice times.

"You're famous now," Kaushal said, grinning.

"Yes," said Jyotish, all smiles. "There are bathrooms in the middle of our wing, by the way. *And* in the opposite wing."

Firoz muttered something and I asked about practice times. Jyotish said we could leave right away, so we went back to change into shorts and T-shirts. When they knocked on our door, we all walked over to the student president's room. It was double the size of ours, and a small group of Minto students sitting in it, talking, turned and eyed us as we entered. Tensing up for a second, conscious of my short pants despite the dark hairiness of my stocky, uncovered legs, I wondered if any of the whistlers were present. But no one so much as mentioned the incident, and Jyotish asked the president where the badminton hall was. To our surprise, he and the others stood up as they were, in flowing kurta-pajamas, saying they would take us there themselves.

"No, no," Jyotish said, also in Hindi. "No need for that. Just show us how to go there."

"Ji, nahin," the president insisted, as courteous as ever. It was my first conscious look at the smooth, full face that, in its later, almost unrecognizably heated incarnation, would burn into my memory. "You are our guests. We'll accompany you to the hall—it will give us much pleasure to watch you play. And please tell us when your matches are, so we can come and give you encouragement."

"Okay, thanks," Jyotish said, noticeably flattered, but laughing a little. "But what if we have to play Patna University in the semifinals?"

"Even if you are playing Ashok Mishra, we will be for you," the president said generously—Patna's Mishra brothers were top-ranked in the East Zone and local favorites.

So we all set out together. Along the way we got a bit of Minto Hostel history: it had been built to serve as barracks for the British army back in 1907 and was named for Lord Minto, the viceroy of India at the time. Minto, they said, was the first to divide the nation's electorate by Hindus and Muslims. After the freedom struggle and bloody Partition, the barracks became a hostel for the arts students of Patna College. Till just a few years back it had accommodated both Hindu and Muslim students. But, as the whole world knew, the two religious groups were destined to be at war till the end of time, so now the Muslims had their own separate Iqbal Hostel. I noticed that Firoz, for once, had nothing to say about that.

At the badminton hall, our history teachers clapped loudly at each, even paltry shot we made, though it was only practice. This spurred us on, and we threw our trained muscles into every resounding long toss or smash, carving out drop shots like great new moons or diving recklessly to recover them. On the way back, the Mintoans praised our athletic skills nonstop in similarly poetic language. It made me uneasy, but our seniors were lapping it up and in a very good mood when we reached the left turn for Minto. They asked our hosts to show us the Ganga.

The Mintoans took us farther up the bathing ghat to a small, open temple by the riverside. One by one, we stepped up to lightly ring a tarnished brass bell hanging from the temple roof. The temple commanded an impressive view of the great river, miles wide at the point we stood, rippling with sunlight. The scent of fresh water wafted into our heads. Little merchant boats with pinkish rectangular sails like those of Chinese junks spotted the immense expanse, while fishing boats poled along closer to shore. Below us, in the shallows, a man had his pant legs folded up and the palms of his hands together to pray. Close by him, another man, with only a cloth wrapped around his waist, washed his clothes on the rocks. Something about the majestic, endlessly stretching vista reached straight into my soul. When we exclaimed in wonder at the ancient gray giant flowing so calmly below us, our hosts were as puffed up as if we'd praised them personally. It feeds half the country, they said, but when it is in flood, *nothing* can stand in front of it.

The next morning, Jyotish and Kaushal went off somewhere together, leaving us to do as we wished before practice at five. On our way out, Firoz and I asked some Minto seniors at the base of the stairs if there was anything to see in Patna.

"Go to Gandhi Maidan," one of them said, turning to us. "Our oval is the biggest of all cities', exactly in the middle of Patna."

"And don't buy tickets on the bus," said another, a clean-shaven, husky fellow almost as dark skinned as myself, with the beginning protrusion of a belly above his pants. "Just say you are from Minto."

I couldn't understand what he meant—*don't* buy tickets—but Firoz's mind was on other things.

"What about drinks?" he asked in his jovial fashion, hardly the orthodox Muslim. "Any place we can get beer with our lunch?" Morarji Desai was prime minister back then, and many cities enforced prohibition on Sundays at least, if not all week.

"For drinks go to Pink Pussycat—it is near the maidan." The loose-bellied Mintoan's gaze had a heavy-lidded intensity that insisted you take him seriously even when he uttered words like Pink Pussycat. "And if there is any problem, just tell them you are staying with us in Minto; tell them that Mahesh sent you there."

We thanked him and left. At the main road, Ashok Rajpath, we caught a Patna city bus to Gandhi Maidan. Getting our tickets from the conductor, I remembered the Minto senior's strange advice about not paying, but felt it was hardly worth trying to save a measly fifteen paise. I asked Firoz what he thought the Mintoan had meant, and he said, "No, no; he didn't say don't *pay*—he said don't go by bus. One hundred percent. He wanted us to walk and see Patna properly or something." His tone implied he had a tape recorder's recollection of the Mahesh fellow's words.

The park was large but not remarkably large, and there was no way of telling just how geometrically centered it was within Patna. A black statue of Gandhi in midstep leaned its walking stick on a polished white granite pedestal whose plaque proclaimed him the father of the nation. Around the statue were scattered twenty to thirty vagrants—some still asleep on the ground under chadars, others sitting up in waist-wrapped lungis, scratching unshaven faces. A road fronting stores and movie halls and fruit and vegetable stalls circled the field, meeting other roads streaming with autorikshas and cycle rikshas, more three-wheelers than cars. Above one crossing flashed a hot-pink neon sign, its tube bent in the shape of a sleek cat on her hindquarters, a long cigarette holder sticking out of her mouth.

We crossed to the restaurant beneath the sign. In a dimly lighted room, we took one of several unoccupied tables. A waiter in a black suit came over with a menu and asked in English if we wanted snacks or lunch.

"Bring us beer first," Firoz said, "with some nuts or wafers. Then we'll have lunch."

The waiter smiled politely. "No beer, sir," he said. "There is prohibition in all of Bihar, you don't know?"

"Every day?" I asked.

"Yes, every day."

"What, yaar!" Firoz said, uncharacteristically peevish. "Just because Morarji likes to drink his own piss, we have to suffer as well." The prime minister was a proponent of urine therapy— reputedly quite healthy—and an opponent of alcohol. So some funny contretemps had arisen on his diplomatic tours abroad, when host politicians proposed toasts.

"But we're staying in Minto Hostel," I said to the waiter, remembering what the Mintoan, Mahesh, had advised us to say.

"You are from Minto?" the waiter responded, raising his eyebrows.

"Ya, and Mahesh told us to come here for beer."

The man nodded immediately, knowingly, on hearing the name, a sudden deference replacing his politely superior attitude.

"Okay, sir, very good. Wait one second."

Instant results! I was impressed by how well our namedropping had worked. He went off and spoke to the man at the front desk, then came quickly back and requested us to follow him. Padding like pussycats along the dark corridor between the dining room and the kitchen, we came to a door set unobtrusively in a corner, and, passing through, experienced a burst of light. We'd emerged onto a small lawn with only the sky for a roof but walled in on all sides. Three square tables occupied much of the grass. Triumphantly, we sat at one and ordered two chilled bottles of Rosy Pelican—the name went well with Pink Pussycat—then leaned back in our chairs, popped peanuts into our mouths, and said cheers to our surprising friends at Minto whose influence had opened the hidden door for us.

After some heavily aromatic, thickly gravied koftas, we walked the crowded footpath of the ring road and swung onto Ashok Rajpath toward the college area. Soon a blue single-decker went past, going our way. We ran after it and, when it slowed in traffic, caught hold of the rear ladder leading up to the roof, lifted our feet to the rungs, and rode along, enjoying the warm wind and the adventure. When the bus came presently to a bus stop, we almost decided to stay on its back, but changed our minds, went around to the rear doorway and climbed into the crammed interior instead. The khaki-uniformed conductor, a long, slim, eel-like fellow, peered suspiciously at us over other passengers' heads as we came around from behind the bus to climb the steps. He pulled the overhead cord to ring the signal for the driver, and the bus roared off again.

"What, you'd climbed up on the ladder?" he asked us in Hindi, as we grabbed hold of metal handles and balanced ourselves in the jouncing corridor. The ladder had been more stable. And more roomy.

"What?" I said with my best blank look, while Firoz just shrugged. The conductor couldn't have done much, in any case, but he muttered something about dishonest students.

"Which stop?" he asked, very brusque, fingering thick bunches of paper tickets in his metal dispenser, each bunch a different denomination in various pastels.

"Minto Hostel," I said, offering an eight-anna coin, and was surprised to see his face change drastically. The aggressiveness disappeared completely, and a cautious, almost scared look took its place.

"Minto?" he repeated.

"Yes," I said, growing impatient.

"You have to use the Patna Market stop," he said, quite stiff and polite now. "I will show you."

And he ripped off two green fifteen-paisa tickets. I took the twenty-paisa change, put it in my pocket, and looked out the windows into the passing streets of Patna, wondering why on earth so many people knew of Minto and reacted to its mention.

———————

This morning, more than twelve years after that bus ride to Minto, I returned to Patna on a one-day business visit—wooden inlay work on decorative items, a Bihari specialty. Once the order was finalized, I felt like seeing Minto again, ready to rethink the

Mintoan enigma an older and better judge of human nature. Something in me has always said that if I could understand them, I could understand myself; if I could understand them, I could understand our country in all its callow bombast and hoary wisdom; if I could understand them, I could understand the world. So, picking up the newspaper lying on my hotel-room table, I went out and caught a riksha. No buses for me this time.

The rikshavala said he'd have to take a roundabout route to Patna College—a procession was crowding the regular road. I said that was okay, and we started off.

"This procession is for what reason?" I asked the pedaling rikshavala in Hindi.

"Many people are dying from sickness," he said, turning his head slightly. "Everybody is scared, and the government is not doing anything. That is why this procession has been brought out."

Unfolding the Patna edition of the *Times*, I looked over the headlines. The first one on the left said, CITY PANIC-STRICKEN AS MYSTERY DISEASE CLAIMS 60. The article informed me that Patna is threatened by what's thought to be Japanese encephalitis but might also be meningitis or brain fever.

The riksha rolled past an avenue of large teak trees flapping elephant-ear leaves, and I saw that Gandhi Maidan was unchanged, Gandhiji still leaning tiredly, the park dwellers lying aimlessly around the base. But more of them this time, I thought, liquor bottles openly by their sides. I couldn't spot the Pink Pussycat anywhere. When I asked the rikshavala about it, he said there was no such restaurant, though he thought he'd heard the name once. Just as well—only me this time, no good-natured joker for company. Long while since I've seen Firoz, let alone the jovial side of him. We had too many arguments following first the Ayodhya mosque-versus-temple controversy, then the mosque's destruction by Hindu extremists, and finally the Bombay riots and bombings. Over such cataclysmic events, even the closest of friends take sides, feel betrayed, grow distant. . . .

I read on. The article's writer blamed the mysterious outbreak on unhygienic street conditions. Hundreds of pigs lived quite happily on the streetside garbage and sewage in normal times, but now many a porker had been found dead. The pigs were suspected to be carriers—mistakenly, it seemed to me, since encephalitis is spread by mosquitos—and were being rounded up and taken to a pig camp on the outskirts of the city. Shouts and threats had flared up between localities vying for municipal sweepers. Inevitably, fisticuffs broke out between the factions. One fellow grew so wild, he pulled out a pistol and shot another man in the face.

A voice screamed in the street, and I pulled my head quickly out of the paper. The shrieks were loud and angry, yet deeply afraid. They had a strange tonal quality. But I knew why as soon as I saw where they came from. A huge black-bristled hog was being roped onto a pole, screeching his lungs out through a tied-down snout! We passed on through a small market radiating sharp green smells above the deep richness of horse droppings. The rikshavala steered us around a string of horse-drawn vege-table carts and back to the main roads. When we reached the college area, I told him to cut through to the Ganga, then drop me at the top of the ghat.

The small temple still stood on the riverbank, but from its floor beneath the blackened brass bell rose a phallic stone Shiva lingam that I had no recollection of, upstanding, smoothly rounded, a stone cobra draped across its head. The Ganga itself was not the gray in my memory, but a vast, muddied brown, close to the color of my skin.

I walked down the slope and turned onto the path leading back to Minto. And there it was, as solemn and brick red as before, but larger than I'd remembered. As if it had grown in the intervening years, pushed outward. Peering through the tall verticals of an iron gate into the courtyard, I saw that the wash stalls, on the other hand, had vanished, leaving a bare patch on the grass. Be-yond the open rectangle, the hostel's corridors were mostly still, only once a student rounding the stairs. He looked small and unimpressive, distant against my still vivid mental imprint of the student president and the man called Mahesh. But when he turned to look outside, all the distance couldn't hide his quick frown as he caught sight of the lone, silent observer at the gate. I shook my head at his brusque, inquiring hand gesture and, to reassure him, turned slowly away. Even so, he strode into the courtyard—kicking at a yelping pye-dog, its coat splotched like the skin of an overripe banana—and out to the gate.

When the man, a sturdy young, slick-haired fellow with a curl to his upper lip, reached the gate and opened it, I stayed outside but told him of my college-days' visit to Minto. What had happened to the wash stalls? I asked, and he laughed unpleasantly. Why? he said. Did I want to go to the toilet? His expression was coarse and leering. I asked about the Mintoans' MD routine and learned it was still practiced. Once more—across the span of a dozen years—I was invited to attend. I felt tempted to watch from a distance but decided even that might be undignified for a married man in his thirties. Just as I thought to inquire about the price of bus tickets for students these days, I felt a dull sting on my arm and slapped at it. A mosquito droned away in a contemptuous spiral, and my heart began to thud as though I'd run full speed up the ghat. . . .

The modern-day Mintoan reached out and clapped his hands hard. When he opened them I saw the small splash of red and black. He sneered at my expression and flicked the insect away, wiped his palms on his pants. I stood there talking to him, ignoring the sting, until I'd pushed back thoughts of mysterious plagues. Then I said goodbye and caught a riksha to my hotel. I have the urge now, alone in my room, to scratch the mosquito bite.

On the afternoon of our encounter with the bus conductor, many years ago, I was examining the puzzle of the Mintoans consciously for the first time. At the Patna Market stop the conductor only pointed from us to the open door of the bus, without a word. We nodded thanks anyway and got off. Once under the minty cover of the ashok trees, I took a good look at the hostel but saw nothing to account for its residents' fame.

The beer and food was signaling from our sated stomachs to our brains, so we climbed to our room for a nap. At about 4:30 we changed for practice and staggered over to Jyotish and Kaushal's room. The four of us set off with racquets in hand, and ran into some of our Minto acquaintances on their way out. I looked for the Mahesh fellow to thank, but he was not among them.

"Going for practice?" asked the now easily recognizable president, showing off his English for a change, his full, friendly, sleekly mustached face lighting up with obvious liking for us. "This time, I am sorry, we will not be able to come. We are going for MD."

"MD?" Kaushal asked.

"Yes. You don't know MD? You don't have MD in Dharampur?"

We looked blankly at each other and shook our heads; no medical program at ISI, if that was what he meant.

"No," said Kaushal. "What is MD?"

"MD is Maal Darshan," the president said, grinning, and we smiled as well, getting a whiff of what it meant. "Viewing of prime goods. You see, at five o'clock all the women come back from college to Sir Ganesh Dutt Girls' Hostel—we call it by the short form, GDS. So we go and stand there to see how they are looking that day."

"Only to see?" Jyotish asked, obviously expecting more than that.

"Sometimes we also tell them something, but they pretend that they did not hear. We say that they are beautiful, or that they should come to our hostel at night, but they don't look at us; they go straight into GDS. Then they look out from the windows to see if we are still there. Sometimes they come down again before six o'clock—that is their curfew time before study period—and they go past us to the Ganga to see if we will say something to them. But if we go near, they walk faster and go away."

Firoz said we should start MD outside Jhansi Hall, our women's hostel, when we went back to Dharampur. And we all laughed.

"But one time I was too fast for the girl," supplied another member of the group proudly, clearly encouraged by our appreciation. "I pressed her bottom with both my hands before she ran away."

He took a second to gauge our somewhat stupefied reaction, then he lapsed into Hindi. But the emphatic words that issued from his mouth were hardly the refined ones we'd come to expect.

"That was an arse worth taking!"

Logically or not, I felt *my* backside's muscles tighten reflexively, the Mintoans' admiring appraisals of it still fresh in my memory. Again I had the feeling that I couldn't quite fathom our hosts: the extreme politeness and courtesy, the generosity with which they supported our team, the doors that opened at the mention of their names, the wary look on the bus conductor's face . . . And now this MD business. It brought all my earlier uneasiness flooding back.

"Maybe you would like to come for MD with us?" continued the leering Mintoan, in English again, making squeezing motions with his hands. He was a lanky character whose face showed he was tickled at the unsettling effect of his frank pronouncements. "This time if I pass that girl, I will not let her go without feeling her breasts!"

"No, no," Jyotish said hastily. "We have to practice for our match. Sorry."

"We will definitely come for your match tomorrow," the student president said, smiling encouragingly, as they turned toward the women's hostel while we continued down the ghat. And the next day, they came to the badminton stadium in full force, applauding every point we made. We were drawn against a strong, reputed team from Gorakhpur, but ours was the best ISI team in a long time and we felt we could win. It was the first time ISI had reached the East Zone final eight, so there was no pressure on us. Jyotish, an athletic and stylish former junior champ of Bengal, played a captain's match to win his singles, but he and Kaushal went down fighting at doubles. And Kaushal dropped his singles. When Firoz and I took court for doubles, the Mintoan group in the stands broke into especially noisy cheers.

Something about their raucous calls took sudden hold of us— we hurled our racquets at the white-feathered shuttle like Red Indians on horseback launching feathered lances. The smashed bird whizzed off our catgut at a hundred miles an hour. Our shots cracked like gunfire around the stadium walls, our rubber soles screeched across wooden flooring. We were partners back then, working in unison, weaving in and out from back to front and side to side like electrons around a nucleus. The pair from Gorakhpur came back strongly in the second game, but we surged home in the third, leaving us tied at two matches all when Firoz went back on court for the final singles.

Our Minto friends came to their feet and clapped as hard as they could when the umpire announced him as so-and-so from

ISI. As they cheered him on vociferously after every single point, I reflected on how well they had treated us, as if we were their very own team. And I felt myself warm to them again. When Firoz, already spent from doubles, lost narrowly in the third game, they were more disappointed than we were, and swore that the linesmen had cheated.

Sweaty and frustrated, we walked back with them to Minto. They recalled every moment of the tie, described it in detail, and praised our play till it sounded as if we'd won. If nothing else, it made Firoz, who had begun to blame himself for the loss, feel a bit better. The student president then ceremoniously invited us to visit his room that afternoon. Jyotish accepted for all of us. We climbed slowly up to our quarters, stripped off our smelly outfits, and trudged over to the bathrooms. The cold shower water restored a quota of my energy, and I heard Jyotish call out from his cubicle.

"Okay, you two—Ravi, Firoz—what do you want to do now? Our return reservations are only on Saturday, so if we go today we have to go unreserved. Kaushal and I are going to stay till Saturday and see Patna properly, but if you want to go I'll give you your tickets."

I thought for a bit. For one thing, I didn't feel like traveling all night in the unreserved bogie without so much as a berth to sleep on. Also, if we returned immediately, we'd have to go to class on Thursday, while if we stayed, we could take a boat ride on the Ganga or something. So when Firoz's voice said, "Ravi, if you're staying, I'll stay," I said all right, let's stay.

When, changed and fresh, we entered the student president's room, he and the other Mintoans were still full of praise, dwelling once more on our fantastic performance, insisting that if a team could beat us as Gorakhpur had, it would definitely win the tournament. I didn't think Gorakhpur could get past its very next match with Patna, but it was good to hear we hadn't disgraced ISI.

Relaxed completely in my chair, thinking of the free days ahead, I had begun to ask about boat rides on the Ganga, when someone charged in through the door like a warhorse, stamped to a halt, and glared around the room.

His dark face was flushed, gleaming with sweat. It was the slack-bellied Minto senior, Mahesh, whose name had brought us the forbidden beer. His heavy-lidded eyes fixed themselves on the president, a slimmer, lighter-skinned man, lounging against a propped-up pillow on the bed in a sand-colored kurta-pajama. His face, I remember distinctly, had a sleek fullness around a cultivated mustache, the almost brown hairs of which curled just over the top edge of his lip in two sleek fringes.

"Do you know," the newcomer shouted in Hindi at him, in a voice hoarse with emotion, "that the bus conductors on Ashok Rajpath are making us buy tickets again?"

"What?" the president cried, sitting up, obviously outraged, and there were loud, indignant exclamations from the others. "Telling us to buy tickets?"

Here was the ticket mystery again, and this time I could see that my teammates were as confused as I was.

"You don't buy tickets in a bus?" Jyotish asked, also in Hindi.

"Definitely not." The president sent a stony glance at the man he'd treated like a god only minutes ago. "Transport charges are included in our college fees—everyone knows it! Why should we pay on top of that?"

Turning again to the newcomer, he asked, "What happened? Tell us."

"I got on the bus and sat down," said the man named Mahesh. He was breathing hard, clearly more from anger than exertion, and his story came out in choppy bursts. "The conductor came and asked, 'Where do you want to go?' I told him, 'I'm a student.' He said, 'So what?' I said, 'So I don't need a ticket.' He said, 'All people have to buy tickets.' I said, 'Not college students.' He said, 'That's only in university buses, not *public* transport!' I said, 'You don't know me—I'm from *Minto* Hostel.' He rang the bell and said, 'I don't want to know all that. Either buy a ticket or get down.' The bus stopped. I grew angry and said, 'I *will not buy*!'

"Everyone was watching the show. . . . He said loudly, 'Then get down—you're keeping the whole bus waiting.' And people started to grumble. So I got up and said, 'I'm going, but you'll regret it.' He said, 'Go, go; don't give me threats,' and rang the bell as I was still getting down. I came here on foot, after that."

An angry buzz ran around the room when he finished speaking, and the student president began to curse at the top of his voice. It was the first time we'd heard gaali from a Mintoan.

"Sister-fucker! Bastard! Must be a new conductor."

"Yes," confirmed Mahesh, still lowering out of those heavy-lidded eyes, but, his somewhat quieter tone indicated, not unappeased. "I'd never seen him before."

"What does he look like?"

"Like the mule he is; thinks he's a big man because he has a big, twirled mustache."

"There is only one path to take," the president said, looking weightily around, and I can see his expression as clearly as if the years were minutes. That smooth, full face was suddenly bloated with anger, with bitterness. "We have to teach them a lesson again. We will have to set three or four buses on fire!"

We sat there as quiet as possible, not sure if our hearing had deceived us. But all around rose loud, excited agreement—it was a matter of *honor*; they'd been too patient with those canine bastards. They pulled their chairs nearer to the bed and started to make plans. From the rapid conversation it was clear they had gone on a rampage through Patna before, setting public buses on fire. And that some buses had burned until only a charred, smoking frame remained. Now they plunged into arguments and colorful discussion on when, where, and how to set new fires. Nothing more sophisticated than wooden firebrands made of petrol-soaked cloth wrapped around one end. Off dashed someone to cut up a river pole and someone else to the petrol pump with a can. One fellow fished out a gold-plated cigarette lighter, struck it with a deft click, and watched the slim blue spearhead burn.

The four of us sat there, stealing looks at each other out of faces that recalled for me the bus conductor's expression when I mentioned Minto. Then Jyotish leaned over to Kaushal and said something in an undertone. Kaushal nodded. Jyotish stepped across to Firoz and me and said quietly, "We're going this evening."

The two of us nodded. No question.

He moved up to the absorbed group at the president's bed, then waited patiently. Seconds ticked by, but at last our hosts felt Jyotish's presence and looked up from their deadly discussion.

"Okay," he said very, very casually in Hindi, inclining his head almost in slow motion. "We have to get our baggage ready—

need to catch the Howrah Mail. . . . Much thanks for the hospitality you showed us."

The student president, his face still all puffed up and wild, rose immediately from the bed and, even as our captain started backward, took hold of his hand and shook it warmly. The Mintoan's face changed once more: the enraged expression was literally wiped off—he looked moved, he sounded sentimental.

"It has given us *much* happiness that you stayed with us," he said. I have rarely heard anything sound more from the heart. "We will remember you, and the noble artistry you displayed."

And there were approving murmurs and nods from the other arsonists and regretful hands raised as we left the room. . . .

We packed rapidly, were mutely grateful to run into no one on our way out of Minto. A quick walk down the ghat to Ashok Rajpath brought us to bus stops crammed with prospective passengers. Visions of stalled blue buses flaming furiously in the middle of the road leapt and flared before my eyes. The gaseous, shifting oranges and reds whooshed into all-consuming, sky-climbing proportions, as if our entire nation had been laid out to burn on a gargantuan funeral pyre.

Firoz waved his hands around and shouted to the waiting men and women, "Don't go by bus! Don't go by bus!" They stared at him as if he were mad. Some of them turned to each other, their shoulders lifted, palms spread, tittering nervously. Kaushal, looking worried, put a hand to Firoz's back to ease him along. A few uncertain steps along the footpath and we caught a taxi to the railway station.

On the Howrah Mail, we stood all the way to Dharampur in the rolling corridor of a heavily congested, unreserved bogie, clutching metal handles that hung from the compartment ceiling, mesmerized by the ceaseless *tukaduk-tukaduk-tukaduk* of the wheels. Shoulder to shoulder and back to front with other passengers, we breathed steady whiffs of their sweat as we swayed through the night. But when the sunlight came streaming through the windows next morning like clarified butter, I found I had fallen asleep standing up.

Who's Your Authority?

Either just returned from heavenly travel or bound for it, disinterested fliers brushed by the redheaded woman in a saffron sari offering pamphlets. But she maintained a cheerful smile. Only Judy Mulchand, her travel suit and long brown hair both mussed from overnight flight, stayed her course within the teeming maze that is Detroit Metropolitan Airport, despite her husband's muttered instructions to avoid the importunate figure.

"Oh, don't be rude now, Nitin," said Judy, her sympathies stirred. "She's looking right at us."

The woman, her carroty hair and light skin out of place above the very thing, her Indian dress, that stood her out from the

American crowd, took a small step toward them as they neared the pillar by which she stood.

"Hello," she said, still smiling pleasantly at the short couple, one of whom, at any rate, was not evading eye contact. "How are you today?"

Judy nodded just as pleasantly and said, "Good, thanks," even as her husband picked up the pace, pushing the luggage trolley ahead of him. It clattered a little over the flooring, and the carry-ons bounced above the suitcases. But the woman, managing somehow to do it unobtrusively and speaking again, moved over just enough that Judy stopped to listen, forcing Nitin Mulchand to halt as well.

In fact, processing his swarthy appearance through light blue eyes, the woman was addressing him now, the palms of her hands put together in greeting and in praise of her God. "Hare Krishna. You look like you might already be acquainted with the Bhagavad-Gita."

And she fished a couple of booklets from her cloth shoulder bag, holding them out. One was titled *Introduction to Bhagavad-Gita*, its cover painting depicting the haloed, ash blue Lord Krishna at the reins of Arjun's golden war chariot. The other said *The Krishna Consciousness Movement Is Authorized* in bold red against a picture of creamy temple domes aspiring skyward. For some reason, the second title provoked a muted snort from the stocky Nitin.

"Yes," he said, anything but gracious, as Judy took the booklets, switching her daughter's carrier to her left hand. "My grandfather is an expert on not only the Gita but the Vedas and Puranas as well."

"Wonderful," said the woman, her redhead's freckles only adding to the anomalous nature of her appearance. She paused for a second while the announcement of a flight arrival crackled above them, a floating, omnipresent, androgynous voice. Then, "What part of India are you from?"

"Bangalore."

"Oh, I have a friend who lives in Bangalore. He tells me it's a beautiful city. We have a center there."

"Yes, I know. At Rajajinagar."

"I think so, yes. Have you been to it?"

"No."

"We have a beautiful center right here in Detroit," she said, persevering gently past Nitin's terse replies but turning to Judy, who was leafing through the pamphlets.

"Really? I didn't know that." Judy was careful not to sound overenthusiastic, yet found it hard to be cold. Not only was this the first American she'd spoken to in a month, but like herself the woman had a connection to India.

"Oh, yes. It's a lovely, enormous old mansion—peacocks roaming the grounds, just heaven on earth. You ought to visit us some day. It's a mile or two from Grosse Pointe; the number and address are at the end of the book. On special days we even have feasts for the public. Mouthwatering, really."

"Thank you," said Judy. "We might just do that."

"Great." Mission accomplished, the woman relaxed and looked over the trio before her, homing in on the carrier in Judy's hands. "Well, what a cute little boy the two of you have."

Her eyes flicked from the child's face to Judy's to Nitin's then back to Judy's. They were the same, yet not the same. All three had rounded features and dark hair, the adults perhaps brought together by the charm of facial similarity. But the man's skin tone was almost wooden Indian in its darkness, his wife's pink, and the child's a creamy tan.

"Girl," said Judy, ignoring some restless shuffling sounds beside her, looking down instead at her daughter resting quietly amid fluffed blues and greens. "My husband doesn't believe in gender identification by baby clothes."

"Mm-hm. Thanks for the material," interjected Nitin, taking quick advantage of the reference to himself, "but we're in a bit of a hurry actually. Our relatives must be waiting."

"I won't keep you any longer," said the woman, spreading her hands as if to let go of them. "The books are free, but if you'd like to contribute something. . . . Maybe if you have some rupees left over from your trip . . . ?"

She left the suggestion unfinished, looking hopefully at them, her eyes level with Nitin's, and he relented; this person was not at all like Isvara dasa after all, really quite sensible in her approach.

"Sure," he said, taking out two ten-rupee notes, knowing he couldn't convert them in the States anyway and it would probably be years before they went to India again, the way Judy had hated everything once her stomach went haywire.

"Thank you." The woman folded the notes over a roll of others, which she dropped back into a corner of her satchel, then pulled out a notepad. "And if you write down your address here, we could let you know in advance about the feast days."

"That's okay, I know when . . . ," Nitin began, but his wife had already dropped the pamphlets into Nina's carrier and was scribbling on the pad.

"Wonderful. We'll look forward to seeing you there. Hare Krishna," said the woman, cocking her head in synchrony with the salutation and stepping back against the pillar as they moved on.

Not really in search, of course, for nonexistent relatives, they located their parked Celica after a minute or two around the lot. Nitin checked the tires and loaded up, while Judy strapped Nina's carrier into the back seat. Then they pulled out onto I-94. The open, ordered highway felt strange after a month on roads where countless cars and autos and cycles and handcarts and buses and trucks streamed almost on top of each other.

Nitin, who was driving, said, "So our trip's over—big flop for you, it seems. Why you didn't listen to me and drink only the boiled water in the refrigerator I don't know. That, too, after all the trouble we took to even brush our *teeth* with bottled water."

Judy shifted uncomfortably—she was still experiencing twinges of the diarrhea-dysentery that had dogged her for the last seventeen torturous days, days when life quite literally stunk, and was wishing the airport was closer to home. But a feeling of wild relief to be back on American ground was sweeping over her, to have put thousands of miles between her and a country that in its extreme levels of noise, dirt, crowding, and poverty had often jarred her senses to the point of migraine. Miles between herself and in-laws, sweet though they were in their own way, who still clearly thought of her as a hopeless outsider. And that after they'd dragged out *their* earlier visit to an interminable five months! Not that it hadn't had its advantages—Amma's inclination to take over the kitchen area had suited Judy just fine, and after Nina was delivered it had been nice, with Mom back in Harrison again (having taken a bagload of pictures: "She has my eyes!"), to be able to leave the baby with Papa and Amma and visit the fitness center or go out with Nitin. But it wasn't her house anymore, and the worst part was that Nitin had wanted them to stay even longer, asked them repeatedly over the last month and a half to extend their trip, till she'd felt like gagging him. It bothered her that he considered it a matter of course rather than discussion that in his parents' old age—not so many years away, realistically—they would come to live with their son and his family.

"Nitin, for the last time, I thought I *was* drinking the boiled water. How in heaven's name should I know that the bottles on the side rack were meant for the rest of the family? And second, it's convenient but simplistic to say I had a bad time only because of that, though it was extremely inconsiderate of you to make me sit through Deepika's entire wedding reception with a smile pasted on my lips when you knew I had the runs and had asked you to take me home."

Nitin—having no defense other than that, caught up in the old, deeply missed sounds and smells and colors, he had underestimated the severity of her problem—did not respond for a while. Finally he said, "They explained the thing about the different bottles to us right from the start, Judy. They don't need boiled water; they're immune to the viruses. Anyway, now we're back and we can drink anything anywhere. I don't believe the first American we run into is a Hare Krishna! Did you see the way that woman was looking at Nina and then at us? I can't stand it when people do that! I'd have imagined children like Nina are common enough among the Krishnas themselves."

But, not for the first time, he'd started something, then found Judy unprepared to drop it at a moment of his choosing.

"Well, it's no worse than your mother being so glad Nina's 'fairer' than you are, or how everyone implied that a daughter was fine but we ought to get working on a son. Or—and really this was the worst—everyone assuming that Nina would be brought up a Hindu."

He sent a sharp look at her before turning back to the highway. "Why shouldn't they assume that? Her father is a Hindu; a child's faith is always determined by her father's faith."

The usually vivacious object of their discussion was still fast asleep in her miniature car seat in the rear, clearly worn out from the thirty-odd hours of travel and some energetic screaming on the plane.

Judy's voice was tightly controlled. "I thought we'd agreed back in Harrison that, if we married and had children, they could grow up and decide for themselves which faith to follow, if they *had* to follow just one. Why do you think I've never insisted on Nina's being baptized?"

He was silent again, remembering the agreement, reached only too easily in seemingly irretrievable times of closeness, when their relationship was never routine and their difference was a source of arousal. She'd loved to cup her smaller, pink hand around the back of his meaty, dark one, saying it was how they must look when nested in bed. *He'd* loved her for things like that and had no problem at the time resolving the issue of their issues exactly as she'd described. A half-baked pact, he now felt. . . . Why should the continuance of traditions begun five thousand years ago be forced to hinge on the whim of an easily influenced teenager, particularly when the dominant, surrounding influences were unfairly weighted? Too bad he didn't care for the Hare Krishnas, come to think of it.

"You shouldn't have given that Krishna woman our address," he muttered. "Wait and see how they pester us now."

"Oh, Nitin, don't make a big deal out of it. So we get a few invitations in the mail; it's up to us whether we go or not. There'd even be peacocks, it seems, for Nina to play with when she gets bigger. *I* think it might be fun."

"I don't. You can go if you want."

She directed a glance at him that shifted from exasperation to curiosity at the set look on his rounded face.

"Why're you so against them? There's a picture of them in the pamphlet, distributing food to rows and rows of poor families in India. And they're spreading *your* religion, after all; isn't that good?"

"Now who's being simplistic? Did I say they're not 'good' people? I'm not 'against' them—I just put twenty bucks in their treasury. . . . And I don't think they're Hindus, exactly; more of an offshoot. Krishna Consciousness—what they call their faith— is a term they coined themselves. Anyhow, I had a weird experience with one of them back in Harrison. Before I met you. And the title of the pamphlet, the word 'authorized,' reminded me of it—they have authorization on their brains!"

"Oh. I read about it in the pamphlet—it was just something about the courts' recognizing their movement as a bona fide religion. The rulings 'authorized' them to keep doing their thing in public, that's all. In any case, I didn't know there was a Hare Krishna center in Harrison."

"Sure. Somewhere behind the Edgemoor strip mall, just an old wooden house in a residential area, with the dining and living rooms combined into a reception hall. Remember my pal Veer and his hippie neighbors? I went there with Doug once—he knew someone who'd become a Hare Krishna."

"So what happened?"

"I'll tell you," he said, taking the exit for I-275 and heading north. "Veer and I were over at Doug's little studio one Sunday afternoon, and he brought out this little paperback book given to him by his Hare Krishna friend Michael to read. Michael had changed his name to Isvara dasa (meaning servant of God), Doug said, and had been trying to talk him into becoming a Hare Krishna as well. This was back in '81, when the Krishnas were getting to be really well known. The book was a transcript of question-and-answer sessions between disciples (or I think they called them devotees) and the Indian guru who started the movement, a Swami Prabhupada."

"That's who the first booklet is by, I think," said Judy, reaching behind to pluck the booklets from Nina's carrier. "Yes. 'By His Divine Grace A. C. Bhaktivedanta Swami Prabhupada, Founder-Acarya of the International Society for Krishna Consciousness.' Quite a mouthful."

"Right. Doug asked us if he was a big deal in India, and we said *we'd* never heard his name, but then neither of us was into religious stuff. We'd heard of ISKCON and the Hare Krishnas, of course. Well, let me tell you, he may or may not have been a big deal then, but *now* they've even brought out a stamp in his name! I saw it, two–three weeks ago, on one of Deepika's letters. He might be one up on Darwin there, I imagine."

"Darwin?"

"Ya. *I* haven't seen a stamp with Darwin on it—have you? Anyway, the book had a very impressive write-up on the Swami's lifetime accomplishments—translated Sanskrit scriptures by the volume into English, wrote scores of books himself, came to the States without a dime in the '60s on a mission from *his* guru to spread the Vedic knowledge in the West. He struggled for a while, apparently, but formed the society and fostered it until it became a worldwide thing, then passed away in the late '70s, only a few years before the time I'm talking about. All of which made us feel quite good about this learned, gutsy old Indian who'd influenced so many Westerners—in a way he'd done all Indians proud. And, as you pointed out, he was spreading our religious teachings among Americans.

"At that point, Doug said, 'All right, but take a look at something he says and tell me what you guys think of it.'

"He turned the pages until he found the one he wanted, folding the corner down before passing it to us, and the two of us hunched over it together, our eyebrows climbing as we read. I don't remember it word for word, but the key lines the guru delivered were against Darwin's theory of evolution, under the clever heading 'Darwinism Extinct.' Something like this: 'The cow has the quality of goodness, the lion that of passion, and the monkey that of ignorance. According to Darwin, his father is a monkey.... [Laughter among devotees.] So his theory is foolish.'"

"You're kidding!" said Judy, startled out of the intrigued silence into which she had fallen.

"No, I'm serious."

"But that's absurd."

"Ya, I know. That's what started the whole thing. Both Veer and I were grad students, after all, very much products of the scientific school, so we were quite shocked at the offhand and insulting way the wise old guru had dismissed a theory so solidly backed up by evidence over the years that we thought of it as fact. Our pride in him changed to suspicion. Also embarrassment in front of Doug. We were sick and tired of the narrow exposure the media gave Westerners of an India bogged down in outdated views and orthodox customs, only featured on the American news when a train was derailed by a cow lying across the tracks or when some illiterate, evil-minded swine in cahoots with his mother murdered his wife in the worst conceivable way and tried to pass it off as sati—you remember how many times people asked you if Indians didn't burn their wives alive? And here was a man of learning giving our American friend reason to believe that even the best of Indians refused to move with the times.

"'That's nonsense!' I said to Doug. Then, leaving the guru out of it out of respect for the dead, I continued, 'Darwin never said his *father* was a monkey; he only—'

"Doug didn't even let me finish. He may not have so much as completed high school (dropped out when his band looked to be really headed somewhere), but his G.K. was pretty good. 'Yes, I know,' he said. 'It's kind of humorous, though—I laughed and laughed when I first read it. That's how he meant it, I think: get a laugh out of his audience.'

"But Veer looked as disgusted as I was. 'I don't see anything funny about it,' he said.

"Doug said he'd noticed we weren't amused, and wanted to know why. After I explained, he had an idea. Twice or thrice a week, he said, the Hare Krishna center held a sort of program in the evening, open to the public. It was followed up by a free dinner, so Doug and the other players in his band (being not very flush with money) wound up attending once in a while just for the food. As it happened, Sunday was one of the days, so he suggested we go, take the book with us, show the passage to Michael—or Isvara dasa—and ask him about it.

"I said fine, I had no assignments due and a free dinner would be good. Veer said no thanks, he had too much grading left to waste time on a nonissue, so around six he went back to his place next door, while we carried on in Doug's precious, silken old Ford, magic-carpeting all the way across tiny Harrison."

"I remember that Ford," said Judy, her mind speeding back over the years.

"Well, when we got to the center and walked up on the wooden porch, there was a bunch of shoes outside the door, and we added our sneakers to it before knocking and entering. Just inside the door, a group of male Hare Krishnas in various faded shades of saffron (cotton kurtas or even dyed T-shirts) were hopping from foot to foot to the rhythm of cymbals and a Plexiglas mridangam—you've seen it, a sort of long, horizontal bongo with a drumskin stretched over each end, but usually made of wood. It looked ridiculous to me—a *Plexiglas* mridangam. They were chanting, 'Hare Krishna, Hare Krishna, Krishna Krishna, Hare Hare,' while a woman in a sari lit incense sticks at a recessed altar, in front of statues of a handsome, black-tressed, flute-playing Krishna next to Radha all decked out in jewelry.

"Two of the men smiled at us without interrupting their chant and motioned us in. The fragrant incense hit me immediately, and I went all loose with nostalgia and homesickness. People were sitting on the floor along the long walls of the hall, facing the group up front, and we found a spot for two on the polished hardwood without any problems—the place was still filling up. Mostly Americans: young student types and an older lot that included mainstream couples as well as flower power like Doug, who, if you remember, had long enough Goldilocks hair (not to mention his beard) to supply all the Hare Krishnas in the room. The only Indians, apart from myself, were a family of three, a little boy nodding his head from side to side and clapping in time to the chant.

"By the time it ended, the long walls were completely lined with listeners and as the short wall opposite the altar began to fill, I became suddenly aware of the weight of another presence in the room, watching impassively. Against that wall was a sort of throne—large, plush, gilded chair on a low podium—and seated cross-legged on that throne was a big, colorful figure I recognized from a photo in the book to be Swami Prabhupada, bald-headed, wrapped in long golden robes, a marigolds-and-roses garland as thick as my arm around his neck, his hands resting composedly on his knees. It took a second or two just looking at an incredible face—broad, spreading nose, huge ears, earlobes reaching almost to a square jawline hung with the folds of age, bitter-chocolate skin, half-closed heavy eyes, and the widest mouth in history (tight-lipped, corners turned sharply down) running the breadth of the face—it really took me a couple of beats to realize I was looking at a life-sized, realistically painted statue, like a waxwork in Madame Tussaud's. But once I'd noticed it, that figure seemed to dominate the room, even when I turned back to the chanters at the other end."

"Mm," said Judy, flipping to the back of one of the pamphlets and showing Nitin a full-page photograph. "That really is an awesome face. Kind of old and beautiful and powerful at the same time."

"Ya," he said, shifting his eyes back to the highway, easing the Celica up to sixty-five. "Well, the chanters had finished, and were seating themselves on the floor to listen to an older and obviously senior Hare Krishna on a raised dais conduct a reading from a translation by Swami Prabhupada himself of the Bhagavad-Gita, the Song of God. The atmosphere was calm, relaxing, and I just leaned back against the wall like everyone, at peace, listening to thoughts that were first expressed four to five thousand years ago.

"It didn't last, my peace—the reader moved on to a passage where Krishna speaks to Arjun of creation, of the origin of not just species but all things, and says very clearly that everything springs from Himself.

"The reading shifted to other passages, but Doug looked at me and I looked at him, and my mind was again on the swami's verdict on Darwin and his theory. I kept wondering if Krishna's assertion in any way prohibited the idea of evolution. Not necessarily, I decided, but almost involuntarily looked over at the figure in the rear. I had the eerie feeling that the great face had grown even heavier in its disapproval.

"When the reading was over, Doug said, so only I could hear, 'Here comes the best part,' and the Hare Krishnas brought out steel thalis filled with vegetarian food, and laid one on the floor in front of each visitor along with water in stainless-steel glasses. It was good, tasty food on Indian lines, but relatively low spiced, with a couple of unusual items like some mashed-banana stuffing in a large bell pepper. Doug, munching away happily, had no idea what it was, but said it had been on the menu before. We were about halfway through when one of the Hare Krishnas, who now seemed to be circulating en masse, came over and sat down on the floor with us, saying, 'Hello, Doug. Good to see you.'

"Doug responded with a 'Hello, Michael,' at which a pained look came over the Hare Krishna's clean-shaven, Caucasian face, so Doug gestured at me and said, 'I brought an Indian friend of mine along. Nitin, this is Isvara dasa. I know him from our high school days, so I still forget at times and call him by his old name.'

"'That's all right, Doug,' Isvara dasa said, then smiled at me, folded his hands in a namaste, and said, 'Hare Krishna. Welcome.'

"I said thanks, putting the plate down to do a namaste as well. He had a sharp, earnest face, and I could tell up close that the hair roots carpeting his shaved scalp were brown. Doug and he made some conversation about people they'd known in school, and I thought, After all this fellow is an American since birth, a Hare Krishna only recently; he's been exposed to the same notions of science that Veer and I have, went to the same school Doug did. He'll be willing enough, among friends, to admit he believes in Darwin.

"Doug seemed in no hurry to bring up the topic, so I picked up the book, which he'd laid by his side to eat, and began to flip through it, searching for the page with the folded corner.

"Isvara dasa smiled at Doug and said, 'I see you are exposing your friend to the wisdom of our spiritual master.'

"'Ya,' I said, taking hold of the opportunity. 'I was really impressed by all his learning. But there's a passage in here that seems quite strange to me.'

"The smile went away at that, and he looked at me as if I'd given him a whiff of the real me. 'Which passage is that?' he asked, and I passed the book to him, opened at the Darwin's-father-is-a-monkey page.

"He read it without blinking, then looked up at me with a face that had turned as cold as the stainless-steel glasses, saying, 'What was it that you found so strange?'

"I'd begun to feel a bit uncomfortable by then, but I said, 'The portion about Darwin, I mean.'

"'What about it?' he asked, and I was certain now that his tone was hostile. 'It's perfectly true. Darwin's theory of evolution is just that—a manmade theory. It means nothing when we have the word of Krishna Himself that all species were created by Him.'

"You know me, Judy; I'm not what you would call a religious person, but I hardly wanted to go against the teachings of the Gita. My family would consider that blasphemy—I grew up hearing my grandfather tell the ancient stories of the Mahabharata, where Krishna encourages Arjun with the words of the Gita. So it was a good thing I'd been thinking about this during the reading, and I said to him, 'But why should creation by a God keep a species from evolving afterward? Why couldn't evolution be part of the creative plan?'

"He shook his head. 'It is, but not in the sense Darwin imagined. The *soul* evolves, from its dwelling in the bodies of lower animal species to those of higher forms, into the human body, finally, of a perfect devotee of Krishna. After that it returns to Godhead.'

"At this point I became aware of something in his way of speaking that I'd also noticed in the senior Hare Krishna's reading of the Gita but had put down to the language of the translation. There was a slightly monotone element to his intonation—whether conscious or unconscious I don't know—that came across as somewhat Indian. I know I should have been flattered, but instead it increased the sense of disorientation I felt at listening to a Westerner lecture me about successive reincarnation. At the same time, I could sense that *he* was feeling in a way betrayed by someone who, of all people in the room, Indian like his swami, should have been very much in agreement with him. And here I was, instead, questioning his beloved guru. I sent a quick glance at the waxen old watcher on the throne, felt his gaze sit like a deadweight on me, and looked away only after a conscious effort.

"Maybe Doug sensed some of this, because he finally stepped in, tossing his golden mane, 'But isn't Darwin's version of evolution pretty much a proven thing?'

"'Exactly,' I said, eager to have his support. 'There's the solid evidence of fossils, after all.'

"This time when Isvara dasa looked at me, I could tell from the narrowing of his eyes that he saw something else at stake here— the loss of Doug as a potential Hare Krishna. What chance was there of convincing Doug to join up if he, Isvara dasa, could not defeat the arguments of a *Hindu* who disagreed with his guru's teachings?

"So he said, '*Fossil* is just a big word for old bones, nothing more. Bones cannot tell you that the ape species developed into the human species. If that had happened, there would no longer be an ape species. But both species exist side by side today, so where is your great evolution theory?'

"I should have said to him that *both* apes and men are supposed to have evolved from the same ancestral species, not one from the other, but I was baffled just to hear someone dispute fossils and I wasn't thinking too clearly. There were other little conversation groups going in the room, where the Krishnas had squatted next to people attending, but they all seemed to be proceeding by smiles and nods.

"'I don't know about all that,' I said, really nonplussed at this point and ready to shift to some steady ground on which we could easily agree, 'but anyway your guru was joking, right, when he quoted Darwin as saying his own *father* was a monkey? It was just a way of putting it, obviously.'

"And this is where I got the biggest shock of the evening, Judy. It was one thing for him to defend his beliefs, but he refused point-blank to see what Doug and even the laughing devotees in the transcript had seen immediately, that the old swami had been in a facetious mood and had stated his position in a manner calculated to entertain his audience, even if smugly insulting of Darwin.

"Isvara dasa just tightened his lips, shook his head firmly, and said, 'No; it is absolutely true. Srila Prabhupada would not have said it otherwise. He is the spiritual representative of Lord Krishna.'

"At which point, Doug jumped back in. 'But he *can't* have meant it literally!' he said in exasperation.

"'That's exactly what I'm trying to get across,' I said. 'Are you saying Darwin actually said his *own father* was a monkey?'

"Isvara dasa glared at me as if I was a demon attacking his swami, and in a way I felt the same about him!

"'Do you know for a fact that he did not?' he asked.

"'Of course,' I said. 'All he said was that man is descended from an apelike ancestor—I don't even see how two people in *this century* can be arguing about that.'

"I still don't see, Judy, but it didn't faze him.

"'Just how well do you know Darwin's teachings?' he asked.

"'Pretty well,' I said.

"'Pretty, pretty, pretty,' he imitated with a sneer, letting me know what he thought of my unconsciously American way of putting it. 'Have you read everything he ever wrote?'

"'Maybe not everything,' I said, 'but enough!' I hadn't so much as read *Origin of Species* but had no intention of telling him. I read it soon afterward, I can tell you.

"'Well,' he said. 'Darwin wrote many volumes. On what authority can you tell me that somewhere within them he does not say it?'

"'On what *authority*?' I repeated, feeling sidetracked.

"'Yes,' he said, sitting up very straight over his crossed legs. 'My authority is Krishna. Who is *yours*?'

"I started to say, 'I don't need—' but he wouldn't let me finish, just repeated (as if to say, 'Case closed!'), 'My authority is *Krishna*; who's yours?'

"And once he had found that magic mantra, he just kept flinging it at me, no matter what I tried to say, even before I finished saying it. No use bringing up Darwin or the scientific community—how could they compare with Krishna as authorities? It was that simple in his mind, Judy—he had divine backing, I had only human or none."

"Mm," said Judy. An uneasy feeling had come over her.

"And I know you're sitting there thinking I was every bit as hidebound in my scientific ways as he was, but God knows (if God exists) I didn't try to jam his frequencies. It was too weird, listening to this Westerner (no offense, sweetheart; you're an honorary Easterner) throw the name of Krishna in my face. The empty thalis had been collected, the fragrance of turmeric and curds was still around us, and a couple of sweet-looking Hare Krishna women with their saris drawn over their heads came around asking for contributions in return for the meal. Doug just shook his head and smiled his equally innocent smile at them. But even as I dropped a buck in the box and the visitors began to slowly filter away, we were still going back and forth with Isvara dasa and his authority mantra.

"'What about how people crossbreed flowers to develop new kinds?' the bearded flower child asked.

"'*My* authority is *Krishna*; who's yours?'

"'Or how new generations of insects become immune to insecticides?' I tried, being the pest I am.

"'My authority is Krishna; *who is yours*?'

"It's not as if there weren't any answers to our questions, Judy—I did some reading up on stuff like that afterward, his whole attitude had me so rattled, and there are those who say that crossbred strains are natural dead ends in that they're often sterile. Like mules. It's just that he was too smug about his all-purpose response to go back to logical argument. And through it all I was aware of that silent presence looking on from the back of the room, the great mouth that couldn't open to speak for itself anymore, except—like Darwin—from the pages of books.

"We were both, by then, totally fed up with Isvara dasa (if he ever had a chance of converting Doug, he'd lost it, assuming Doug could have brought himself to cut off his hair in the first place). Things were getting loud and starting to catch the attention of other Krishnas, though they stayed at a polite distance. It must have struck Isvara dasa, this 'servant of God,' then, that he wasn't playing the part of the serene and accepting holy man too well. . . .

"Doug had his yellow beard stuck out aggressively, and was saying, 'You can't even think for yourself half the time, man. And don't try to tell me Krishna is your authority—only for the hundredth time—'cause Krishna sure as hell didn't say Darwin's father was a monkey. Your piece of *waxwork* back there did!'

"At which, Isvara dasa suddenly changed around and said, 'I accept whatever you say. *You* are my authority.'

"Can you believe that? That abrupt three-sixty took the gas out of our tanks for a full second: I couldn't understand it. But Doug was too carried away to let it go. 'Is that right?' he said, still fuming. 'So I'm your authority now?'

" 'Yes,' Isvara dasa said quietly, and with some dignity, I have to admit now, though at the time I decided it was a sudden lack of stomach. 'You are my authority.' He'd clearly found a semi-new mantra and was going to stick with it, maybe for another half hour.

" 'Well, then,' Doug said, obviously in no mood to be a merciful God, 'I'm telling you, as your authority, that you're an idiot! Always were, now that I think about it.'

"Poor Isvara dasa just nodded stoically and said, 'I accept that. You are my authority. . . .'

"And this time there was really no more to say, so we got up and walked out, ignoring the still polite 'Hare Krishnas' spoken at the doorway, leaving the book behind.

"And that, quite simply, is why I don't feel all that comfortable around Hare Krishnas," said Nitin, winding things up as the Celica angled away on the Farmington Hills exit ramp and Nina, feeling the centrifugal force, began to mewl and cough in her car seat. "Maybe I just ran into the wrong one. Or else, they seem to have evolved a bit, ha ha, going by the airport lady—I'll tell you what, I don't mind giving the Detroit center a try if you still want. You're right, I can see Nina playing with the peacocks all day. And no harm exposing her to more of the Hindu ethos than she'd get otherwise—you know how it's Christian this and Christian that all around us. No harm sampling some of those feasts ourselves either. When we told Veer about our visit to the Harrison center, he thought I'd been wrong to eat their food and then question their beliefs—clear case of an ungrateful and impolite guest. But Doug said nonsense, that fool Michael was the one without manners, an overbearing, insulting host. So I don't know. What do you think?"

Judy sighed and shifted on the seat. Relieved that their Celica was only minutes now from the Fredericksburg division and a fresh-smelling toilet, she looked out at the stubby junipers flipping by the exit ramp. Visiting the Krishna center didn't seem such a good idea anymore—she decided to skirt Nitin's sudden switch to promotion of it. Disturbing thoughts and images were thronging her head, limned on the windshield like ghosts across the trees. She saw Nina, her brown legs and hair grown long, running up the aisle of Harrison's old Methodist church. And on a creaky front pew, Judy's own mother all wrinkled around cottony eyes, smiling proudly to see her granddaughter at service. For a moment Judy could hear, as if she'd attended that very Sunday, the reverend's calm yet resonant intonations. She remembered a sermon he'd preached from the Gospel of John: there were many mansions in his Father's house, said Christ. But he also told Thomas that he alone was the way—no one came to the Father except through him. . . . She sighed again and, despite what was brewing in her, some of the reverend's gentleness crept into her voice as she answered Nitin.

"You were just being you," she said, putting a hand to his shoulder. But she turned involuntarily to check on her daughter.

Keeping Time

Still time, thought Miss Davar, adjusting pearl
gray glasses on a bony nose and about ears hidden by straggly,
graying hair, as she peered through the window of her living
room. The light made her squint and there was no sign of the
Commissariat boy as yet, so she drew the curtain and returned to
her lemon tarts and her teacup. The tea, a nice Brooke Bond
blend, had lost some of its heat to the already warm room, whose
temperature must have been changed by an immeasurably small
increment. The tarts from Horseshoe were a diabetic threat, but
they brought back mornings when Papa was still alive and money
seemed plentiful. She stretched out a crumpled area on her house

dress, then let it go and watched the print fabric wrinkle up again. Too late now to iron it. She would put on another dress after Zubin Commissariat's lesson; the boy would certainly not notice a few wrinkles.

In any case, it mattered less to her how she looked nowadays—too old for little vanities. And too much of a misfit. My, how nice everything had been before the British had left; the whole country had just gone downhill after that. Parsis were hardly looked up to anymore. Far from being knighted, at times they were even made fun of by other Indians. Oy, Bawaji, kem Bawaji. It was very annoying. And it had been very wrong of Papa to have slowly spent all their money (mostly Mama's inheritance) and not even told her it was nearly gone. After all those years she had stayed with him and not married anyone—even when Jamshed Wacha and Rusi Masani had been so keen, such fair, handsome boys. It galled her to remember how Papa's worthless friends from the Parsi Gymkhana had shown up with long faces at the Towers of Silence, after stealing his money every evening at card tables. Old Edulji Bharucha, constantly borrowing from Papa and the others, never giving it back, taking his debts to the towers himself when she had tried to collect. All so humiliating. Invited by Rusi to his wedding (as if she'd go—how she'd cried herself to sleep that night), running into him and Armaiti, at concerts or other functions, chattering away brightly with their beautiful children and now their grandchildren! Oh, hullo Nergis. Darlings, say hullo to your Nergis Aunty. Buddhi spinster Nergis Aunty.

"My goodness, Nergis," Vera would say, pulling away from her own bright brood to spend a minute with her old Presentation Convent school chum. "How well he's aged. Remember when he was desperately in love with you? Roses, chocolates, books, what not?"

"So long ago, Vera." Putting on her most-uninterested face. "Only *you* remember these things."

Yes, Vera always remembered her. Looked out for her so sweetly after Papa died. Their flat was not something he could spend, thank God; what would have happened to her if she had no place to stay? She would have had to throw herself completely on Vera, and that would have meant taking even an old friendship too far. So nice of Vera to find her a pupil from time to time; the Commissariat boy was only the latest. But the numbers had grown smaller as the years went by—not too many people wanted their children to play the piano nowadays. Even Parsis had started to send them to Bharat Natyam or sitar classes instead. At one time there had been nine children coming to her every week, and now this boy Zubin, Vera's grandnephew, was the only one. Only one pupil, every Saturday morning.

And she knew very well that, if he had the choice, he would not come either. He always looked so sulky as he sat on the stool, staring down at the yellowed ivory keys, doing nothing until she popped her head out of the bedroom and told him to practice his scales. He would run through them then, stopping after every five or six to get off the stool and pretend to turn it up or down. She wished she still had girl pupils; boys were so fidgety. And if you weren't strict with them, they took advantage and didn't do their homework. She was quite sure that if his mother Thriti did not happen to be Vera's niece, Zubin Commissariat would have stopped coming a long time ago.

But though he was definitely lazy, she had to admit he was quite clever for his age. At eight he had been able to play Bartok's "Village Dance" without any mistakes, at nine he could do Schubert's "Moment Musical No. 3," and now she had him playing Bach and Chopin at ten. She picked up a crumb of lemon tart from the tea table and placed it on the edge of the saucer. If he did well at the contest next week, that would show the Commissariats how much he had learned.

"I'm tired of you making such a fuss every time, Zubin," said his mother, creamy odors emanating as always from her supple, milky, rounded limbs. "You know you have to go—what will Vera Aunty say otherwise?"

"Make Vera Aunty go then." He set his face against her feminine charms and maternal authority, both of which would, ordinarily, have helped her have the last word with him. "Why do I have to suffer just because Miss Davar is *her* friend?"

"Don't be silly, Zubin. 'Suffer!' My God, as if we're torturing you. Any other boy would be grateful to learn the piano."

"I've learned already," he said. "I can play on my own—why should I keep on going to that skinny old woman?"

"Shh. Don't say such things. I'll talk about it with Daddy—but you go quietly now or I'll tell him you're acting very naughty."

The promise to discuss the matter with his father was an unexpected concession, and Zubin was filled with hope as he went down the stairs. It was warm and sunny outside, smelling of grass. People were playing cricket in the Oval Maidan, punctuating light weekend traffic noises with springy *thock* sounds of willow bat meeting leather-wrapped cork ball. Rajiv and Yezdi and two other boys came running out of Empress Court carrying a ball and a bat. They saw him with his music books, and Yezdi started to laugh and point at him.

He turned away from them and hurried along the footpath. But once he was out of range of their voices he slowed down almost to a stroll, looking up at the palm trees and twisting around to check the time on Bombay's Big Ben, the Rajabhai Tower. He was five minutes late already, so there was no point hurrying. Let Miss Davar wait; it served her right. He smiled, remembering Schubert's "March Militaire" and her face that day a year ago.

As usual she had given him the piece to read for homework without even playing it for him. How was he supposed to know what a piece sounded like if she never played more than one or two phrases? It irritated him to have to struggle at the piano while she just sat on the side and watched, leaning over once in a blue moon to play only one hand of a few bars, her long, meatless fingers picking up and coming down stiffly like mechanical hammers. "March Militaire" had both hands playing complicated chords at the same time, not simply a melody line for the right hand. And he was supposed to read it by himself and try to play it at home!

So when she asked him to play it the next Saturday, he just sat and looked at the thickly notated sheet of music on the upright black Bechstein, wondering whether the mustiness in his nose came from the piano or from her.

"Did you do your homework, Zubin?" she asked. As if he didn't get enough homework from school.

"I don't know how it's supposed to sound," he said.

She raised an eyebrow at that. "The music is there in front of you; what more do you want? Play one hand at a time first."

He stumbled through the treble first and then the bass.

"Now put both together."

He sat there sullenly.

"What's the matter?" she asked.

"I can't play both hands until I hear how it sounds together."

"Just try," she said. "What has happened to you today?"

"I have to hear how it sounds first," he repeated, keeping his hands down on his lap. "You never play it, so I don't know how it sounds."

She went red in the face.

"You insolent boy," she said, her voice rising quickly. "Are you trying to say that *I* cannot play the piece? Is that what you are trying to say?"

"I can't play it if you don't show me how it sounds," he said, refusing to incriminate himself, mindful of his father's temper should word get back home.

"You think I cannot play it?" she screeched, her angular face twisting, brown eyes flaring behind her spectacles. "Get off!"

She practically pushed him off the stool and, furiously smoothing her dress beneath her, settled onto it herself. Then, to his utter surprise, she yanked her pearl-rimmed glasses off and stuck her face to within an inch of the sheet of music on the stand.

And with her face skimming the very surface of the paper to scan each line, she pounded at the keys with a fury that shocked him, never looking down at them, her bony fingers crashing down, chord after chord, whether the music was marked piano or forte, crescendo or diminuendo. Hard, pointed sounds sprang from the Bechstein to rock fiercely about the brown walls, encircling both of them.

When she had finished, the notes still dying, he stood there stunned. He watched as she sat back, unseeing, breathing hard, until at last she groped for her glasses and put them on. Then she got up and sat on the side chair again.

"Try it now," she said.

And he did, his efforts tinny and weak after the red downpour. He'd never challenged her to play again, but that one time was worth remembering.

Now he could see the bandstand ahead and was tempted to run across the street and buy a glass of sugarcane juice from the hawker's stand at the edge of the Oval. He felt the yellow green froth tickle his upper lip, could almost taste the iced sweetness. But the clock tower said 9:15 already, as he came to the doorway of Moonlight—he had better go in. He looked up for a second at the brown plastered wall with cracks spreading like the veins in Miss Davar's hands, then stepped into the dinginess around the lift shaft and the staircase. He rang the bell at her front door and waited to hear her voice answer the two-noted chime before twisting the huge brass knob with both hands.

She called out again from inside the bedroom as he walked over to the piano. "Why are you so late, Zubin? Now I have to stay here until 10:15. You think I have nothing to do after ten o'clock except sit here with you?"

He did not try to answer.

"Please have the manners to come on time from now on," she continued, popping her head through the ruby bead-curtain of the bedroom door to throw a severe look at him through her specs. The beads clinked and jingled against each other. "Start your scales."

He started his scales. They bored him, and he got up in between to twirl the stool higher. When she came out, she had on a loose-fitting, crumpled housedress as usual, and hardly looked like she was going anywhere after ten.

———

Such an inconsiderate boy, thought Miss Davar, irritated by the absence of contrition on the offending face, oval and disproportionately large, as its youthful owner wound up his B minor and looked up at her.

"How are your mummy-daddy?" she asked.

"Fine," he said.

"Have you practiced properly for the contest?" she continued, crossing over to her chair by the side of his stool.

"Yes."

"Aren't you excited?"

He shrugged.

What a strange boy he was. Last April, she recalled, he had refused to sing the second verse of a song she had picked for his
school's music competition. Only the second verse, but he would
not say why. He simply said, with a stubborn look on his face,
that he would not sing it. And that was that. And then she had realized why—the second verse had the word *bosom* in it. So she
had to pick another song, just because of that. Who would have
thought boys so young could be conscious of such things? It had
made *her* conscious again, after all those years, of her own rather
deflated chest. How she had secretly thrilled, when Rusi Masani
and Jimmy Wacha were courting her, to catch their quick down-
ward glances!

"Well, you should be excited—wouldn't you like to win?"

"Yes," he said.

She let some air out through her nose. "Okay, in any case, let's
see how well you have practiced."

She leaned across to open the elongated wooden pyramid of the
metronome on top of the Bechstein. Squinting at the gradations,
she slid the weight carefully up the length of the pendulum and
set it going: *tick-tock tick-tock tick-tock*. So steady and depend-
able, like the Rock of Gibraltar.

He lowered the stand for the music sheets. Then he turned to
Schumann's "Traumerei" and started to play.

She listened carefully. At first she was relieved—there was no
doubt he had been practicing. The boy must be eager, after all,
just didn't want to show it. There were absolutely no mistakes,
and he was keeping perfect time. But as she continued to listen, a
doubt crept into her mind. He was clearly observing the four-
four time and the markings for loud and soft, and yet . . . there
was a stiffness, and something flat about the tone. As if a Baked
Alaska had been taken out too soon to develop a delicate browning. (Ages since she'd had any—it would probably send her into
diabetic coma.)

Still, that was not the point for a children's competition. What
was the matter with her? She could hardly expect a ten-year-
old child to play the piece with the touch of a Rubinstein. And
"Traumerei" had become so commonplace at the contests; she
should have picked something else. In any case, it was too late to

talk about such obscure things, on the eve of the contest. It would only confuse the boy.

"Good," she said when he finished. "But don't stop practicing until Friday itself, or you'll start making mistakes again."

He nodded silently, and the metronome continued to mark time.

The next Saturday, Miss Davar sipped her morning tea—nice and hot for now, but bound to cool off. Unless she were to gulp it down with the horrible slurping noises some people made. She wondered how the Commissariat boy had done at the contest. So little enthusiasm—just like his parents. She shook her head, remembering the ruination of her choir project. Vera had got the Commissariats and several other couples to join, and they had all started to come to Moonlight for practice every Tuesday evening. Miss Davar had led the choir, of course.

"Once we become good," she said to them as they stood in two rows before her, the men in their bush shirts mostly, salt-and-pepper hairs curling over their forearms, some of the women in light, gaily colored chiffon saris, but most in dresses, "we can give concerts in Bombay first. Then we'll get invited to sing in other cities. And then when we're famous enough we can tour the world, give concerts everywhere. Just think—London, Vienna, Philadelphia, Tokyo! Won't that be terrific?"

But later, poring over new scores during a break, from behind the faint varnish smells of Mama's hand-carved walnut partition she had overheard the Commissariats whispering.

"Talking to us like little children!" said Thriti. Even through the whisper her voice was like the boy's, though his would probably break after a year or two and Miss Davar would have to pick songs to suit its new range.

"I know," said Darius Commissariat, whose forceful tenor normally rang through and beyond the small flat. "Round-the-world tour, my foot! Some hopes she has."

They had been the first to back out. And then the Katgaras and Paymasters had followed suit, so her neatly assembled choir had become a shambles. No wonder the children had no ambition. Give the child a famous name and expect everything else to follow without the hard work—that was how people were nowadays.

She put her cup down and drew the curtain a little. There he was now, strolling along, looking all over the place, but actually five minutes early this time. He was not such a bad boy, after all; maybe he had even done well in the contest. She dabbed at her mouth with her handkerchief, unlatched the front door, and hurried off into the bedroom, careful not to set the bead curtain clinking.

"Come in, Zubin," she called out when he knocked.

Perched on the edge of the bed, she heard him walk over to the piano and give the stool a whirl. Then there was silence. Now he would waste time until she told him to play his scales. No, how surprising, he had started to play. Very softly, he had started to play "Traumerei." The tempo seemed slower than usual—he had not started the metronome! She rose, about to call out, when the music began to build and she stopped to listen.

My, how strange—how differently he was playing it today. He was still keeping time, but now there was an underlying surge and ebb as the phrases unfolded, a lift and fall, a melancholy to the sound. It pulled at her like a gentle tide. The melody poured steadily from the aging Bechstein into the house, and a sadness took hold of her and closed her eyes.

When the music ceased and the house grew quiet again, she stood still until the sadness passed. Random pictures—of Vera's slow smile, of herself in plaits behind her mother's powder blue frock, of Papa doffing his sand-colored sola topee, of Edulji dealing rummy hands from paisley-patterned packs when she was still a child welcome among the men at the Parsi Gym—came and went in overlapped confusion, followed by images of Rusi Masani putting his hand on hers as it rested on caramelized ivory keys and of Papa rocking slowly in his chair, mouth open, softly snoring. Mama's voice came through with all the forgotten desperation in it: "Don't I have *any* say in what we do?" She had wanted to go out to dinner for a change, but Papa, who had been to the gym already for his cards, said he would rather just eat at home as usual, and Miss Davar, Nergis, had said, "Yes, Mama, let's just stay home now," to avoid any unpleasantness.

Mama's question when it came had drifted uneasily in a

strained, almost resentful silence, the answer so obvious. She had never asked it again. Now Rusi's face floated back to Miss Davar in all its bold etching, his tall frame immaculately suited in gray, a Darcy irretrievable after she'd turned him down to start with, then asked him to wait once too often, so bitter in his threats—carried out eventually—to marry Armaiti Seervai.

Then the pictures became murky, and she walked into the hall.

"Did you play it like that in the contest?" she asked, crossing over to the side chair.

"No," he said, shaking his head reassuringly. Why, the boy was actually trying to be nice today. "I played it the same as in practice. Only at home yesterday, after the contest, the piece changed in my mind—the way it sounded. I don't know why. And I wanted to play it differently."

"That's too bad," she said, a dry note creeping in. There was no need to ask how the contest had gone, then. "You would have won the contest if you had played it like that."

"Oh," he said, clearly startled.

She watched him turn away in confusion and reach for the plain white envelope he had placed on top of the piano. Inside it, she knew, was her monthly payment.

He gave it to her and said, "Mummy told me there's a letter for you also, in the envelope."

A letter? She opened the envelope and pulled out the thin, folded sheet of crackly white paper, not bothering to check the orange twenty-rupee notes. Taking her glasses off, she laid them on her lap. Then she unfolded the page, brought it to three or four inches from her face, and started to read.

"Yes," she said vaguely when she finished, and lifted her head to scan the lines again.

Dear Miss Davar,

How are you? Hope everything is fine. I'm sending the money with Zubin in advance, as usual. Thank you for teaching him so well. But for quite some time he has been insisting that he does not want to learn any more. You know that Darius and I would have liked it if he continued, but we do not want to force him. So this will be his last month of piano lessons.

How is the choir progressing? Please say hullo to Vera Aunty.

Thank you for teaching Zubin all these years.

Yours sincerely,

Thriti Commissariat

"Yes," Miss Davar said again, her head nodding of its own accord. She folded the note along its creases back into the envelope, then put on her spectacles.

Getting to her feet at last she said, "I have to write a thank-you letter to your mummy, Zubin." The words dragged and she pushed to bring them out at a normal pace. "Give it to her when you go back home."

"Okay," he said, still looking bemused.

She went into the bedroom and sat on the bed for a while. *We do not want to force him.* . . . So that was how she had spent the last twenty-five years, teaching children under compulsion.

She turned to the rolltop desk to put the envelope in her purse and look for the letter pad, dimly aware that the boy was just sitting there in the hall instead of practicing. The desktop creaked on its way up, then clicked into place as she settled in the chair. Finding the letter pad, she opened it. Only two pages left; she would have to get a new one. No hurry—just Vera to write to. And the dhobi would bring back her linen on Thursday and have to be paid. She reached over sideways and tucked the plain yellow bedsheet in where it had slipped out at the corner, then put her nose to it. It felt cool to the touch, smelled fresh enough. There was no point sending the clothes out anymore; she could wash everything herself.

Taking up her Sheaffer, she checked its window for ink. The silver nib scratched a turquoise zigzag across the blotting paper before a dim sense of oppression made her look around. The house had become very still.

It was so quiet she did not have to raise her voice.

"Play your scales, Zubin," she said.

He began to run through the scales, and she started to write.

The
Mark
Twain
Overlook

If a small town too, like the little man, will have its ten minutes in the sun, then Muscatine, Iowa, has already seen its ten. It had a near miss once before. Back in 1854, Mark Twain spent a summer there and is still counted by Muscatine folk, warm-hearted and lively people in a wintry climate, as the town's most famous inhabitant ever. Some of its street names today are Samuel Clemens Road, Becky Thatcher Road, and Aunt Polly Lane. But the fact is, he was a little-heard-of news writer reporting for his brother Orion's Journal then, and moved on down the Mississippi well before his characters charmed their way into print. His fame reflected no light whatsoever on the quiet lumber center. It was not until the end of the century, really, that fortune in the shape of a rough brown river clam finally relaxed its jaws to smile widely on Muscatine for a while.

By the time Zubin Commissariat found his way there about a decade from the end of the next century, only traces were left of Muscatine's brief heyday. There was an unlikely sounding pearl button museum on the corner of Iowa Avenue and Second Street not far from his apartment house, but he walked by without really noticing it, on the opposite side of the road, going down to Riverside Park in the evenings. Winter was on the way, generating more than a nip already against his bare arms and face too used to year-round warmth in Bombay. The skies were clouded a rocky gray. Downtown buildings were variously brown-toned and the streets discouragingly barren on weekends. At Bandag, where he was on a year's contract to help convert an accounts receivable package, the regular, i.e. permanent, programmers said Muscatine had a population of 20,000 on weekdays, when people came in to their jobs, but only 3,000 on weekends, when they drove off to nearby hometowns.

At the park, the river air was clean and increasingly sharp. At winter's peak, when snow covered the grass and piled against the base of gold-lacquered statues at either end, the breath went down Zubin's airpipe like a sword. One statue was of a stag, the other of a Mascoutin Indian, both nobly posed, the heavily antlered stag looking inland, the Indian out over water. The Mississippi rounded the bend sluggishly, reflecting the sky in its gray except for a border of brown below trees along the far, Illinois shore. Zubin often had the park to himself in winter, and the border turned green before he found someone to walk with him. Her name was Christina Lopez.

The apex, of course, was the sunset together at the overlook and the epiphany afterward. While this is a story about Zubin Commissariat, Christina Lopez, and, not least, Muscatine, it's not a story of Zubin *and* Christina *in* Muscatine, except in passing. A woman hankering to get herself and a possessive daughter out of a small town; a man moving through, unwilling to be her vehicle. Clear enough that it would end. Zubin just didn't anticipate exactly how. His reluctance, despite prompting, to utter the *love* word became one loose rail on the track. The *marriage* word then had to appear, wrapped in Christina's most seductive perfumes and dresses and home-cooked dinners (with Monique away at her grandparents'), and was also sidestepped. He assumed then that the final switch, sending their cars off on separate tracks, would be thrown by the event of his contract's coming to an end at Bandag. But Christina threw it instead, much ahead—she was not one to stay behind and turn nun.

She found a teaching position at a middle school in New Orleans, not very far from her Texas roots, cooked one more dinner for Zubin, then, all excited, told him of the offer and her intention to move there with Monique the next term. Would he like to join them? Finding a programming job in New Orleans should not be a problem, she would think. Now that he was no longer her train out of Muscatine (need never and may never have been seen as such, he had to concede), he was left with the option of either agreeing to go or asking her—them—to come with him instead to wherever his next contract took him. A section of his mind would have liked some stable center in a roving life, and he felt enough for Christina that in intimate times he'd wished he could have used the *love* word without misleading her. But another section was not sure quite how much, other than black hair and disgust for the Buchanan right, they had in common. And yet another section was strongly reluctant to become Monique's instant and unwanted daddy.

So he was glad for Christina in her good fortune but, instead of shuffling unreadably once more, straightforwardly declined to join her in Louisiana. She, in turn, didn't wait to shut things down between them (he'd hoped to delay that until she actually left). He avoided the park and D. C. Arnold's after they broke up, so time hung on his hands in the evenings and weekends after work. His new dream, born on the day of the overlook, grew in his head, and he began to walk down Iowa Avenue daily to the Musser Public Library. Within its light-brown brick walls and on complicatedly lettered shelves were stacked a hundred and forty thousand worlds to explore, worlds he'd ignored since leaving college at Powai. It amazed him that it cost nothing to get his own bar-coded library card, just a show of I.D. to the woman in the front desk rectangle, and that there was no limit to the number of books (or compact discs or videos) he could check out, if he could get them read and returned in two weeks.

He met Christina at D. C. Arnold's, a bar he often strolled over to after dinner on Saturdays. It had live bands on stage, often repeat groups, playing the staple hard rock of KIIK 104, Kick One-oh-Four to the Davenport deejays. The heavy beat relaxed him, pounding out the muscles of his eyes, arms, and neck, strained from hours in front of the monitor. He was a painfully slow drinker, nursing a Bud till it was lukewarm and flat, wetting his drooping black mustache (whence his nickname Pablo in college days at IIT, Powai), leaving his table to get a second, which usually lasted to when the band played its final set and it was time to go. Christina said she'd watched him at his routine several evenings before the one on which she'd picked a table next to his, then waited to flash him a smile.

When she did, it was ivory white. Skin that spoke of honey even in a winter-spring creaminess. Glossed lips and black hair curling in to the red. Echoes of castanets, banjos, midnight serenades. Months later in September, at the Viva México Fiesta, he watched her dance to such music, cotton skirt calf-length in purple floral patterns flaring around her hips when she twirled, wrapping around them when she stopped. When they danced to slow numbers at D. C. Arnold's she was voluptuous, shifting against him in slumberous rhythms. Sitting by an enormous grounded anchor in Riverside Park, they watched boats rock within the safe harbor to a similar lilt, and he was reminded of a song, "South of the Border," his father sang in Bombay to his mother's piano accompaniment. The song's speaker sang of a girl he'd left behind in Mexico, then returned to, only to find she'd turned nun in his absence.

South of the border, I rode back one day.
There in a veil of white by candlelight she knelt to pray.
The mission bells told me that I mustn't stay
South of the border, down Mexico way.

He especially liked the pun on "tolled," and Christina, who hadn't noticed it, was impressed with his facility in the language. By then in his fourth American year and beyond irrational umbrage — why should an Indian's good English be occasion for surprise? — at such reactions, he told her of his Jesuit school in Bombay, from where the Indian School-Leaving Certificate final papers went all the way to Cambridge in England for correction. His, so the padres had said in approval, had earned him among the highest English Literature marks ever posted by a Bombayite in the I.S.C. A certificate of scholastic achievement signed by none other than Indira Gandhi had arrived later in the mail, only to be mislaid over the years by his parents and lost. The thought of their carelessness still irked him. Only much later would he realize he was perpetuating the stereotype while protesting against it — "good English" was a relative term whose definition varied from India to Australia to Jamaica to England to Canada to America. And also across time: Chaucer would be practically unintelligible if he were to speak today.

Christina smiled at Zubin's boasting and teased him about it, but she was clearly pleased he thought her worth the effort. Unaccustomed to having American girls either approach him at a bar or stay interested once he opened his patently un-American mouth, he'd wondered at the time why she'd picked him but had put it down eventually, and cynically, to a combination of things. For one, his near-Mexican looks. For another, his apparent general disinterest in the women at the bar — likely, though not calculated, to pique their interest. For a third, simple supply and demand: fewer "good men" either around or still available in a small town.

"So, what's a South-of-the-Border girl doing west of the Mississippi?" he asked, humming the tune.

"What's an Indian doing in America?" she retorted, though she knew of his contract at Bandag and of the Bombay computer consultancy that had stationed him there. India was a new but burgeoning power in tailor-made business applications software, and he was one of a thousand young, highly educated consultants rented at lowball rates by American companies to program their systems. The import of contract programmers had reached dimensions, in fact, that sparked controversy all the way onto investigative shows such as 60 Minutes. The central assertion was not a new one: work that might otherwise have employed needy Americans had gone instead to foreigners.

"Case of supply and demand," he replied, stopping short of making the parallel to Mexican field-workers, particularly the low dollar allowances paid to consultants by their Indian head offices, compared to what American counterparts earned. "But..."

He flipped a thumb at the Mascoutin statue. Its subject had hair down to his shoulders, eagle features, a string of bear claws around his neck, an animal skin hanging down his back. His chest was bare over buckskin leggings, one foot raised against golden rock. Both he and the stag, thought Zubin, look almost like trophies.

"I've heard that at one time there were only Indians here," he continued, wondering if she'd be as prickly or defensive or guilt-ridden over the makings of her nation as some Americans he'd encountered on contract in Michigan and Florida. Sometimes he'd felt sorry for them. He could see what it was from their point of view: a no-win situation of the inescapable, unending variety. Whether you changed gaming laws to benefit Indians or religious-freedom laws to deny them peyote "for their own good," it all harked back to one thing. Even when you built statues to them. Or maybe especially then. And not only did that one thing have nothing to do with any of your actions, with the actions of any American of this century, but it had everything to do with what you were, it was the foundation, no less, of your identity and existence, and others denied your humanity because of it. . . . Zubin had learned that it was also, consequently, unwelcome subject matter, particularly if coming from a foreigner. Mainstream America was tired of such issues.

But Christina only laughed, a xylophonic affair. "We're named after you, then. That's where Muscatine got its name, from the Mascoutin Indians."

"I was wondering," he said. "Sounds almost the same."

She nodded. "Though some people say it's from a word in Mascoutin that means burning island."

"Burning island?"

"Mm, yes." She had a way of cocking her chin to the left and sending her eyes to the right when she was being mysterious. "I'll have to take you to a certain spot one of these evenings. Remind me."

He drank in fiction to some extent indiscriminately, drawn by back-cover summaries but also by writing that seemed a cut above thrillers he'd read in college. By the time, four years later on a fresh contract in Minneapolis, he began to write himself, he had a curious, uneven, eclectic mix under his belt: Vonnegut, Dinesen, Joyce, Hardy, Saroyan, Raucher, Rawlings, Kerouac, Austen, Rossner, Chekhov, Malamud, McCullers, Pirsig, Remarque, Welty, Steinbeck, Eliot, Salinger, Le Guin, all mingled there, like it or not. The exposure, somehow, had not undermined his belief that he too could write if he put his mind to it. In fact, he felt driven to it by a surfeit of books about Western—as in white—characters, felt a lessening desire and ability to constantly live (vicariously) the life of the Other, a growing need to read stories about himself and those most like him.

He had a hard time finding them—only the name Rushdie had visibility above such stories. Skimming *Midnight's Children*, Zubin was put off, despite its instant brilliance, by what he thought at the time was a supercilious attitude. Distinctions between narrators and authors were as yet unclear to him. So he put it away. He went through a long phase when he could not finish books, losing interest in the journeys of American or English characters so divergent from his own, unable anymore to generate the necessary curiosity about their destinations. Eventually he came to know of the Desais, Sidhwas, Singhs, Naipauls, Mistrys, Seths, Mehtas, Ganesans, Kangas, and Mukherjees, discovered Tagore, even rediscovered the gentle Narayan of his schooldays, but often only because he encountered them on the shelves at Nalanda or Crossroads when, every three years or so, he went back to Bombay.

In the interim he explored the lives of black American characters created by the Hurstons, Baldwins, Bambaras, Angelous,

Wrights, McPhersons, Morrisons, Naylors, Johnsons, Walkers, Ellisons, Reeds, and Widemans, finding relief mainly in the non-whiteness of their perspectives. Yet their perspectives were not quite *his* (something of a middle ground: brown). When Huck and Jim got separated, journeying down the Mississippi, it was more by the dense fog that surrounded them than by the invisible island that subsequently came up between them. "Nothing don't look natural nor sound natural in a fog." And black characters, while not white, were also not Indian. So when Zubin hit upon a rare anomaly, Hesse's *Siddhartha*, white author writing about Indians, even if idealized, "noble" ones, he was very taken with it and also with the protagonist's dogged quest for meaning. In a burst of adventurousness that had been building within him since the day of the overlook and was not uninspired by fictional exploits, he finally chucked programming, left the writing of code to go write his own stories.

He leaned back against the anchor. Its gray metal had baked in the midwestern sun all afternoon, and the warmth came through his shirt. The boats and their masts or cabins swayed left and right, left and right, in lazy, rhythmic regularity that put him in mind of the metronome his piano teacher in Bombay had always insisted on, except that there was a relaxed, unhurried, yet elastic nature to their movement.

"You're my guide, today," he said idly, tossing the words burning island *around in his head, "showing off your hometown."*

"Your guide can't stand her hometown!" she responded in a burst that took him by surprise.

His face must have shown it; she eased back on the ire. "That's probably an exaggeration. Muscatine's fine, as small towns go; I just get this way sometimes. You would too, if you'd lived all your life in a provincial little hole, with the prospect of rotting there for the remainder."

He made a sympathetic throat sound, twisted toward her, listened closely.

"We've been here for generations. My grandparents were not even born when their families moved up from San Antonio. Not

quite south of the border, to answer your question, but El Paso before San Antonio, they tell me, and Juárez before El Paso."

Why San Antonio to Muscatine, of all places, was the question left unanswered. Only in his later romance with the Musser Public Library did he learn that Texas-based Mexicans would come up to Iowa once a year to pick summer tomato crops. Some stayed on after the season rather than shuttle back and forth, until Muscatine was eventually seven to ten percent Mexican American. Tomato-picking ancestry could easily have been a detail a sixth-grade teacher chose not to supply unless she had to. Christina came close only on one other occasion, when they found mutual satisfaction and new depths of scorn shredding Pat Buchanan politics like chicken for tamales. Into America, river of many fish, had flowed two noticeably swollen tributaries, their slithery inhabitants taking too much feed from those in the mainstream and giving back, allegedly, too little. One stream, old and great, wound down from the nearby Sierra Madres, sometimes spilling over manmade barriers. The other, recent, smaller, trickled in all the way from the Himalayas. When fish from the two rivulets fell into the same pond, they found they had notes to compare.

At Riverside Park by the Mississippi, Christina was not yet done with small towns.

"Mom and Dad seem happy to live out their lives here, and I guess I could manage that too, if it was just me. But I don't want that for Monique. I want her to have all the possibilities in the world, not the twenty-three or so in Muscatine. I don't know too many people still south of thirty years wouldn't get out of here if they had the chance."

Her father, earth faced and coal eyed in a photograph on her dresser, had helped produce corn spirits at Grain Processing Corp., her mother, unsmiling in the same, fair skinned and plump, was still a secretary at Heinz. Her ex-husband she rarely spoke of, except to mention he'd never trusted her with the accounts. Even after five years of marriage — could Zubin imagine? Her daughter, Monique, was fragile and silk-haired at seven, and the second time they'd met she sent a look at him, when Christina was at the refrigerator, that said I hate your guts. She'd meant him to see it.

*He wasn't sure he liked where he thought the conversation was
going, so he said, "I know what you're saying, but I grew up in a
big city; it's no paradise. Muscatine's closer, in fact. But I want to
see this burning island of yours."*

*"How about tonight?" She was ready to shelve the topic
too. "Come get me at 6:30, and I'll show you the Mark Twain
Overlook."*

"The Mark Twain Overlook?"

"Uh-huh. Didn't you know he lived here?"

"Mark Twain lived in Muscatine?"

*"For all of one summer," she said, looking pert again. "Then
he came to his senses."*

For a long while it was no less fascinating an occupation than
he'd anticipated. The activity itself, at the time, was close to
God's: people and settings bloomed from his fingertips. He put
lives in motion and watched them play out, unconscious of more
than the intoxication of having stories to follow (and shape) that
for a change contained characters he not only could relate to
but were in some way him, all of them, beautiful, ugly, woman,
man, child, aged, turtle, dog, Parsi, Sikh, Muslim, Hindu, Taoist,
Christian, black, brown, even white, the Other he'd grown so
weary of from overexposure. All born of his mind and its sense of
the world, after all, and molded by it. Madame Bovary *c'est moi*,
how true, he thought. How he loved them. Later he felt that had
he kept things that way, written always in a vacuum for himself,
been his own and only reader, he might still have had access to
the original thrill. But he also knew it would have been a head-in-
the-sand kind of bliss.

When he joined creative writing workshops around Minneapolis and St. Paul, the bubble was punctured but not quite burst. To
have the private workings of his mind aired in the hearing of others was a mixed thrill and took some squirming to get used to.
This was not helped by the groups' being almost a hundred
percent white American (three out of five middle-aged or older
women, the rest assorted). In a curious inversion now, his Indian
protagonists became the Other that *his* readers did not identify

with. Matters of race, religion, gender, and politics that he'd learned to censor in his conversations demanded expression and a presence in his writing, as did his divided sense of self and place, and he felt down to his bones the silences into which they were read out aloud by workshop leaders. Nevertheless, he experienced a sense of release at the airing of them, added to the surprising new clarity of thought that writing about them had produced. At reading's end, however, he found that his darlings drew as much criticism as praise. Mark Twain once said, if you want a writer to adore you, tell him you adore his work. Few in the workshops seemed to know that or, if they did, seemed needy of Zubin's adoration.

But hardest to handle were the terrible discrepancies that inexplicably arose between what he'd transmitted in black and white and what the listeners, his readers, seemed to have received. Twain also remarked that the difference between the almost-right word and the right word is the difference between a lightning bug and lightning. Zubin was uninformed at the time but eventually came to know of Derrida's merry band of deconstructionists and that inescapable condition of man's existence in language: the slippage between *each and every* signifier and what it signifies. Whether as seemingly simple a one as "red" or as clearly complex as "love"—it didn't matter. They were all just arbitrarily assigned names that inadequately represented the actuality. He was still writing code! He worked at making his manuscripts as clear and hard and incontrovertibly defined as polished diamonds, only to discover again and again the distortion his ideas suffered in being rendered through words, as if images refracted by the diamonds became obscured in a dazzle of light. It took him a while to see in this the potential for multiple interpretation rather than misinterpretation, that the dazzle could enrich rather than obscure the image. But in the meantime, a consciousness of his writing had descended upon him.

He demanded more and more of himself as a writer, was less and less easily satisfied or fulfilled by his efforts. Yet if the joy had gone out of the activity to an extent, he looked instead to enjoy a less easily obtained but therefore higher pleasure at the end of repeated rewrites: from having created a product of indisputable quality. The measure was relative, of course—quality can only be gauged through comparison—and the most immediate comparisons available were comforting. Nine out of ten pieces turned in by his fellow workshoppers seemed rather simplistic to him, and he wondered (a) if they really couldn't see that themselves and (b) why they stayed at it.

The last was not a question he had to ask of himself. As yet. The episodes of his novel had begun, relatively, to flow again—he was surer of what he wanted of his writing and how to get there. This was not to say he found it easy going. As a programmer he'd written complex programs, the code of each sometimes filling a hundred-plus pages of printout, each preformatted line of which had to work logically with the ten thousand others or the whole fell to the ground. It amazed him that the task of writing them seemed a simple one now, compared with the staggering complexity of making the hundred thousand words of a novel hold together, which they had to do in a billion rational *and* irrational ways, some of them as subtle as a whisper, others completely intuitive and unstatable, if it was to be any good at all. Whenever, from then on, he heard the casual assertion that anybody can write a book if he wants to, Zubin was reminded of the times he'd heard people deprecate the achievements of famous sportsmen with the words, "Well, if we had nothing to do but practice all day long . . ." and began to understand the enormity of his easy assumption, on a night now five years in the past at Diamond Dave's, that he had what it took to write one. And he realized better the compliment implicit in Christina's faith that he could even write a good one.

Fifty years after Twain left it, Muscatine came to have its ten minutes in the sun. The town sits on a bend in the Mississippi, and over time a large number of mussels came to collect on the riverbed where the flow changes direction. A German immigrant and adventurer, John Boepple, hatched the idea of mining the shiny, color-streaked interior of the shells for material to make buttons. The pearl button industry was seeded this way, and it thrived. In 1905 alone, a billion and a half pearl buttons slid, skittering, out of Muscatine factories, more than a third of the world's button production. The town's infrastructure grew proportionately too: hotels and inns, parks, schools, art galleries, emporiums, and cafes with striped awnings shot up everywhere, bright offspring of the new economy. Muscatine, vigorously alive and bustling like never before, came to be known as the pearl button capital of the world.

But capitals go down with their empires, and the pearl button empire was not meant to last. Paddleboats anchored to the surface of the Mississippi gave way to prop planes buzzing its skies, hemlines flew higher too, and the great material of the century, plastic, largely unsung but spreading even to the shores of the Ganga and the Yangtze Kiang, made its way to Huck Finn's river as surely as Twain's road beyond Muscatine had led to literary fame. Buttons could now be molded in plastic perfection, and pearl buttons were soon merely quaint, redundant artifacts. Their twilight meant also the setting of Muscatine's ten-minute sun, hotel rooms fell empty, and the boomtown became again the quiet backwater it had been before John Boepple's tidal brain wave.

———

At times Zubin felt a fleeting regret that Christina was gone from his life. That he'd let her go, more accurately. Maybe he'd been wrong to see an ulterior motive behind her affections, and maybe by now Monique would have grown to accept him. He'd dated sporadically since then—in Detroit and Minneapolis, not in Muscatine—but nothing had ever developed. And now he could hardly afford to date anymore, let alone think of settling down.

Every day his endeavor lengthened, his savings were running out. Programming may not have fulfilled him, but it had certainly paid the bills. He cringed a little now when anyone popped the innocent but inevitable question, "What do you do?" The reply, "I write," brought on excited queries about books the inquirer might find in the stores, and when he shook his head and admitted he was only yet working on his first one, he was deflated by the change in their eyes, though they fought noticeably to keep it out of their faces. Once at a neighbor's barbecue, an auburn-haired girl with whom he'd felt he was making progress up till then didn't spare him the logical follow-up: "Oh . . . So, do you do anything besides write?" He shook his head again, his face freezing up, and could only shrug his shoulders at her wry, "That must be nice. . . ."

So eventually he found a part-time programming job, lived entirely on one-dollar TV dinners, and moved to a cheaper complex. Food, rent, and gasoline (he still had his paid-off Cavalier, having decided against selling it to get a bicycle) became his only expenses. He missed the security and comforts of his earlier lifestyle but was content: the realization of his dream seemed a short drive away now, and it was worth the trade-offs.

In the evening when Zubin went over, Monique was only a squeaky voice saying bye to her mom from an inner room. Christina looked edible in a green crepe dress over black fishnet that showed almost to her thighs. She smiled at the way he eyed her as he drove. A peachlike perfume expanded till it filled the car. She directing, they went down Mulberry past the county courthouse — a handsomely white-pillared and clock-towered affair — onto Second Street. Just off U.S. 61, she pointed him toward the river up a short climb that leveled off and opened out into a little picnic area, replete with charcoal grills. Pulling up, he looked expectantly around, then at her.

"You'll see," she said, pointing to a plaque off in the corner. "But we have to wait till the sun goes down."

They got out of the Cavalier. A low, two-rail wooden fence looped the perimeter just where, to their left, grassy slopes fell off toward the river. The Mississippi was a bland, steel blue; it took the bend placidly. Puffs of breeze came up to them and dusted their faces. They pressed up against the waist-high top rail, their eyes tracking a long narrow bridge that reached over to Illinois in an arc so slight it paralleled the earth's curvature. A bridge between two states. If not for the truss above its cantilevered center span, it might have been a Roman aqueduct, held up every so often by verticals. At right angles to it ran the line of the breakwater rubble, walling off the safe harbor where the sailboats and motorboats and small yachts still rocked to Mexican rhythms. To the front and right the town buildings spread, whites and browns blent to gray, a couple of rectangular hangars stretched out in the foreground.

"It's not that bad," she said almost to herself, left hip turned in to the rail, and, without knowing what it was to grow up in a small town, he knew she must be thinking of all the years she'd passed, every one of them in Muscatine. The perspective from such a height, looking over the whole, would prompt such thoughts. Leaving her still steeped in them, he visited the plaque. It spoke of a Great River Road from Canada to the Gulf of Mexico, curving three thousand miles up and down the Mississippi. The plaque quoted Mark Twain on Muscatine: "I remember Muscatine for its sunsets. I have never seen any on either side of the ocean that equaled them."

Some endorsement, thought Zubin, turning back to look for the celebrated orb. It had dipped toward the back of town, the blinding tip of a celestial welding rod, still high enough that only quick, oblique glances were possible. He skirted the Cavalier to Christina's side, padding over grass, and saw her smile come on with new reflected lights deepening to tones of red as they spoke. All of Muscatine was acquiring those tones, even as it turned steadily darker. Dreary streets and buildings colored and dissolved in soft effulgent glows. The countryside behind and around town fell into an expectant dusk; there was a hesitation in the air, something clearly on the way.

When it came, though, Zubin was stunned by its beauty. Thinking back later, he tried to isolate each color, but failed. At the Musser Public Library, he tracked Twain's quotation to his riverboat travels account, Life on the Mississippi, and found that the lookout's namesake had had no such problems. The passage, more specific than on the plaque, spoke of Muscatine's summer sunsets, adding:

> They used the broad, smooth river as a canvas, and painted on it every imaginable dream of color, from the mottled daintiness and delicacies of the opal, all the way up, through cumulative intensities, to blinding purple and crimson conflagrations. . . .

Watching with Christina, Zubin was conscious of her hand and of a universal blush, a heated orange glow that lay upon all

the darkened forestry and shot through low-flying stratus in lu-
minous pinks. At center, the white-hot sphere had swelled to gi-
ant proportions. It was close to the horizon by now, could almost
be looked at directly. A funnel of light hung shimmering beneath
it in tornadolike swirls that reached deep into the river. When at
last the sun touched the trees, it lit orange and yellow fires along
their tops, and Zubin saw how the Indian name for Muscatine
might have come about.

<hr>

As things turned out, his dream came close to materializing. The pace of his writing, always less than blazing, slowed as he entered the last phase of the book—delivering satisfactory closure (or nonclosure, whichever worked) seemed the hardest part yet. But he let each chapter trickle in, having learned not to force it. And when he was only a page or two away and knew how it should go, he waited the three days to St. Patrick's, wanting an auspicious day on which to type THE END. Apart from a little controversy raised by someone who wanted closure as of a coffin's, the final workshop reading was a minor triumph, and after some tinkering he had a novel manuscript to publish.

But he soon learned that between writing a book manuscript and publishing it stands the least enjoyable task: selling it. Excerpts he sent to magazines, literary or glossy, came back after months of silence, accompanied by impersonal, form-letter rejections or an occasional comment. Nor, he was told, could an unknown writer send an unagented novel manuscript directly to a book publisher any longer and expect it to be read by an editor; it just got thrown in something comfortingly called the slush pile. Queries to literary agents in New York sometimes got as far as an invitation to send the first fifty to hundred pages of his manuscript, but no one wanted to take it on.

His belief in the book was unshakable, though, so he saw breaking through as only a matter of time and kept stubbornly at it. After a year or so in which reworked excerpts began to earn pen-written notes of guarded praise and regret from magazine editors, things seemed to turn around all at once. Two acceptances arrived in quick succession, from an Indian glossy he'd located in

Chicago and a not-unknown literary magazine out of California. Barely had he gotten word from the latter than an agent called with abundant praise, in a modified Yiddish accent, of the book manuscript, offering to market it to New York publishers.

Zubin couldn't keep his voice from shaking as he accepted terms on commissions et cetera. From all he'd heard, getting an agent was the difficult part—once you had one, your book was as good as published. Now, finally, he had validation. When the dread question, "What do you do?" was popped, he could point to publications, produce copies, casually drop the words, "my agent in New York," speak of the book, and *look forward* to the change in expression. Not skepticism, not the damning, barely concealed, "What a fool," but belief and respect. Not resentment, not "How come he gets to sit on his ass and pretend he's a big-shot writer, when we have to work *our* asses off day after day in the real world?" No—admiration, this time, and even excitement. He found himself moved by the willingness of all kinds of virtual strangers to vicariously enjoy his adventure.

Christina seemed to see paradise too at the overlook, but it's not paradise that burns. The passage out of Life on the Mississippi *differed in one more way from the shortened form on the plaque and on tourism brochures at the Musser. In full it read, "And I remember Muscatine — still more pleasantly — for its summer sunsets." Still more pleasantly than what? In text leading up to the passage, Zubin found two other remembrances. "I lived there awhile, many years ago," Twain first wrote, "but the place, now [as the riverboat passed it years later], had a rather unfamiliar look; so I suppose it has clear outgrown the town which I used to know. In fact, I know it has; for I remember it as a small place. . . ."*

His second, most prominent memory, was vintage Twain:

> *But I remember it best for a lunatic who caught me out in the fields, one Sunday, and extracted a butcher-knife from his boot and prepared to carve me up with it, unless I acknowledged him to be the only son of the Devil. I tried to*

compromise on an acknowledgment that he was the only
member of the family I had met; but that did not satisfy him;
he wouldn't have any half-measures; I must say he was the
sole and only son of the Devil—and he whetted his knife on
his boot. It did not seem worth while to make trouble about
a little thing like that; so I swung round to his view of the
matter and saved my skin whole. Shortly afterward, he went
to visit his father; and as he has not turned up since, I trust he
is there yet.

Clearly, Christina was not the only native of Muscatine who'd
thought her hometown less than heaven.

He called his agent at the turn of each month, resisting the
urge every day to call earlier. The list of publishing houses his
novel had been circulated to grew each time, but so did the number of those who had sent it back. No reasons given, usually, but
he'd been trained by the magazine submission process to handle
the silence in which rejection often came wrapped. Once again he
felt it was only a matter of time before the breakthrough, though
clearly he needed to accept what he'd already suspected: New
York was not going to think his novel so marketable as to clamor
and contend for it. The *real* bottom line, he told himself, was that
it was well worth publishing and someone would eventually want
to do that.

Occasionally the agent passed on in the mail an editor's comment, and while it bothered Zubin to read, say, from one publishing house that his narrative was too linear for the editor (what
would a nonlinear *Siddhartha* have been like, for instance, despite the book's denial of linear time?) but from another that his
indirect narrative strategy (whatever that meant) was confusing,
he couldn't help but be stirred by the almost surreal notion that
his manuscript had been in the hands of so-and-so at Knopf (was
the K silent or pronounced?). Even as it began to register very,
very slowly—so clearly could he visualize the printed book
now, down to the cover picture: two trains on a collision course
along the inwardly angled tracks of a vanishing perspective, one

a rough, old, dust brown, and clanking Western Railway steam engine belching smoke, the other a sleek, red-white-and-blue, pristinely bright and sharp-edged Amtrak streaking along effortlessly, above them the title *Culture Crash*—that he might fall just short of the tape, he saw too that it was against the odds he'd come within such clear sight of it. He wondered again what kept some of the workshoppers coming back Tuesday evening after Tuesday evening, toiling over new manuscripts to bring in, when all their writing before had gotten nowhere even with their empathizing peers. Was it their ability to hope? Or to fool themselves? Was it the need to create, to find a voice, to clarify one's thinking, all or any of the built-in rewards he'd recognized along the way? Would they be enough for him without the end reward, the voice unheard? He'd begun work on his next novel, but found himself struggling for focus now.

When the agent called to say apologetically that he'd put a fresh list of rejections in the mail and, after almost a year of sending the manuscript out, was about to give up, Zubin said, "I don't blame you," and meant it. He'd run out of steam. He stopped writing altogether. When the list came, there was only one note enclosed with it. Later he'd realize it was the kindest one, but at the time it made him bitter. The editor sent the standard regrets and added that the agent's client had "the tools to write a first-rate book." Clearly, this one had struck her as *less* than first-rate. Zubin felt himself accused of having failed to deliver the one thing he believed he had: a "good book"!

Indignation galvanized him out of apathy and his one-bedroom into the bookstores. In what way, he wanted to know, had his book failed to measure up? Right away he was further embittered by a scan of the trash, as he perceived it, lining the shelves. Romance and horror of the most lurid variety had *not* been barred from publication on the grounds of being second- or even third-rate! Served him well for writing something serious. And for being naïve enough to think that what was not done in conversation would be acceptable matter for public printing. Or that Americans would want to read—and live—the lives of Indian characters who were not the comical store-clerk stereotypes that sent them subliminal reassurances of their own sophistication. Writing about race and color only brought a writer trouble—

even the Hurstons and Twains had found that out. *Huckleberry* got just a lukewarm reception when it first came out in 1884, unlike other books Twain had written. Hurston had to quit writing, died a housemaid—dear God, for a Hurston to be reduced to that—and was buried in an unmarked grave long before *Their Eyes Were Watching God* was resurrected and took its place as an American classic.

Such thoughts were comforting—they took the onus for failure off him—so he held on to them for close to a year. To his surprise, he found himself still drawn to his Brother on occasion (his burnout on computers had stopped him from even getting his own P.C.) to work on the new book, writing about much the same things he'd done before, without knowing what kept him at it. He had to return full time to programming, however. It felt like a capitulation, though he wasn't sure to whom or what he was bowing. Certainty of any kind had gone out of his life and way of thinking, but so had ambition of any kind, and he was a relaxed, looser version of his former self.

He read too, when he found the time, and now more than ever had difficulty finishing books he started. He was too conscious of the writing and its flaws or excellences to think the story was real. Even if the style drew no attention to itself, he knew only too well now that it was all, each sentence, each word, coming out of the mind of some writer, someone human and imperfect, and that at each fork in the story line the protagonist might just as easily have gone the other way. It was the same with movies anymore, though documentaries almost worked. Nonfiction too, or simply journalistic reporting, held him better. But the writing still intervened, distorted what had actually occurred in ways that were now painfully apparent to him. Only live television allowed him to any extent, inasmuch as he could sift the choreographed from the spontaneous and true, to suspend disbelief. The moment-to-moment progression of even a tennis match, developing *as* he watched, was far more unpredictable and its nuances more honest and unmanipulated than any man-made plot. It struck him, too, that each match was an episode in each round, each round a chapter in each tournament, each tournament one book (whose ending might only be hazarded, as in the best of detective novels) of many volumes, all populated by recurring characters whom, over time, the spectator/reader came to know intimately. If he wanted the complexity of more than one-on-one interaction between characters, he could step up to doubles, or better still to a football game within a season of games. Action on- and off-court blurred: Graf and Seles battled for Grand Slam titles even as Seles took a knife between the shoulderblades from a Graf fan, or a few volumes later Graf, who'd once laughed a shy schoolgirl's laugh when asked if she might pose for *Playboy*, made a pensive appearance in *Sports Illustrated's* swimsuit issue instead. Zubin could believe in it all—because it was happening in front of his eyes—and watch for developments across the years. He could even reread a chapter between Connors and Lendl, say, watch their expressions or lack thereof, feel the uncontrolled, subtle shifts in momentum, and enjoy the true drama of it.

Over a corner table at Diamond Dave's, the night of the sunset, Christina had leaned toward Zubin with a twist of her shoulders and a quirky smile that made her brown eyes fizz.

"So your father sang and your mother played piano. What did you do?"

"Me?" he said. "I did both. Took piano lessons when I was a kid, but it bored me. So I quit."

"Mm-hm. Could you play now, if I found you a baby grand?"

"It's been a while," he said warily, and wondered where in Muscatine a grand piano might exist. Then, feeling the lameness, "I wasn't too bad at the time, though. My teacher — sweet old lady but all scales and by the book — told me once I could've won a contest."

"Oh, please," she said, dimpling. "You win contests!"

He bridled at that and fell to smoothing his mustache down, though he knew her trick of teasing to the point of insult. It was her way of upping sexual tension. She'd rock him that night like those boats in the safe harbor. Their waitress came by, her bust looking to come through a maroon T-shirt, chatting them up, busily laying out dinner (veal parmigiana for him, heavy with cheese and tomato, blackened chicken salad for Christina). Her fingernails, Zubin noticed for some reason as the plates came down, matched the T-shirt perfectly.

"I had some definite artistic potential, let me tell you," he said, picking up after a minute, good humor refueled by the smells and the food. "I'd make up little pieces of my own that were pretty good for a ten-year-old, I think."

"And where did it go — that potential?"

Good question. . . . The only keys his fingers played anymore were on the terminals at Bandag, recoding old accounts-receivable programs. Not even creative the way programming could be, designing new systems. And, unlike several programmers he knew who weren't alive unless they were thinking tech, he'd never been one to get excited about it, always happy to leave the job behind at five (or nine, if he weren't so lucky). Was he meant to write code for the rest of his life? His smile died. What kind of dreary existence was that? He felt then that he was meant instead for the beautiful things: sunsets coloring the world, islands burning, delicate readings of dreams — for Schumann's "Traumerei," of course, not COBOL and C and PASCAL.

"I think it's still there," he said, back on earth, surprised and a bit excited. He was seized by a Tom Sawyerish urge to stand on his hands for this beautiful tease, convince her of the possibilities he suddenly sensed in himself, and celebrate them with her.

"I think it's been just sitting there," he continued, putting his knife down, "waiting for I don't know what."

She let out a small laugh, easy but not unexcited, and he could tell in her eyes that he was reaching her.

"Is it still music? Or something else?" she asked in almost sibling understanding, leaning forward, little tease to her tone anymore. When he watched her dance at the fiesta in September, all color and verve, he thought it natural she'd been so quick to grasp what was happening inside him.

"No . . . ," he said, casting about for what it was and reeling it in. "Not music . . . I think I'll write a book sometime! Like Mark Twain. That's why I have to wait — till I've lived enough. So I know more about things."

As they sat in contemplation of the idea, slippery as yet, still dripping birth fluids, slowly it took on form and an encouraging solidity. Then Christina moved.

"I can see it," she said, putting her hand out to cover his on the table, her dark eyes bright by now like her father's in the picture on the dresser. She liked the idea, clearly, liked what she saw it doing to him, liked his confidence that he could make it happen. "I can see you writing a good book."

His disenchantment with fiction notwithstanding, the return to reading even fragments of books did, inevitably, cause him to encounter and acknowledge the iconoclastic, literary stuff coming out of ethnic authors, the Alexies, Erdriches, Kincaids, Hijueloses, Roys, Changs, Diazes, Lewises, Ansas, Kureishis, Tharoors, Divakarunis, Cisneroses, Kamanis, Alvarezes, Lahiris, Gilbs, Chandras, Sharmas, Lees, Vergheses, Jins, and Jens. (In reading Indian authors, every once in a while he had the eerie, stomach-tightening experience of encountering some of his own material, done depressingly better than he remembered doing in his book.) They'd certainly managed to be published. Yes, it was harder to break into literary-book print than into the genres, but only because readers bought fewer literary books, whether mainstream or ethnic, than thrillers. (As for those who read the literary stuff, Zubin could now go on *amazon.com* and scan page after page of readers' comments posted on specific books. He was left amazed and shamed by the eagerness with which hundreds of amateur reviewers embraced ethnic literature—they so clearly belied his own stereotype of the Other.) It was simple business mechanics, supply and demand once more. But clearly if your work was good approaching brilliant (just good was no longer good enough—too much of that already floating around) you could do it, and do it writing about anything.

That excuse gone, he had to look again at his novel. And, as if disemboweled by magic, it was a different beast from the vital one he'd remembered. *Naïve, affected, derivative, romanticized, sketchy, faint-hearted,* even *simplistic*—the adjective he'd thought applied only to the other workshoppers' manuscripts— were some of the descriptors that came to his shocked mind. His fiction resembled the rich, complex realities he'd wanted to convey (and thought he had) as a stick figure resembles a human (that maddening slippage again). He'd been looking through a fog himself, apparently. Hoping against hope, he pulled out the two excerpts that had gotten into magazines, but reading them made him wince, and all the more because they were out now in the public domain and there was nothing he could do about their mediocrities. Finally, unavoidably, he knew that the editor at Putnam or wherever had been right. He had *not* managed to do what Christina and he had been so sure he could: write a good book.

When the shock wore off, he redoubled his efforts at the word processor every evening after work. He'd make his next book a good one if it killed him. He'd make it a great one. That was the gift those tactfully silent rejections had given him: the chance to make his appearance in print something to be proud of. It was all part of a learning curve along which he'd already seen himself make strides, and he intended to stay at it for as long as it took. On the micro level, he spent hours at each point of his work considering the direction of, and crafting, only the next sentence or two, determined to be satisfied with nothing less than what, say, Chekhov or Tagore might have accepted into his own manuscripts. When he read such passages back, they felt tangibly better, and he was encouraged. On the macro level, he was impressed by John Gardner's simple but ingenious insight in *The Art of Fiction* that "the writer struggles to achieve one specific large effect, what can only be called the effect we are used to getting from good novels," and that "the writer unfamiliar with the highest effects possible [as achieved by the very best works of literature] is virtually doomed to search out lesser effects."

Embarking on a search for the higher effects, he found himself dizzied by the densities of an Updike or Doctorow, the cerebrations of a Borges or Kundera, the inventiveness of a Barthelme or Brautigan, the erudition of a Byatt or Atwood, the unlimited imagination of a Marquez or Calvino, and felt himself drawn on, fascinated, accumulating awe like a ferret that senses the presence of a large form in the brush but feels impelled to investigate. One day he opened a short-fiction anthology to Gordimer's "Siblings" and was immersed in her virtuoso, do-it-all style, in the rich, voluptuous, deeply ambiguous life that sprang fearlessly, full bodied and quivering, from the page. And the simple truth exploded in his head that he would *never*, graft how he might, write even a paragraph that measured up to the brilliance of the gifted.

Everything after that was anticlimactic. It was as if, accustomed to getting A's in undergrad coursework, he'd entered the graduate program only to find he could never do better than B's, that in truth he was, had been all along, would always remain, a B student. All his life thus far he'd believed that he could accomplish anything he was of a mind to if he put in the requisite effort for as long as it took. Ranking high in school, cracking the IIT entrance exam, graduating high enough to be drafted by Tata Consultancy Services, becoming a well-paid computer consultant at Fortune 100 companies: all these had followed as if naturally and inevitably his setting of aspirations and exerting toward their achievement. So to finally acknowledge the mountain he didn't have the *legs* to climb, its peaks tantalizingly visible but unreachable, was a shock to his system.

He consoled himself with the recognition that even the Gordimers and Marquezes didn't, in fact couldn't, always measure up to even their *own* best stuff. Not all of Gordimer was a "Siblings," and he'd read a story by Updike recently that, while good, was neither a *Rabbit* nor "The Christian Roommates." How often, after all, could you ask of someone that she create magic? If on the near slope of the learning curve, his, there was the unattainability of the summit, perhaps on the far side was an inevitable falling off. At least they only had to handle going from A+ to A, and there was always the prospect of hitting A+ again. He left the couch and went off to Barnes and Noble in his Cavalier to look for *A Soldier's Embrace*, the 1980 collection by Gordimer for which she'd written "Siblings" and in which maybe she'd reached *her* upper limits.

But it was not on the shelf with other books by her, and, when the perky young salesclerk pulled it up on her screen, she had to shake her head and tell him sorry, they couldn't even order it—it was out of print. . . . He nodded blankly and went back among the books, pulled something by Boyle about East and West off its shelf and settled into one of the cozy chairs. But he couldn't read, just sat there looking around: all those thousands of books—an absolute flood of words—by so many brilliant writers. Only a minute fraction, really, of the total numbers increasing exponentially each decade, helped by the spread of word processors and workshops, fighting an ever more chancy battle (supply and demand all over again) for attention and recognition. For their ten minutes of sun. And each of them, bar a handful, destined to drop out of sight.

Even the great ones, could they realistically expect to last forever? Who was to say Homer's was truly survival of the fittest? The all-recording Alexandrian library, possibly containing greater genius than Homer's, eventually burned to the ground the way Alexander had once torched Persian writings. Look far enough down the road and who survived might all come down to chance, someone's personal e-book or CD-ROM collection dug up after millenniums. Maybe all a writer, any writer, could do was make his work as good as he possibly could and get it out there, enter it in the lottery. The thought was less comforting than depressing; he put Boyle back and left.

Home seemed uninviting, too closed and hushed, so he got onto 35 West and headed for one of his favorite places, Minnehaha Falls. The sun, cooled to orange and heavy, was setting over it when he left the car and walked into the park by Minnehaha Creek. It had been a wet year, and the water foamed and shimmered down to the glen fifty feet below and on into the Mississippi. Above the falls, out of the stream's grays and blues rose the bronze, gleaming statue of Hiawatha and Minnehaha, and as always it reminded him of Longfellow's "Song," on the one hand, and the statue of the lone Mascoutin back in Riverside Park, on the other. No small-town setting, this, however. Only a spin away rose familiar pedestrian skyways and office towers in a business world he hadn't been able to escape. A world so boundless, in fact, that it even, for all practical purposes, ran the arts. Not as clearly labeled as an island that burns, but one of *his* hells.

Right where he was was good enough: not on the Mississippi itself but by a creek that fed it. The river for the Mark Twains, a tributary for aspiring writers. The thought relaxed him. He lowered himself to damp grass and watched the sun go down. The question rose in his mind, would he keep on writing, and he put it immediately to rest. No question. He still wasn't sure why, exactly, but he now had a felt knowledge of what brought his workshop companions back week after week, and he had some ideas.

He'd read an article in which an author (Welty or Porter or O'Connor, he couldn't remember who) said she wrote because, quite simply, it was what she did best. He thought maybe, rather, it was the best thing she did. He'd also heard of someone who'd said he couldn't *not* write. It seemed to Zubin that people sometimes wrote to find their way out of personal hells, and perhaps only after they did that could they not write. Had Christina, for instance, been a writer, she'd have written about people who felt trapped in small towns. She'd probably spoken of it in her dances, in fact, if he'd just had the vocabulary to follow. It was all right, though—he might have learned more of her story, but most likely he'd have misinterpreted it. Misunderstood her as they'd misunderstood each other a hundred other times. Slippage, more slippage, and yet more slippage. Inescapable. Unending. Every last bit of communication through history set in code, and each piece of code with its own built-in bug, just waiting to blow some program up! The only story you could hope to know to any real degree of completeness or accuracy, from the inside out—from deeper inside than language could go—and so in all its stunning complexity and truth, was your own. It may not have been as important to you as your daughter's, say, but it was the story to whose internal details you had the most (and most direct) access. Writing from the data banks of *his* own story had helped him approach some hazy understanding of it, and, in circular fashion, his writings had eventually become a part of his life story. He'd even come to see things he'd written actually happen around or to him. In the final analysis, he felt he'd become the person he now was, and his story the story it was, because he wrote. One writer, he surmised, might bargain his soul away like Faust, to write, while another might find his, writing. Sometimes he wasn't sure which of the two he was. In all likelihood, both.

The sun was ready to go, and he watched it light the stream, feeling no urge, at last, to put words to the image. Someday he might yet write that good book, but until it took hold of him he'd just live things for a bit. He was moved by the thought that in Muscatine too, at this time, the sun was setting on the Mississippi, and, at the other end of the Great River Road, in New Orleans as well, a place he'd never been to but was somehow connected with because of Christina. At times he toyed with the idea of tracking her down in the Big Easy. When her day to leave Muscatine had drawn near, he'd made a call and was surprised at her quick agreement to have one last dinner. She'd heard of a great new place in Iowa City, so they drove the forty-or-so miles there, one of his three visits to the congenial university town. Its sunlit campus parks and umbrella-shaded food stalls had warmed him to it. Only years later had he learned of its famous University of Iowa Writers' Workshop. His old friend the Musser Public Library, just a stroll down Iowa Avenue in Muscatine, was all he'd needed at the time, and he went on and on to Christina about it.

The Thai restaurant off-campus was nice; they sat in the right angle of an aquarium, and the rainbow-colored fish swimming about them made the evening seem surreal. She was the thinnest he'd ever seen her, maybe too thin—beautiful still, but in a different way. (He'd grown heavier, he knew; it showed in his face when he shaved around the mustache.) He could tell from her talk that she was excited and sad. Bourbon Street and Mardi Gras up ahead (no more real winters), Watermelon Jamboree and Viva México already dropping behind. And for him? Well, completion of his contract at Bandag, first of all, then on to the next one. Oh. Where? Wherever; there was talk of either Michigan or Minnesota at his head office. Winters either way. She said no to dessert, and they left. In the Cavalier, doing fifty on Route 22, they ran out of things to talk about. A loaded silence ensued, till finally she rolled her window down. Then the darkening air rushing past made it hard to hear anyway.

Back in Muscatine, pulling into her division with their headlights streaming, he thought for a moment she might ask him in despite Monique. But, instead, she invited him to come visit her in New Orleans. Long way off, he thought, polite thing to say. So he responded with a nod and a "sure, love to" that meant nothing. It was exactly the kind of connotation to which he'd restricted his use of the *love* word. She hesitated still. Then fleetingly across her face a tired look had passed. At the time he couldn't figure it out, but now he felt it had spelled frustration of

The Mark Twain Overlook 209

some kind. With all the slippage, maybe. At any rate, she'd just turned and gone in, hadn't even kissed him good-bye.

When finally the dampness began to seep through his jeans, he got up to leave. Minnehaha Park was all shadows by then. The creek had changed to silver.

The Iowa Short Fiction Award and John Simmons Short Fiction Award Winners

2001
Ticket to Minto: Stories of India and America,
Sohrab Homi Fracis
Judge: Susan Power

2001
Fire Road, Donald Anderson
Judge: Susan Power

2000
Articles of Faith,
Elizabeth Oness
Judge: Elizabeth McCracken

2000
Troublemakers, John McNally
Judge: Elizabeth McCracken

1999
House Fires, Nancy Reisman
Judge: Marilynne Robinson

1999
Out of the Girls' Room and into the Night, Thisbe Nissen
Judge: Marilynne Robinson

1998
Friendly Fire,
Kathryn Chetkovich
Judge: Stuart Dybek

1998
The River of Lost Voices: Stories from Guatemala, Mark Brazaitis
Judge: Stuart Dybek

1997
Thank You for Being Concerned and Sensitive, Jim Henry
Judge: Ann Beattie

1997
Within the Lighted City,
Lisa Lenzo
Judge: Ann Beattie

1996
Hints of His Mortality,
David Borofka
Judge: Oscar Hijuelos

1996
Western Electric,
Don Zancanella
Judge: Oscar Hijuelos

1995
Listening to Mozart,
Charles Wyatt
Judge: Ethan Canin

1995
May You Live in Interesting Times, Tereze Glück
Judge: Ethan Canin

1994
The Good Doctor,
Susan Onthank Mates
Judge: Joy Williams

1994
Igloo among Palms,
Rod Val Moore
Judge: Joy Williams

1993
Happiness, Ann Harleman
Judge: Francine Prose

1993
Macauley's Thumb,
Lex Williford
Judge: Francine Prose

1993
Where Love Leaves Us,
Renée Manfredi
Judge: Francine Prose

1992
My Body to You,
Elizabeth Searle
Judge: James Salter

1992
Imaginary Men, Enid Shomer
Judge: James Salter

1991
The Ant Generator,
Elizabeth Harris
Judge: Marilynne Robinson

1991
Traps, Sondra Spatt Olsen
Judge: Marilynne Robinson

1990
A Hole in the Language,
Marly Swick
Judge: Jayne Anne Phillips

1989
Lent: The Slow Fast,
Starkey Flythe, Jr.
Judge: Gail Godwin

1989
Line of Fall, Miles Wilson
Judge: Gail Godwin

1988
The Long White,
Sharon Dilworth
Judge: Robert Stone

1988
The Venus Tree,
Michael Pritchett
Judge: Robert Stone

1987
Fruit of the Month,
Abby Frucht
Judge: Alison Lurie

1987
Star Game, Lucia Nevai
Judge: Alison Lurie

1986
Eminent Domain, Dan O'Brien
Judge: Iowa Writers' Workshop

1986
Resurrectionists,
Russell Working
Judge: Tobias Wolff

1985
Dancing in the Movies,
Robert Boswell
Judge: Tim O'Brien

1984
Old Wives' Tales,
Susan M. Dodd
Judge: Frederick Busch

1983
Heart Failure, Ivy Goodman
Judge: Alice Adams

1982
Shiny Objects, Dianne Benedict
Judge: Raymond Carver

1981
The Phototropic Woman,
Annabel Thomas
Judge: Doris Grumbach

1980
Impossible Appetites,
James Fetler
Judge: Francine du Plessix Gray

1979
Fly Away Home, Mary Hedin
Judge: John Gardner

1978
A Nest of Hooks, Lon Otto
Judge: Stanley Elkin

1977
The Women in the Mirror,
Pat Carr
Judge: Leonard Michaels

1976
The Black Velvet Girl,
C. E. Poverman
Judge: Donald Barthelme

1975
*Harry Belten and the
Mendelssohn Violin Concerto,*
Barry Targan
Judge: George P. Garrett

1974
*After the First Death There Is
No Other,* Natalie L. M. Petesch
Judge: William H. Gass

1973
The Itinerary of Beggars,
H. E. Francis
Judge: John Hawkes

1972
The Burning and Other Stories,
Jack Cady
Judge: Joyce Carol Oates

1971
*Old Morals, Small Continents,
Darker Times,*
Philip F. O'Connor
Judge: George P. Elliott

1970
The Beach Umbrella,
Cyrus Colter
Judges: Vance Bourjaily
and Kurt Vonnegut, Jr.

Ivy Bigbee

Originally from Bombay, Sohrab Homi
Fracis teaches literature at the University
of North Florida and is a fiction and
poetry editor at the *State Street Review*.
He was awarded the 1999–2000 Florida
Individual Artist Fellowship in Literature/
Fiction, and his work has appeared in
*Other Voices, India Currents, Weber
Studies,* the *Antigonish Review,* and
the *Toronto Review of Contemporary
Literature Abroad.*